THE HERO CHRONICLES
SECRETS

THE HERO CHRONICLES
SECRETS

BY TIM METTEY

KENWOOD PUBLISHING GROUP
www.kenwoodpublishinggroup.com
Cincinnati, Ohio

ISBN-10: 0-9858340-6-4
ISBN-13: 978-0-9858340-6-7

ACKNOWLEDGEMENTS

When I first started school, it was discovered that I had a learning disability that affected my reading and writing, making school very difficult.

Several people in my life stuck by me and helped me along the way. Thank you to my mom and dad for not treating me differently and pushing me to excel; my wonderful teachers and tutors (Mrs. Rush, Mrs. Richardson, Mrs. Stark, Mrs. Lacks, Mrs. Wolfe, Mrs. Kitchen), who spent countless hours helping me; my friend Karen, who encouraged me with her excitement for what I was doing and told me the story was good even when I wasn't sure; and my editing team for getting my book ready to be published. Also, if it weren't for my wife, Chanin, I would have never put my thoughts down to make this book happen. No matter what I faced, she just simply told me to write, and so I did.

Lastly, I would like to thank the men, women, and children who have risked something for others. These true heroes are represented in our police officers, firefighters, EMTs, first responders, military, and many others not listed. These individuals risk their lives every day for us, and for that I thank them.

I hope this book shows that no matter what struggles you may face, anything is possible. I am living proof of that.

THAT DAY
CHAPTER ONE

October 10

"Randy, you better get over here or you'll miss the bus," I yelled across the street. Randy was walking out of his front door, breakfast in hand, late as usual. The bus brakes squealed at the stop sign just up the street. Randy darted over the lawn and across the street just in front of the bus.

"Randy, I have told you a million times—don't run out in front of the bus. Next time I will have to report you," said our bus driver, Mrs. Burgeous, with a stern look as we scrambled aboard.

Mrs. Burgeous had short grey hair that looked like a neatly placed beehive. She was always nice to me, mostly because I followed her rules. Randy sat two seats behind me. I sat in the very front seat, right behind Mrs. Burgeous and next to a tall blonde girl named Lindsey. She was two grades older than me and was at least a head taller. She was normally talkative, but today she wasn't paying any attention to me. She just stared out the window toward the sky, listening to music.

"Good morning, Alex. How are you today?" Mrs. Burgeous was looking at me in the big mirror that bus drivers use to see what is happening on the bus.

"Well, Mrs. Burgeous, I'm excited for school today."

"Well, bless my stars! That has to be a first. Why are you excited?" she asked.

"Not really sure. Just feels like it is going to be a great day. And, the school is serving pizza and fries for lunch."

She laughed. "Well, that sounds like a good reason to be excited, and I bet you have gym today also."

"Yes, I do. How did you know?"

"I'm a good guesser," she said with a big smile. I leaned back and noticed that Lindsey was staring at me, looking very serious.

"Alex, did you see the clouds with the lights in them?"

Before I could answer, Randy blurted out from behind us, "What lights, Lindsey?"

Lindsey didn't turn to acknowledge him. She just stared at me, waiting for my answer. "No, I didn't see anything like that," I said.

"Well, there are strange lights in the sky that look like clouds with rainbows trapped inside. I hope I can see them better when I get to school." She looked back out her window up toward the sky. I leaned over closer to her, but from my seat I couldn't see anything.

The bus slowed down over the two speed bumps right before the E.H. Greene School's parking lot. I was always jealous of the kids in the back of the bus because the speed bumps sent them flying into the air.

"Okay, fifth graders, this is your stop," Mrs. Burgeous said loudly. The brakes squealed, slowing us to a stop right between two other buses. I got up and stood in the aisle, waiting to get off. I was first in line with Randy right behind me.

"So do you think we will see those lights that Lindsey was talking about?" Randy asked.

I shrugged my shoulders. "Not sure." I looked over at Lindsey. She was still in her seat looking out the window, fixed on getting another glimpse of the clouds. Mrs. Burgeous opened the doors to the bus, and I quickly got off.

Before I had a chance to look up, Randy was pointing at the sky. "Look at those things! Cool!"

I looked up and saw them. Lindsey was right about what they looked like—clouds with swirling rainbows trapped inside.

DING! DING! DING! DING!

The high-pitched bell rang and I hurried to class.

**

Paying attention in class was harder than usual. Everyone was talking about the lights, and I couldn't stop thinking about them either. My teacher, Ms. Rush, was the only other thought that entered my mind. She was so beautiful. I wished for her to be my girlfriend. I daydreamed of picking her up in a shiny red sports car and taking her to a nice restaurant like Applebee's or somewhere like that. If only I was older.

"Mr. Taylor. Mr. Taylor?" Ms. Rush's voice shattered my daydream. "Could you please tell me the capital of Ohio?"

I looked down at my book, hoping the answer would jump off the page at me, but nothing.

"Mr. Taylor, please pay more attention next time. Anyone else?" She looked around the room. Several hands jumped into the air around me. "Ms. McBride?"

"The capital of Ohio is Columbus." Tina McBride was a big time brown-noser. She always knew the answers to all the questions and never did anything wrong. If only I sat by her, I would at least get some help during tests.

"Very good," Ms. Rush said.

DING! DING! DING! DING!

The bell rang for recess. I hurried to the front of the line to go outside. We walked down the long hall lined with our red lockers and then out the door to the playground. The rest of the school was already outside at recess. Instead of playing, everyone was standing and looking up at the dazzling rainbow clouds. The teachers were gazing along with us. Some of them had cameras and were taking pictures of the sky.

"Mark Siegel, Tina McBride, and Alex Taylor, please report to Ms. Rush's classroom," blared the outdoor PA. *What did I do now?* I thought as I walked through the doors back inside. Down the hall from me were Mark and Tina. I ran to catch up with them.

"Are we in trouble?" I asked.

"Well there's no way I'm in trouble," Tina said, "but you and Mark probably are." I glanced at Mark, and we both gave her a nasty look. We all walked into Ms. Rush's class. She was sitting at her desk in the front of the room. She looked up with a big smile and waved us toward her. I was relieved to see her smiling.

Right then the ground started to shake, knocking us sideways. Ms. Rush's expression turned to one of complete terror. The walls and floor began to move violently in different directions, and there was a loud sound like a train coming down the hall behind us. The ceiling and walls started to fall in on us. A metal beam fell and grazed my leg, cutting through my pants and into my shin. I turned and ran toward the exit. I was being thrown in every direction, weaving in and out of parts of the ceiling. The lockers had come alive, shifting back and forth, dancing off the walls. Several of them had worked their way into the middle of the hall, making it difficult to get through. The intense sounds were like nothing I had ever heard. I was right next to the exit when a large piece of the wall fell. I jumped over it and went through the shattered door to the outside. I got away from the building and turned back to see it still shaking.

"We made it!" I yelled, but I was alone. Tina, Mark, and Ms. Rush were still inside.

MOVING

CHAPTER TWO

Almost Five Years Later

The doorbell rang. I opened the door just wide enough to see who was there.

"Is your mother home, young man?" A short elderly woman stood before me, hunched over, holding a walker for support.

"Yes, she is. Just a minute, please." I shut the door. Cora was standing right next to me.

"There is an old lady outside who wants to see you," I whispered.

Cora opened the door. "Well, hello, Mrs. Phillips. It's so good of you to come on such short notice." Cora turned to me. "Nicholas, please finish packing your room." She walked out onto the porch, shutting the door behind her. Mrs. Phillips must be the new owner of this house, free of charge.

I had been calling Cora "Mom" for years, but it was still weird to say it or hear others say it; she's actually my mom's

6

sister. Before I started calling her Mom, she insisted on being called Cora. Not Aunt Cora, Auntie, or anything else—just plain Cora. I still call her that when no one else is around, but in front of others I always call her Mom, because that's how it has to be for now.

I looked at the large window in my room and could clearly see my reflection in it. I barely recognized the person I saw. I was no longer a little kid. I was now stuck somewhere between a kid and an adult. My hair color had changed from blond to sandy brown. I had grown at least a foot over the past five years and was skinnier than when I was younger. No matter how much I ate, I didn't gain weight. I was hoping I would grow taller than the average 5'9" that I was, but there was no sign of me growing taller any time soon. So average is what I would have to settle for.

I looked past my reflection at the moving truck sitting in the driveway with boxes stacked neatly around it. I hated moving. Every year for the last five years, we have moved on August 10, which was tomorrow. I was getting really tired of it.

"Nicholas, please come down here and help me," Cora yelled from the bottom of the stairs. I looked out the window one last time and walked through my empty bedroom and down the stairs.

"Grab those boxes by the door and put them in the truck. I would like to leave at 5 a.m. sharp tomorrow morning."

I had changed a lot over the last five years, but Cora hadn't at all. She was still slender and beautiful like she had been plucked out of a fashion and beauty magazine. The only thing that changed was her blonde hair—every other day a new style or color, but each as beautiful as the last. I was finally taller than her, but she still seemed larger than life. Always in control. Perfect in every way.

We had perfected a routine that made moving easier for us. We would pack the evening before and leave early the next morning. This would eliminate any questions from people as to why we were moving. This was one of the ways we stayed unnoticed. I put the rest of the boxes into the truck.

"So what do you want to get to eat tonight?" Cora asked.

"I don't care. You pick."

"Nicholas, don't be that way. I know you don't like to move, but you know why we have to. Let's go to Rukker's. I know you like that place, and you can drive! You need to practice more so you can get your license when we get to our new home." She tossed the keys to me. She definitely was trying to cheer me up because we never drove the truck into town unless it was absolutely necessary.

The drive into town was normally a treat, but tonight it wasn't. It was just another sad reminder that I would be gone tomorrow, never to return to this town.

Rukker's was packed. It had its normal line of cars waiting around the corner for the drive-thru. This was the first place where Cora and I ate when we moved here exactly a year ago. It was an odd choice because it's literally covered in used gum all over the outside. Cora had her standards and this did not pass. But it was our little tradition on the last night to always eat at the same place where we had first eaten when we moved to that town. When we moved here, Rukker's was that restaurant. I don't know why Cora wanted me to pick where to eat tonight, because I knew this was where we would go.

I pulled into the packed parking lot and found a spot.

"Nicholas, I'll wait in the truck," Cora said, staring at her pink leather planner that had all of our life in it. All of our important information was in there. It was what she used to organize our lives.

"What do you want me to get you?" I asked.

"I'll take a Rukker Burger, no pickles or mustard, please."

"Do you want something to drink?"

"Oh yes," she looked up, "a chocolate shake. Can't forget that!"

The line inside was as long as the one outside. I made eye contact with Andy. He was short and skinny with red hair and a lot of freckles. Andy was the closest thing I had to a friend here. I had made sure that I gave him no reason to be friends with me, but he was persistent, and so he was my first "kind of" friend in a long time.

"Hey, Nick! I get a break in five! Don't worry about the line; I'll place your order and meet you out back. The usual for you and your mom, right?" Andy said it so loudly that the entire line turned back to look at me. Red-faced, I nodded yes and walked out the front door. I got back to our truck, not sure if he was going to get our order right, but it was better than all of those people staring at me while I told him what we wanted.

"Food will be ready in a couple minutes," I said. Cora nodded, barely even noticing I was there. She was still staring at her planner, deep in thought. After a couple of minutes, I walked to the back of the restaurant. Andy was standing there with a bag of food and a large chocolate shake.

"Here's your food, and I even remembered your mom's chocolate shake that she loves so much! So what are you doing tonight, Nick?" Andy asked, giving me a punch on the arm.

"Well, nothing really," I quickly replied, avoiding eye contact and hoping he wouldn't suspect anything.

"What's wrong with you, man? You look like your cat just died or something." Andy laughed at his own joke. I didn't know what to say. Cora never let me tell anyone that we were moving. She thought it made things easier not to tell anyone so that there wouldn't be a lot of questions for me.

"Well, I got bad news, Andy. I'm moving tomorrow." The words just came out. I don't know what I was thinking or why I told him. Cora was going to kill me.

"What? You're messin', right?"

"No, seriously, my mom got transferred. They want her to be there as soon as possible. The moving truck is already packed and ready to go first thing in the morning."

Andy grinned at me. "Well, I guess we will have to make this a night you will never forget then, won't we buddy?"

"No, I can't," I said. I took my bag of food from him and grabbed the chocolate shake sitting on the wall next to him.

"Um, yes you can and yes you will and that's that! I'll be by at 8:00 to pick you up."

"Do you know where I live?" I asked.

"Eh, I'll figure it out," he replied.

Andy walked in the back door, leaving me alone holding the bag of food. I stood there for a minute stunned. I felt a sudden wave of panic set in. What was I going to tell Cora? I had broken one of the main rules.

Driving back home with Cora was complete torture. I almost ran two stop signs. I hoped that she wouldn't look up from her planner to talk to me. Hiding anything from her was next to impossible. Her motherly instincts had become fine-tuned over the years.

We got home and Cora continued to study her planner as we walked in. I put the bag of food on the table in the empty kitchen.

"Nicholas, where's my shake?"

"Ugh, I forgot to bring it in. It's in the truck. Sorry, Cora, I'll go get it."

She looked up from her planner. "Nicholas, is there something wrong? You've been acting strange the whole ride home."

"No, everything is fine. I just hate moving day."

"I know you do, but everything will be fine." She walked up to me and put her hand on my face. "I promise."

We sat in silence eating our food.

"Andy got our food for us for free?"

"Yes!" I said a little too loudly.

"Well, that sure was nice of him." She smiled, but then went back to reading her planner.

We continued to eat in silence. Right when I had worked up the courage to tell her about my conversation with Andy, she said, "Nicholas, we are moving about two hours from our hometown this time. It's a pretty nice town, and the school is incredible."

The doorbell rang. Cora jumped to her feet, nearly knocking over her chair.

"Cora, it's Andy," I called to her before she reached the door.

"Andy's here?" Cora asked as she opened the door. "Good evening, Andy. What can I do for you?"

"Hello, Ms. Keller. I'm here to take Nick out for, you know, one last night of fun!" His words were like fingernails going down a chalkboard, causing me to wince at each word.

"Last night of fun?" Cora said, sounding surprised. She opened the door wider so we could both stand in the doorway facing Andy.

"Mom, I told Andy that we're moving." I didn't look at her, fearing that her look would turn me to stone.

"Yeah, we're going to have a little party for Nick," Andy chimed in.

Cora paused for a moment. It seemed like the longest couple of seconds of my life.

"Well, okay. You boys have a great time. Nicholas—"

I looked up at her.

"Make sure you are home by 5 a.m." She smiled and winked.

"Don't worry, Ms. K. I'll get him home early enough." Andy laughed, grabbed my arm, and pulled me out the door.

What just happened? Why didn't she send Andy home and then lecture me about how she was just trying to protect me? This had to be some sort of test and I had just failed miserably.

Then something else popped into my head—we are moving two hours from our hometown. Cora is moving us closer to our hometown, the one place she insisted we always had to stay as far away from as possible. With the entire country to choose from, she chose a place only two hours away. What was going on? My head began to hurt thinking about Cora's sudden change of personality and rules. I turned my attention back to Andy.

"I know you're not having a party for me. You've only known I was moving for a couple of hours."

"Did I say *have* a party? I meant *crash* a party!"

"Whose?"

"Marshall Jenkins!" He grinned mischievously.

"Wait a minute. He's a senior, and the last time I checked, we were lowly freshmen."

"We aren't exactly going in," he said with that same grin.

"So what are we going to do, just sit on the stairs and watch them? Oh boy, I think I'd rather pack."

"Nick, leave it to me. We'll have fun. Trust me!"

The night was extremely hot and muggy. The clouds that covered the sky trapped in the heat, making it unbearable for an August night. The humidity was stifling. The thick dark clouds hid the remaining light from the sunset and any light from the moon or stars. It became dark quickly.

The thirty-minute walk to Marshall's house took a lot less time than usual because Andy would randomly ring the doorbell of houses, which resulted in a mad dash not to get caught. The darkness that the clouds provided helped, because before people answered their doors, we were running down the street, swallowed by the night. It was very childish, but fun. I had missed out on all of this type of stuff over the last five years.

Marshall's house had cars everywhere—in the front yard, in the driveway, and up and down the street. All of the lights were on in the large two-story brick home. Andy ducked down and ran toward the back of the house. I followed him. Andy was hiding behind two large bushes along the back fence where the light of the house didn't reach.

"So what now?" I whispered.

"I was just making sure they were all in the backyard."

"Why?" I asked, not sure if I really wanted to hear the answer.

"Because when we smear this toothpaste on their car windows," he said as he pulled out two tubes of wintergreen toothpaste from his pocket, "I don't want any interruptions." He handed me a tube and smiled like he was filming a toothpaste commercial. "It helps fight plaque and bad breathe *and* cleans even the dirtiest of senior trash." He laughed and ran by me.

I followed him to the front where he started smearing the toothpaste all over the car windows. I pretended to smear toothpaste on some of the cars, but only the ones farthest away from the house and Andy. My stomach was hurting horribly, like I had an ulcer burning a hole in it. I was scared of getting caught, which I knew had something to do with how I was feeling.

Andy moved over to a car I recognized, Marshall's black Mustang. Getting back at Marshall for all of the stuff he did to Andy over the years was the real reason why we were here. Getting to prank all of the other cars was a bonus. Andy hated Marshall. He had tormented him for years. And to make matters worse, they had been good friends and neighbors when they were younger.

Andy was like an artist moving around Marshall's Mustang so fluidly, so gracefully, not missing a spot. The wintergreen paste made the car sparkle. I could smell its faint scent in the air. Then Andy started to put some type of round pink circles all over the car. I was too far away to tell what they were, and I was not about to get closer to find out. I ran back to the bushes at the side of the house to wait. A couple of minutes later, Andy joined me.

"What did you put on Marshall's car?" I asked.

"Bologna!"

"What?"

"Bologna! I thought it would complement the toothpaste, and it did! You know bologna polka dots are the new rage in automotive design," he whispered. We both laughed silently.

I turned my attention toward the party in Marshall's backyard. I found myself envious of all those people having a good time together. How fitting. I was in hiding, watching everyone else live life to the fullest. Just like my life. Hiding . . .

Marshall had an incredible deck that covered the entire back of the house, a huge grill, and a hot tub that could easily fit twenty people. Beyond the deck was a regulation-sized basketball court, and beyond that was a huge lake. There was a dock with two large ski boats. Most of the party was either in the lake swimming or on the dock watching. Someone suddenly yelled, "Skinny dipping!" from the deck. A group of guys pulled off all of their clothes, ran naked toward the lake, and jumped off the dock into the water. A wave of laughing and screaming came from the lake.

Andy looked at me like he just had a brilliant idea with the light bulb still shining above his head. "I'm going for their clothes!"

Before I could stop him, he was over the fence. He was like a human vacuum, grabbing every piece of clothing he passed. He was halfway across the back deck when someone shouted, "Look!" from the dock. He was nearly to the other side of the yard by the time they started getting out of the water. He threw the clothes over the fence, hopped over, and disappeared.

I sprinted to the front of the house. Andy was running down the middle of the street, dropping clothes as he went. I ran up to Andy, grabbed him, and pulled him into a side yard a couple of houses down from Marshall's. We slid down into a ditch. Andy was terrified. His face was frozen with fear and he was shaking violently. He was breathing hard, but not loud enough to drown out the angry screams coming from Marshall's front yard. They had just seen their cars and they were mad!

"Let's go!" Andy whispered to me in a shaky, out of breath voice.

"No," I said. "We need to stay here to see which way they'll go before we move."

Cars began to leave one at a time. We waited for twenty minutes. Only two cars remained in the driveway when we finally popped our heads out of the ditch. Andy had calmed down, but he was still shaking.

The last two cars roared to life, and in front of them was a large group of guys. I could barely make out how many there were from where we were hiding. This had to be the search party to track us down.

"We should have run when we had the chance," Andy said. "We would have made it."

"Maybe, but they would have seen us," I said very confidently.

"What do you care? You are moving!" He was right. I would have been gone, never to see them again.

"Well, you were nice enough to throw this great going away party for me. I had to thank you in some way."

Andy flashed a nervous smile. The engine of Marshall's Mustang roared, sending a wave of panic through Andy. His expression changed back to fear, but I didn't feel scared at all. I was calm. I was in complete control, but I didn't know why. I was usually a worrier and this was definitely a time to worry.

The angry mob, minus the torches and pitchforks, got into the cars. Both of the cars went in opposite directions, very slowly down the street. I could feel Andy starting to get up. I easily pinned him down with my arm, making sure he didn't try to run. He squirmed for a second and then stopped.

The car passed by us slowly. Beams of light came from inside the car searching for us. They were almost out of sight before I let go of him.

"Gosh, Nick, next time you want me to stay, just say so! There's no reason to crush me," Andy said, rubbing his chest.

"Sorry, I thought you were going to run for it and blow our cover."

"Well, we better start running now before they come back!" he said.

All of the houses in Marshall's neighborhood had fences in their backyards, so we could only run from front yard to front yard. Then we could duck into the woods at the end of his street.

"Nick, you have to admit that this is one night you'll never forget."

"Yeah, seeing you run down the middle of the street with those clothes was pretty funny. It looked like you had just robbed a laundromat!"

We stopped jogging after a couple of minutes and walked for a while, making sure to stay close to the fronts of the houses to try to stay hidden. Up ahead I saw the woods. We were only about ten houses away when I heard the familiar growl of Marshall's Mustang behind us. We both began to run as fast as we could. If we made it to the tree line, we would be in the clear. The car was not far behind us, and they were gaining on us quickly. The car accelerated. I realized that they were not on the road anymore, but in the front yards. They didn't want to catch us; they wanted to hit us!

Andy was now down by the street for some reason, making him an easy target. I was closer to the front of the houses. The car lunged forward to hit Andy. Suddenly my muscles tensed hard, jerking my body toward Andy with an incredible burst of speed. I was moving as fast as the Mustang, maybe even faster. I yanked him behind a large tree. In that moment, Andy's body was like a rag doll. It moved without any resistance. He had no choice but to do as I wanted.

We kept sprinting toward the tree line. A second later, I heard a sound like an explosion. I turned to see that the car had hit the tree head-on. Pieces like shrapnel from a bomb went flying in different directions. The Mustang was wrapped around the large oak tree. They had swerved to hit us and hit the tree instead.

Andy had already made it into the woods. I stopped. I had to make sure they were okay. The Mustang's doors swung open, and one by one everyone stumbled out of the car onto the lawn. No one looked really hurt; they had some scratches but that was it. Porch lights from several houses flicked on. I ran into the woods to find Andy.

"Hey, Nick! Over here!" He was leaning against a tree. "What were you thinking? Did you want to get caught?"

"No, I was making sure that they weren't hurt."

"Hurt? Are you kidding? They tried to kill us! Did that slip your mind?" He looked disgusted, then turned and started to walk.

We walked in silence for most of the way home. He was mad at me for checking on Marshall and his friends. I would have tried to make him understand, but I was preoccupied with wondering how I had saved him from getting hit by Marshall's Mustang. The question lingered in my mind most of the way home. My muscles were still sore from the sudden explosion of speed.

Five minutes from my house, Andy stopped and turned to me. "Well, have a nice life, Nick. Stop by Rukker's if you're ever in the neighborhood."

"Sure, if I'm in the neighborhood," I said. He smiled and walked off.

I turned toward my house where I knew Cora would be waiting for me. The lecture about how I had broken the rules would be horrible. I wasn't scared about being hit by the car, but walking through the front door made me sick to my stomach. Maybe I should have let the car hit me to save me from what lies ahead.

FACTORY
CHAPTER THREE

I opened the door very slowly, careful not to make a sound. I was praying Cora had fallen asleep while she was waiting to kill me.

"So how was your night?" Cora's question sent me flying across the floor. "Wow! Someone's jumpy!" Cora was standing in the kitchen door, staring at me with her arms crossed. I couldn't tell if she was mad or not.

She turned and walked into the kitchen. I followed her. Cora was packing the last of the glasses into a box.

"We went over to Andy's house," I said.

"Well, that sounds fun, but I thought there was going to be a party." She didn't turn to face me. She just continued packing.

"Oh yeah, after Andy's we went over to a friend's house for the party."

"Oh, okay. It sounds like fun. You should go up and try to get some sleep. I put your toothbrush in the downstairs bathroom, and the inflatable bed is already set up in your room."

"Thanks," I said, dumbfounded. I escaped to the bathroom and shut the door. *Why didn't I get in trouble?* I thought as I was brushing my teeth.

The inflatable mattress was in the middle of my dark, empty room. It was comfortable, but I still couldn't sleep. The ceiling was staring back at me as hard as I was staring up at it.

The next morning came too early. The alarm clock was buzzing a loud, obnoxious buzz. The clock on the floor said 4:30 a.m. Cora must have set it for me.

I was sick. I didn't want to sit up too fast because I was sure I would throw up all over the floor. How come I was always sick? You would think that I'd get used to feeling this way, especially after waking up like this every morning for the last five years. I used to tell Cora about being sick, but it happened so frequently that I just accepted it as part of me and saved her from all the gory details.

The sickness forced me to lie very still, making me unable to move in fear of getting sicker. I searched along the side of the inflatable bed for the only thing that helped me feel better, the only way I could cope with this horrible morning curse. My hand hit something that made a familiar, soothing rattling sound. My Tic Tacs. I popped three into my mouth, and the cool mint flavor started to make me feel better almost instantly. I sat up. On the floor next to me I saw a pair of khaki shorts and my favorite orange Izod shirt that Cora had bought me before school started last year. She must have laid them out for me last night after she was done packing the kitchen. I put my clothes on slowly and deflated the bed, still feeling kind of sick.

I could smell Cora's coffee brewing. The smell turned my stomach, making me feel worse, but I was used to it now after waking up to that smell for the last five years. I'm positive that Starbucks has made most of its money from Cora.

I tenderly ventured down to the kitchen.

"Hey, sleepyhead, how did you sleep?" Cora was leaning against the kitchen counter, drinking her coffee and looking over her planner.

"I don't think I slept."

"Do you want something to eat?" she asked.

The question turned my stomach, again making me grab a couple more Tic Tacs. "No, I'm fine, thanks." She knew I was sick. That's why I had a fresh pack of Tic Tacs next to the bed. She knew me well. "Cora, do we have anything else to put into the truck?"

"No, I did it all last night. Just grab the stuff in your room and anything you have in the bathroom. I'll grab the coffee maker, and we will be on our way."

I walked back upstairs and got the deflated mattress, my clock, and the clothes I had worn the night before. I grabbed my toothbrush from the downstairs bathroom and walked out of the house. I didn't notice last night when I was brushing my teeth, but I had used the same toothpaste Andy had used on the cars at Marshall's party. This brought a smile to my face.

Cora was already outside. She was hooking up the light to the towing trailer for our old Ford truck. "Nicholas, just throw that stuff in the back of the moving truck."

I shoved the stuff in the small space behind the passenger seat and walked back over to where Cora was standing. She took my hand, closed her eyes, and said in a whisper, "God bless this house and the people who will live here. Please guide us, and may we have safe travels to our new home." She squeezed my hand and just like that, we were off. I always wanted to ask her why she prayed the same prayer, but I figured it was something between her and God.

We were leaving town right as the sun rose. The truck bounced every time it hit a crack. The constant jarring reminded me of how my mom used to rock me and sing to me before bed when I was small. I reclined my seat, put my feet up on the dash, and let the truck rock me to sleep.

I was suddenly surrounded by darkness, the same darkness that haunted all my dreams. It was a suffocating, never-ending pressure that covered my entire body, not allowing me to move. I was paralyzed as usual, but this time it was different. The darkness was the same suffocating pressure, but it was like a black smoke surrounding me, not the usual nothingness. I sucked the thick putrid smoke into my lungs. My muscles tensed to fight against it, to expel it out of my lungs. During my struggle, I could feel each muscle in my body pushing against the darkness, and there was a bitter acidic taste in the back of my throat. My lungs seized, and I spit the putrid smoke out, gasping for air.

"Nicholas, are you okay? Wake up! It's just a dream, hon." Cora was shaking me with her free hand. I took a deep breath. The truck air burned my lungs. I gagged, almost vomiting into my lap.

"Nicholas, your Tic Tacs are on the dashboard."

She didn't wait for me to reach for them. She thrust the pack into my hand. I opened it and dumped almost half the pack into my mouth. Cora cracked my window and I leaned up against it. The combination of Tic Tacs and fresh air helped me recover from the dream. I waited a couple of minutes with my eyes closed and then put my seat up.

"Feeling better?"

I nodded, not able to speak yet.

"Well, let's talk about where we are moving. That should get your mind off of being sick and your bad dreams. You are going to love our new place. Well, not that we didn't love the other places, but this place is not a small town. It's bigger." Cora was talking to me like she was talking to one of her girlfriends about some juicy piece of gossip. She continued, "It actually has a mall, movie theaters, and nice restaurants. Can you believe it?" I would have laughed if I had been feeling better.

Cora bought all of our stuff on the Shopping Channel and the Internet. She even got most of our groceries from the Internet, too. So to have a place big enough for her to shop and still be able to blend in sounded like heaven for her. Yet I knew that even though she had those new places nearby, she still wouldn't use them. And the restaurants were nothing; she could do better herself. She was a gourmet cook. So her excitement over these places was more of a hope and dream of hers than a reality.

"Now, the average class size will be around 400 students, not the 100 you have been accustomed to."

"Why are we moving to a bigger town? I thought that there is less chance of people recognizing us and discovering my secret in a small town."

"Well," said Cora, "I wanted to see how we would do in a bigger town. Plus, you need to be around more people."

This went against everything she had taught me for the last five years. We were supposed to live in a small town, not get close to anyone, and blend in. Cora said that small-town folk know how to keep to themselves.

"Who are you, and what have you done with my aunt?" I said, feeling panicked by the sudden change.

She laughed, never looking away from the road. "Honey, I am the same loving, beautiful, intelligent Aunt Cora you've always known. You are getting older, and you know how to keep our secrets, so it is time for more responsibility."

"Well, how do you know I'm ready? I could have messed up everything last night. I told Andy that we were moving, and then I went to a party and we—"

"Shh, Nicholas," Cora hushed me. "Nothing happened, did it?"

"Something could've happened," I said.

"I have to admit it was hard for me to just stand there and bite my tongue. I really wanted to grab your hand, slam the door, and remind you of everything I've taught you for the last five years." A wave of relief washed over me knowing she wanted to stop me. She continued without seeing the smile on my face. "But, I smiled and let you handle the situation, and see, it worked out just fine. Maybe not how I would have done it," she added, "but it still worked out. Some habits are going to be hard to break." Cora grabbed my hand and squeezed. That was her way of telling me that she loved me and everything was all right.

"Cora, what's the name of the city we are moving to?" I asked.

"Winsor, Illinois, home of the Winsor Cougars."

I recognized the name of the town because my dad used to take us camping there. "Do you think it's okay to move so close to the place that we are hiding from, our home?"

"It's a hundred miles away. We will be just fine."

We were close to the halfway mark of our trip when a rest stop appeared up ahead. We pulled off to eat and to stretch our legs. The sky was bright blue with no clouds to be seen. It looked like a Florida sky. A light breeze helped take the edge off the heat of the early morning sun. Cora grabbed the cooler from behind her seat and walked over to the covered picnic area.

The rest stop looked like every other rest stop I had ever seen. There were only a couple of cars and trucks parked at the far end of the lot. In front of the restrooms was an older couple reading what looked like a map. Cora had unpacked my roast beef, pickle, and mustard sandwich and her PB&J. Both sandwiches looked more like small mountains because of the homemade bread she used for them. We each got a bag of pretzels and a bottle of water.

This had been our moving meal for the last five years. I always thought it was funny because I ate the adult-type sandwich and she ate the kid sandwich. Even though it was on fancy bread, it was still PB&J. This lunch was the beginning of our New Year, our January First without the silly New Year's resolutions. We were starting over, moving. No friends or family to call when we got there to say we arrived safely. This was the beginning, the starting over point.

"Cora, I am going to go wash up."

Cora looked up from her sandwich, surveying the entire area and then centering her attention on the older couple.

"Cora, they are a harmless little old couple."

She smiled. "Go ahead."

I walked over to where the couple was standing. The woman looked very frail. She was holding a map. If a strong breeze came along, I was sure she would be carried away. The man was almost double her size and well built for someone of his age. She made eye contact with me and I smiled.

I walked by them and into the bathroom. The water felt so good over my hands. I splashed some on my face.

"Excuse me."

I looked up with water still in my eyes. I grabbed a paper towel and wiped my eyes. The man from outside was right behind me. I spun around.

"Son, my wife wants to ask you a question before you leave. I told her that you would be out eventually, but she insisted on me coming in here and asking you to come out." I was stunned. "Yeah, I know what you are thinking because I'm thinking the same thing, but you don't stay married to the same woman for 48 years by doing what you want to do." He turned and left the bathroom.

There was no other way to get out of the bathroom except the main entrance. I knew that if I ran into any problem with them, Cora would be within shouting distance. I took a deep breath and walked out to face them. "Excuse me, ma'am. Did you need something?"

"Oh, yes, young man. I asked Herbert to make sure I could ask you a question because I didn't want to bother you unless it was okay."

I looked at her husband, and he shrugged his shoulders and looked back at the map that she had been holding before. Just past him on the highway, a sea green pick-up truck had pulled over on the shoulder. I couldn't see who was in it, but I felt uneasy, like I was being watched. The woman leaned in close to me so only I could hear her, bringing my attention back to her.

"You are him?" she whispered. My heart started to race. "I just wanted to say thank you." She stepped back away from me and smiled. I didn't know what to say, so I smiled and turned around, walking toward Cora who was now standing up, staring at me intently. I glanced over my shoulder to see if the truck was still there, but it was gone. When I reached her, my heart had almost stopped racing.

"What was that about?" She was still standing, staring at the couple that was now walking toward their car.

"Cora, it's okay. They just wanted to know if I knew the best way to get to Cincinnati." Cora's body relaxed after a moment and she sat back down across from me.

I had eaten my entire sandwich and was starting on my pretzels when Cora said, "Hey, look at that!" She was pointing at a large billboard on the highway. There was a group of football players, all in green and gold uniforms and not wearing helmets. In the center of them was a tall, blond player holding a football in his hands, definitely the showcased player on the sign. Above them in large black words was "Cougar Football. Winning isn't everything—it's the ONLY thing." Then it hit me. She was not showing me the billboard to get a laugh out of me because of the corny saying, but to show me that it was the school that I would be attending.

"Winsor Cougars. You're sending me to a school where sports, not just any sport, but *football* is this important?"

"You know I would never send you to a sports factory. Winsor is top in the state for its academics. Just because their sports are good, doesn't mean their academics are sub-par."

She packed up the lunch leftovers and cleaned everything on and under the table because she was agitated. She would have weeded around the shelter if we weren't on a schedule.

We continued on our way. Fifty miles from our lunch stop there was another Cougar football sign with another corny sports saying and the same blond male-model of a football player. After about the fifth sign I said, "You know, I can't wait to see the billboards with the chess team on them or the quiz team. I can see their slogan: 'Studying isn't everything—it's the ONLY thing.'" Cora shot me a dirty look, then giggled.

"Hey! We're here!" Cora pointed to a large wooden sign that said "Welcome to Winsor" with a large rainbow painted on it. Then a metal sign over the road read "Winsor Exit Ahead One Mile on the Right."

"Now remember, the first thing we need to do when we get there is—"

"I know. Unpack the boxes quickly into the house, so we can move the truck to the back of the house, so we don't draw any attention."

"As I was saying before I was so rudely interrupted, we need to unpack, go get some dinner, and then go to bed early to get some rest because we have to register you for school tomorrow at 8:00 a.m. sharp."

"So let me guess. We are moving into a two-story house with elaborate landscaping, a wraparound porch, a long driveway, and a place to hide the truck in back. And, the color of the house is going to be a shade of yellow. I almost forgot, no neighbors close by and surrounded by woods."

Cora didn't answer immediately. She was concentrating on the road signs we were passing. "Well, you are all wrong. The house is beige . . . with some yellow accents," she said with a smile. "Okay, we are getting close . . . 2022 . . . 2024, there it is, 2024 Trailwind Drive."

We pulled into the long driveway. It looked like our last house and all the ones before it, which was scary. It looked like someone ripped our old house off its foundation and dropped it right here. Except for the color and some of the landscaping, it was identical. The sun was muted by the large trees that surrounded the house; very little of the sun's light reached the ground. It was only around 5:30 p.m., but it looked like 8:00. Cora must have loved the fact that the trees blocked our view of our neighbors' houses down the road.

"I can't believe they still have the sign in the yard," Cora said. I knew Cora would have told the realtor weeks ago to take any signs out of the yard. That was part of her plan to get us into our new house with no evidence of a house for sale or a "sold" sign in the yard.

"Nicholas, get out and grab that sign." Whenever she said my name with every syllable heard clearly, she was really mad. I got out and pulled the "just sold" sign with a picture of what I guessed was the realtor out of the ground. I put it on the side of the house away from Cora. Cora was already out and undoing the restraints for our truck. She unlatched it and backed it off the tow ramp. I removed the tow bar and rolled up the back door to start unloading. Cora and I swiftly moved all of the labeled boxes inside to the appropriate room in the house. Then we moved in what little furniture we had. We could definitely show up any moving company. We had this moving thing down to a science.

"Nicholas, will you go around to the front door and put out our door mat?"

I carried the mat to the front of the house. Sitting on our doorstep was a basket of cookies and fruit with a big bow and a note that said "Welcome to the Winds."

Cora had moved the truck to the back of the house. She was already inside when I walked through the back door carrying the big basket. Cora was busy unpacking the kitchen. I laid the basket right in the middle of the kitchen table. She caught sight of the basket out of the corner of her eye, and her face turned a deep shade of red. She continued unpacking, ignoring the large welcome basket on the table. She looked like a kid holding her breath until she got her way. It was funny.

I finished putting everything away that went in the family room and bathrooms. Cora and I had decided earlier to get dinner from Ethan's when we were driving through town. It was one of those chain restaurants that exist in every major city around the U.S., serving the best of American cuisine. I knew that exactly a year from now Ethan's would be my last meal here in this town. It was a very depressing thought to know that nothing here would last longer than a year. We got our food and then returned home. The large basket had disappeared off the kitchen table.

After we ate, Cora said, "Goodnight, Nicholas. I am heading up to bed; see you in the morning." She walked upstairs and disappeared into her room. Cora had already pulled down the shades in the house. I locked all the doors, turned off the downstairs lights, and went to bed.

REGISTRATION
CHAPTER FOUR

The next morning was like all the ones before, but just in a new town. I woke up sick, grabbing my Tic Tacs, and Cora was brewing her favorite Starbucks blend.

"Nicholas, do you want any breakfast? I can whip up an omelet or even a Belgian waffle with some homemade blueberry syrup."

I held up my hand to make her stop talking. "Cora, as long as we've been together, when have I ever wanted to eat breakfast?" I said, praying not to get any sicker.

"Well, I was hoping this new house and town would make you feel better, more relaxed."

"Cora, when I feel well enough to eat in the morning, I promise you'll be the first to know."

"Okay then, let's go get you registered," she said, filling her mug with the rest of the coffee from the pot.

Backing out of the driveway, I saw the welcome basket. It was sticking out of our trash bin. Cora must have thrown it out when I wasn't looking. Typical.

Twenty minutes had passed and we were at the school. "Are you sure you got the right place?" I asked. The sign said "Winsor High School," but it had to be a mistake.

"Nicholas, I know it's bigger than the other schools, but—"

"Are you kidding? It's the size of an amusement park," I interrupted.

"It might be bigger than what you are used to, but it's the same as the rest of the schools. This will help you when you go off to college."

The school was not only big, but it was incredibly landscaped. It had a large fountain in the middle of the parking lot, topped by a bronze statue of a man with a football under his arm. The entire parking lot looked freshly blacktopped, and there were a dozen guys painting lines to make up the individual parking spots. When we drove by a crew painting the lines, I could see that each white divider line was not solid, but a group of words. Each line read, "The Home of the Mighty Winsor Cougars." Along with the painting crews, there were dozens of two-man landscaping crews manicuring the grounds. Colorful shrubs and trees lined the parking lot and school. There were even a couple of people polishing the bronze statue. The only things missing from this school were roller coasters and waterslides.

"Okay now, when we get in there, let me do all the talking," Cora said.

"I know. It's the same as last year and every year before that."

"Well, I'm just making sure you remember, smart-aleck."

We parked in the visitors' lot next to the main entrance. The main entrance was just as elaborate as the rest of the school. It was surrounded by large yellow rose bushes all in full bloom. Right in the center of the walkway was a large flagpole with one of the biggest American flags I had ever seen. We crossed the street and stepped onto the slate-like decorative concrete that led from the visitors' lot to the entrance. We walked up to the large glass doors, and they opened automatically. We walked into the main lobby. For how incredible the outside was, the inside of the school was nothing special. It looked like any typical high school. Actually, my last school was nicer. This one had tacky, orange-patterned carpet that you would find in a bank, and the walls were a mix of brick and metal panels painted a sterile off-white.

"Hello. My name is Cora Keller. I'm here to finish registering my son, Nicholas, for school."

The secretary didn't even look up. She spoke in a monotone voice, like a recording from an old answering machine. "Please fill out the green form to the right, and make sure we have proof of your current address and a current physical if the student is going to participate in any extracurricular activities." Then she continued to type, never looking up at us.

"I already filled out the paperwork and sent it in with the physical a month ago," said Cora.

"Oh, well then," the secretary said, looking up, "please have your son go around the corner and down the hall. The Guidance Office is on the right. He needs to meet with his counselor to work on his class schedule, and then he can get his school ID."

"Oh, we already discussed his schedule and sent that in too, so I guess we can get his ID and be on our way."

"Ms. Keller, he has to meet with his counselor. All new students have to when they enroll here."

"We are in a hurry. We have lots of errands to run today to get settled into our new house." Cora sounded uneasy. I knew she didn't want me to be questioned by anyone when she wasn't around.

"Mom, it will be quick since you already sent everything in." I took her hand. She held on to it tightly and gave me a look that said, "Don't tell them anything, and be nothing special."

I walked around the corner and down the hallway. On the right was a sign that said "Guidance Office." I entered through another glass door.

"Hi, my name is Nicholas Keller. I'm a new student. I'm supposed to meet my counselor." The secretary was very old and almost invisible behind her computer screen. Her thick glasses had a long chain around her neck. She stood slowly, using the desk as a crutch. She was unable to stand up completely.

"Please wait right there, young man. I'll go and see if your counselor, Joy Lemmins, is available to see you." She turned slowly and walked down a narrow hall behind her desk. There were several offices on both sides of the hall. She stopped halfway down the hall, glanced in one of the offices, turned around to face me and walked back to me slowly. "Nicholas, Ms. Lemmins is ready to see you."

I walked past her and down the hall. I looked back, and she was already at her desk working.

"Nicholas Keller, right?" The voice was coming out of the office to my left. "Come on in and shut the door."

The door was covered in white paper and had different, colorful shapes and words all over it. It looked like a bulletin board from a kindergarten classroom. Joy Lemmins was standing behind her desk. She was short and stocky with frizzy blonde hair going everywhere. She had thick red-rimmed glasses that framed her round, pale face. If anyone needed to be outside to get some sun, she did. Her office was outrageously decorated. There were lava lamps, strings of beads, and a large red pleather bean bag chair in the corner. I could smell something like sugar cookies, but I couldn't see where it was coming from. Her office looked like a little kid had decorated it.

"Please get cozy, so we can get to know each other." She pointed at the bean bag chair, but I chose the normal chair in front of her desk. Her lips puckered together and then shifted to one side. I guess she wasn't happy with my choice of seating.

She wasn't bothered long, because she sat down and began to speak with a large, toothy smile. "My name is Joy Lemmins. I'm going to be your counselor and friend here at Winsor High, home of the mighty Cougars." Then she let out a small roar and swiped her hand through the air. I guess she was doing her Cougar impression. Scary.

"So where are you from, Nicholas?"

"We just moved here from Tatesville, Ohio."

"Oh goodness, that sounds like a pleasant place. It must be really nice. Was it hard moving away from your friends? That must have broken your wittle heart."

"No, the move has been okay, and my little heart is just fine." What was wrong with this woman? If Cora was in here, I think she would have smacked her by now.

"So why did you move here?"

"My mom was transferred."

"Okay, what company is that?" She had a piece of paper out; it looked like she was taking notes. What was with all of these questions? She knew all of these answers, because they were in my school file. Cora always made sure to give them plenty of information on me so that people would not ask me these types of questions.

"Excuse me, Ms. Lemmins. Not to be rude, but I thought that we were just going to go over my class schedule."

"Oh yes, we are, deary. I was just trying to get to know you better so we can become pals."

Did she just say she wanted to be pals? The look on my face must have given me away.

"Don't you want to be pals?" she asked, like I had just hurt her feelings.

I ignored her question and looked down, hoping to avoid the question altogether. "Sorry, Ms. Lemmins, I just don't like to talk much. I'm kind of shy."

Joy Lemmins was now peering through her red-rimmed glasses down at some papers on her desk. A minute passed and I began to feel uneasy.

"Sooooo, are you on track with your academics?" Before I could answer, she said, "Yes, yes, yes, you are, you are." She wasn't talking to me, but to herself, and the scary thing was that she was answering back. She pulled off her glasses and squinted at me. "Mr. Keller, your classes look fine. You are taking a very difficult class load, but based on your past transcripts it looks like you can handle it. Hmmmmm, but something is missing, missing, missing." Her voice whined and trailed off.

"Ms. Lemmins, I can get whatever you're missing. My mom is out in the lobby." I stood up.

"No, sit down, Nicky. I don't think your mom can help because she doesn't have what I'm looking for. It's not a piece of paper, but something you haven't done." She put her glasses back on, folded her arms, and leaned back in her large chair, nearly tipping it over.

"I haven't done something, Ms. Lemmins?"

"Extracurricular activities is what you haven't done, my boy. You know, a club, a sport, or something. I know you've moved a lot, but you need to think about college. Great grades are only half of the equation." Joy Lemmins continued to ramble on about what colleges are looking for, but I didn't hear her. She was right. I hadn't really done anything but go to school. Then I remembered something I did.

I blurted out, interrupting her ramblings, "I play football. Well, I try to."

"Oh, football," she said like she just smelled some rotten food. "Well, that's not my first choice, but it's a start." The disappointment in her voice was evident. I bet she was hoping for Glee Club or Science Club. "I believe football started a week ago, but I'll see what I can do."

She picked up the phone. I couldn't believe I hadn't noticed it before; her phone was completely covered with multi-colored gems. It shouldn't have surprised me that her phone looked the way it did, because it matched the rest of the room. Crazy.

"Yes, Gregory. I have a new student here who would like to try out for the football squad. Yes, Gregory, I'm well aware that you already started, but he didn't have a choice. He just moved here with his mommy. Yes, he has his physical. Okay, Gregory, that's super-duper, thanks. Yes, yes, I will let Mr. Keller know." She hung up the phone.

"Nicholas, you are all set. You start football tryouts tomorrow at 8:00 a.m. on the practice fields on the side of the school. If that doesn't work out, I would like for you to consider something a little less barbaric. Oh yes, Gregory wants to make sure you are ready for hard work, because if you're not, he said and I quote, 'Don't waste our time by coming in the morning,'" she said in her best rough man voice, and then she growled.

I stood quickly. "Thanks Ms. Lemmins." I grabbed my ID from her desk and hurried out of her office to escape.

Cora was sitting in the lobby looking extremely anxious. Her legs were bouncing up and down.

"Mom, are you ready?"

Cora looked up at me with relief and met me at the front door. "Why were you in there so long? I was going to come in there and get you. I was worried."

"Don't worry. I avoided her questions and tried to blend in, but . . ."

"But what?"

"I have football tryouts tomorrow," I said, not knowing how she would respond.

Cora waited until we were in the truck to say anything else.

"You know you don't have to try out for the football team here." Cora's words stung. She knew the reason why I played, or more accurately, sat on the bench. Dad had been a great football player, captain of the team. So if I couldn't be with him, at least we could have this in common.

"Listen, Nicholas, football is taken more seriously around here. It's not like the other schools. They actually have cuts."

"Cora, I know I'm not good, but I would like to try." I looked out the window, trying to hide my anger mixed with grief. Thinking about my parents made me sad, reminding me of how much I missed them.

**

"What are you watching, Cora?"

She was standing in the middle of the family room, wearing her apron. She was glued to the TV. "I'm watching *Entertainment Now*." Cora rarely watched TV, especially shows that had to do with celebrities and Hollywood types.

"We have a special guest with us today," the female host said. "You may know him as Doc Hollywood. It's the one and only Dr. Chase Letterby." There was a roar of applause from the audience.

"April, it's a pleasure to be here with you as usual." The doctor looked like he had come out of a soap opera.

"So, Dr. Letterby—"

"April, please call me Chase."

The two of them were clearly flirting with each other, not with words, but with their body language—and all on national TV. It made me sick to watch, but Cora was soaking up every moment.

"Okay, Chase, it may shock our viewers to know that you are not a plastic surgeon."

"Yes, you are right, April." He put his hand on her knee. She giggled. "I am not a plastic surgeon, even though I have had to do some plastic surgery in the past. I do a little of everything."

I looked at Cora and she was hanging on his every word.

"Chase, you are too modest. I have heard you can do everything from taking out tonsils to brain surgery."

He just smiled at her and gave a larger-than-life, fake-sounding belly laugh.

"So how did you get the nickname 'Doc Hollywood'?" she asked.

"April, I guess it's because I have helped some celebrities over the years."

"Is it true that you performed a kidney transplant on Prince Matthew of Wales?"

"Well, April, I don't talk about my patients, but I can tell you that I have met him."

They both laughed.

"Cora, why are you watching this garbage?"

"I knew him from college. He was in med school when I was a freshman, but that was a long time ago." She turned off the TV and walked back to the kitchen. She didn't want to talk.

TRYOUTS
CHAPTER FIVE

Cora dropped me off at school at 7:30 the next morning. I had no idea where to go or who to see for tryouts. There were six large practice fields, some with soccer goals, others with football goals. On the other side of the fields were three baseball diamonds that any minor league team would kill to have. Sitting by itself in the distance beside the large parking lot was a stadium. This stadium looked like it was taken straight out of Ancient Rome for the gladiators to fight in. It was a work of art with its large arches and dramatic pillars and columns.

I walked through the rose-covered front entrance and walked up to the same secretary who was there yesterday. "Excuse me, I'm looking for Gregory. I think he's one of the football coaches. I am here for tryouts."

In the same monotone voice as yesterday, she said, "Coach Greg Hoff is on Practice Field One getting ready for football tryouts. It has several bleachers around it." She looked at her watch and said, "The coaches should be having their coaches' meeting right now by the first set of bleachers."

I walked back out the front entrance and headed toward the practice field with the bleachers. The day was already getting hot and the humidity was creeping in. There was a group of coaches standing off to the side of one of the three large sets of bleachers. By the bleachers was a large sign that said "Practice Field 1." The coaches were all listening to a tall, older man. I stood a couple of feet away from the group of coaches, waiting for him to stop talking so I wouldn't interrupt. One of the younger coaches saw me standing there and walked over to me.

"What do you need?"

"I'm Nicholas Keller. I'm here for tryouts."

"Tryouts started last week. Sorry, you are too late." He began to walk away.

"Excuse me. Coach Greg knew I was coming, and he told me to be here at 8:00 a.m."

He turned back to me. "New recruits need to head over to the white trailer outside the locker room to get their football gear," he said, pointing to the side of the school. "And, that's Coach Hoff to you, not Coach Greg." He walked back to the group of coaches still listening intently to the tall, older coach.

I walked to the side of the school where there was a white trailer right up against the building next to a door that read "Locker Entrance." I looked inside the trailer. Football equipment was scattered around, and I noticed some movement in the back.

"Hello. I'm here for practice. I'm a new student," I shouted into the dark trailer. The movement stopped and someone started to come to the front. He was having a hard time getting

45

to the front because there was no clear path through all the equipment. The man that emerged was as tall as he was wide. He was wearing a green Winsor Football visor soaked with sweat. He had a whistle around his thick neck and a name badge that said "Coach Stenger." He stood there staring at me. He was gasping for air like he had just run a marathon. His shirt was also drenched with sweat.

"Are you here for tryouts?" he wheezed.

I nodded my head yes.

"You know tryouts started a week ago?"

"Yes, I know, but I just moved here. My counselor, Joy Lemmins, talked to Coach Gr—Hoff."

"Well then, that's a different story. What grade are you in?" He took a deep breath.

"I'm going to be a tenth grader."

He went back into the trailer, climbing over and through the piles of football equipment. Inside the trailer it had to be at least ten degrees hotter than outside. A few minutes later, after a lot of banging and several curse words, he made his way back to the front carrying football pads, a helmet, and a white jersey.

"Here, put these on," he said. He was even more out of breath than before.

"Where should I go to change?"

"Right here. Just put the equipment on over your clothes."

"What about lockers?"

"You only get to use the lockers if you are already in the program. You have to earn it." He pulled out a small towel and wiped his red face.

I took my equipment to the side of the trailer out of view from Coach Stenger and started to put on my pads. More guys began to show up over the next five minutes to get their equipment from Coach Stenger.

"Hi, I'm Eric," said a voice behind me.

I turned around. Eric was shorter than me by a couple of inches. His long, brown hair was pulled back into a ponytail, and he had a bronze tan.

"I'm Nicholas."

"So are you new to the school?" he asked.

"Yeah, just moved here. And you?"

"No, lived here all my life, but this year my dad is making me try out for the team. Not that I wanted to, but he used to play for Winsor back in his glory days, so he wants to relive his youth through me." Eric shrugged his shoulders. "Well, it's nice to meet you," he said, turning to put on his equipment.

Coach Stenger blew his whistle. "Let's get out to the field, men! Let's go! Let's go!" He took the lead and trotted slowly out toward the field. We all walked behind his slow-paced jog.

The hot August sun was beating down on the field. It had to be over 100 degrees. I felt like I could have a heat stroke at any moment. The cool water from the on-field water station didn't quench my thirst, but it sure made the heat more bearable. I filled my cupped hands with water and dumped it over my head, providing some relief.

There were coaches all over the practice field running different drills. I was assigned a group and told where to go. In the bleachers, people were actually sitting in the heat, watching players go through drills. While everyone else was doing drills, my group wasn't. We were just running on the side of the practice field. Not only were we not taking part in drills, but we had also all been given football equipment that didn't exactly fit. My equipment had to be at least two sizes too big. The jersey hung down to my knees, and every time I made a sharp turn my helmet would almost come off. It looked like I was wearing my older brother's football equipment. Being only 5-foot, 9-inches and 145 pounds didn't help either. I guess this is how they weed out new recruits. Let the equipment beat us to death.

Coach Stenger blew his whistle. We all jogged over to him.

"Okay, men, we only have five spots for the JV squad this year, and by the end of practice today you'll know who made it and who didn't. Now get out there and show us what you got!" Coach Stenger blew his whistle again with spit flying out of it, and we started to run up and down the side of the field again.

We ran for about thirty more minutes. All of the coaches were now together in the middle of the field, including Coach Stenger.

"Huddle up men!" One of the coaches yelled through a megaphone. We all circled around the group of coaches.

"It's time for the annual JV-varsity scrimmage." There was some cheering. The cheers came from the bigger and older guys who apparently were on the varsity team. Most of the younger guys' faces showed no expression; some looked terrified.

"Hey, don't worry about it, Nicholas. Coach Miller does this once a year. All we have to do is survive," Eric whispered to me.

"Who's Coach Miller?" I asked Eric.

"He's the tall coach in the middle holding a clipboard. He's the varsity coach, a legend around here. It's his way or the highway. Did you see the billboards on the way here?"

I nodded my head yes.

"Those billboards were given to Coach Miller by some wealthy alumni to promote his team all over the state."

"Okay coaches, break up the guys into offense and defense. Let's see what they got!" yelled Coach Miller in a deep, powerful voice.

Coach Stenger divided the group of us into offense and defense and put us with the JV squad. I was put on defense. I didn't know how he was dividing us up because we didn't do any specific drills to determine our offensive or defensive skills.

Those of us from Coach Stenger's group stood out because we weren't wearing the nice green practice jerseys that the JV players had on or the incredible gold practice jerseys that the varsity players were wearing. We all were wearing plain old, dirty white jerseys. The JV offense was the first to play against the varsity defense. I was lucky to be with the defensive squad, so at least I could watch first and try to learn something before I went out there to get killed. Eric was on the field playing quarterback in his white jersey, and every time he touched the ball, the varsity defense ran over him, usually leaving him flat on his back.

"Switch!" someone yelled on the sideline. Both units came off the field. It was time for me to get in there, or at least that is what I thought. I stood on the sidelines waiting for my chance, waiting for the coach to put me in. Fifteen minutes had gone by and I still was standing on the sideline. I guess I should have expected this. It was my first day and the rest of our group had been practicing for a week already, if not longer.

"Keller!" shouted Coach Stenger. "Get out there and play middle linebacker."

I ran onto the field. My big helmet bounced around, making it hard to always see. I had no idea where I was supposed to stand to play middle linebacker. After three years of football, I still had very little knowledge of the game. I stood in the center and waited, hoping I was close to the right spot.

"Hut, hut, set, hike," the varsity quarterback yelled. He dropped back and disappeared behind the enormous wall of guys protecting him. Then, out of nowhere, I was hit in the head and knocked to the ground. My helmet popped off immediately. Several hands helped me up; one handed me my helmet.

One guy said, "Don't worry about that. They've been doing that to us for the last twenty minutes." I looked over at the varsity players.

"Man, I didn't see him until I was running over him. They suck!" I recognized who was speaking. It was the tall blond from the Cougar Football billboards. He had his helmet off, showing them how he had knocked me to the ground and using his own helmet to show how mine came off. They were all laughing with him, at me. My body started to become tense; my muscles started to seize. I could feel my muscles pushing and pulling against each other, and then acid erupted in my stomach, sending an intense bitter taste to the back of my throat. My lungs seized and I coughed, gasping for air.

"Okay, let's do it again!" a coach yelled.

Instead of getting sick from the taste, it made me even angrier than I already was. Somewhere in my stomach was a burning sensation, a fire of sorts. It was like nothing I had ever experienced. My heart was pounding so loudly I could barely hear anything around me. Thump, thump, thump. I became very focused. The new sensation in me stopped. Now, all I wanted to do was go after that billboard boy and hurt him for embarrassing me like that.

"Set, fox, 18, set, hike," he yelled and then disappeared again. My muscles tightened so hard, they felt like they were going to pull away from my bones. I couldn't see him, but I knew he was there, right in front of me. I saw a small opening between two of his bodyguards.

I lunged through the hole with such quickness that neither of them moved. He was in my sight. I was moving so fast that he didn't have time to react. I hit him with all of my strength, drove him to the ground, and ran back to where we huddled up before the play. Green jerseys swarmed all over me, jumping up and down, yelling.

"Varsity on the line. You owe me two suicides for that hit Oliver took," Coach Miller yelled.

I jogged over with the rest of the JV squad. Everyone was hitting me on the helmet saying, "Good job! Nice hit!" Coach Stenger gave me a high five. The other coach walked over to us.

"Well, I'm glad Joy called me yesterday, Keller. Great hit. Okay men, good job! Take a knee and watch varsity run; then hit the showers. Good practice."

The bitter taste of acid still lingered and my muscles ached.

We watched varsity run their suicides. When they were finished, we all headed toward the lockers. I jogged over to the white trailer to take off my equipment.

I was so tired that it was hard to take off the oversized equipment. I pulled my shoulder pads and jersey off at the same time. There standing in front of me, blocking out the sun, was a winded Oliver. I felt like I was in *Jack and the Beanstalk*, and I was Jack staring up at the giant.

"Next time," he poked me, "it won't be that easy, JV runt." He pushed past me, and the newfound fire inside me burned red-hot.

SPECTATORS
CHAPTER SIX

"Keller, nice tackle," Coach Hoff yelled from the sideline. They must have seen something in me they liked because I made the JV team after only one day of tryouts. Eric says it's because I flattened Oliver. It must have been, because running the sideline during tryouts wouldn't impress anyone. Eric also made the team but swears his dad paid Coach Hoff.

"Set, hut, hut, hike," Eric yelled from across the line of guys. Eric got the ball and dropped back to throw it. I ran through the JV guys like they were stuck in mud and hit Eric square in the numbers before he could do anything. The ball went flying out of his arms and he hit the dry, hard field with a thud.

"I don't care how much my dad paid Coach Hoff; he should have cut me because getting hit by you in every practice sucks." Eric was slow to get up. I helped him the rest of the way up.

"Good job, men. Hit the showers," Coach Hoff yelled. I had been getting a lot more playing time over the last couple of weeks. I still had no idea what all of the plays were or where to stand on the field, but they kept putting me out there. For the last three years of football, I had never stepped onto the field to do anything other than drills, but now I was part of the team. I had changed—well, not physically, but on the inside. When Oliver laughed at me, it did something to me. It took everything in me to control it at times, especially during practice.

We jogged to the locker rooms. We were on Practice Field Two. It was a lot smaller than Practice Field One, which was the field that varsity used for practice. It wasn't dry like ours was. Their practice field was watered daily, and the lush green grass was nicely groomed with fresh lines painted on it every morning. Every day we had to jog by it to get back to the lockers to change. The three bleachers along the varsity practice field were always filled. It was unbelievable that people would show up on these hot days to watch a football practice—not even a game, a practice. I was on the team, and I wished that I didn't have to be out in the sun, in the scorching August heat. People took pictures, and there was always at least one news crew filming the practice. Wow, this town needed to get a life. We had just jogged past the bleachers when Coach Miller called me over. Eric was next to me and pushed me in the direction of Coach Miller. "You are busted, Keller," he said, running on.

Coach Miller was an imposing figure. For a man in his sixties, he looked like he could play pro football. He was watching the varsity team practice. I jogged up next to him.

"We've been watching you and we like what we see. For the next scrimmage against Moeller, we want you to play with varsity." I was stunned. "How does that sound to you?"

"G-G-Great, Coach! Thanks!" I said, almost bursting with excitement.

"And, Keller, don't let me down." He looked into my eyes.

"I won't, Coach."

Suddenly, I heard a loud metallic crack and spun around. One of the large light towers used by the TV stations was falling out of the bleachers and heading right for us. I pushed Coach Miller out of the way as it crashed and sent pieces of glass and metal everywhere.

"What are you trying to do, kill us?" Coach Miller yelled into the stands. "I am going to ban whoever is responsible for this."

Several news crew members scurried out of the stands. Through the bleachers and the smashed light tower, I saw the same sea green truck that I had seen at the rest stop. I moved to see it better, but it sped away.

"You okay, Keller?"

"I'm fine, Coach."

"Okay then, go get cleaned up while I deal with these hooligans."

I sprinted back to get changed. I couldn't believe I was almost killed. But, at least I was going to break my three-years-of-not-playing streak, and I was going to do it playing with varsity. JV hadn't had a scrimmage yet. Their first one was the same day as varsity's scrimmage. I was looking forward to playing with JV, but the chance to play with varsity was a dream come true.

When I got off the bus, I ran the ten-minute walk to my house. I was so excited to tell Cora the incredible news. I bounded up the walkway and through the front door, slamming it with a loud thud. Cora came running down the stairs.

"Is everything okay? Nicholas, what's the matter?"

"Nothing's the matter. Everything is great. I think I might actually play in the next scrimmage!"

"That's wonderful!" Cora was excited too, because for the last three years she had sat in the stands waiting for something to cheer about. Now she would get her chance. "That is great news!"

"Well, it's just a scrimmage, but I have to start somewhere."

"Nicholas, I am so proud of you."

"Wait, the best part is Coach Miller, you know, the varsity coach, told me he wants me to scrimmage with them!"

Cora's face turned to stone. The air in the room felt like it was sucked out. All of the excitement was gone.

"How can you go from not playing the last three years, to playing with varsity this year? You're just a tenth grader. Is the team really that bad?"

"Gee, thanks! What happened to the excitement?"

She took a deep breath. "No, it has nothing to do with you. I mean, you have never played in a game before at the smaller schools, and now they want you to play varsity for a school that is known for its football team. There will be," she paused and took another deep breath, "a lot of people watching you."

"I finally feel like I fit in somewhere," I said, "and this is how you congratulate me. First you tell me that it would be impossible to make the team, and now that I've made the team and will actually play, you're not even happy."

Cora didn't say anything. She walked into the living room and sat on the couch. She crossed her arms and stared out the front window. Her legs were bouncing around more than her usual nervous twitch.

After a minute, she spoke in a very calm voice. "Nicholas, I'm sorry for how I acted. I am so proud of you—you know that! We will make this work somehow. I can't wait to cheer for you during the game." She got up and walked over to me. I was still standing in the hall rooted to the ground. She gave me a big hug and walked into the kitchen.

I wasn't buying the "I'm proud of you" routine. Why was she acting this way? She was so happy at first, but as soon as I mentioned varsity, everything changed. But why? I knew there would be more people watching, but there would be people watching the JV scrimmage, too.

I retreated to my room after a long, hot shower to escape Cora. She was busy cleaning the already clean house, and from the smell of it, she was cooking an "I'm sorry" dinner. I couldn't stop being angry at her. Nothing I tried to do or think of made me feel any better. I just wanted to be mad. The fire in me was feeding off my anger. I turned on some Simon and Garfunkel. It was my mom's favorite. She would listen to them when she wanted to relax, and I needed to relax. My stomach muscles were in knots from being angry.

The pitter-patter of rain against the window took me by surprise. It was the first time it had rained since we moved. The rain would help the brown, withered plants get back some of their life. Hopefully, it would do the same for me.

There were several claps of thunder off in the distance, and the rain intensified. I turned my music off so I could listen to the storm. When we lived in Oklahoma there were storms every night during the summer. They would put me to sleep.

I turned off my desk lamp, which was in front of my window, so I could see the lightning better. The thick, swirling black clouds that reached up to heaven rolled toward our house. It was getting darker outside. The storm rolled over the top of our house. The black clouds swirled around in the sky until it became pitch black. It was as dark as a starless night, and it was only 6:00 p.m.

The lightning lit up our small backyard and the woods lining it like fireworks on the Fourth of July. I noticed there was something just beyond the tree line. Another flash of light illuminated the tree line again, exposing two silhouettes. There were two people standing down in the trees. I knew somehow that these people, these spectators, were watching me. I didn't know how or why I knew this.

My heart began to race. I wasn't scared, but my body was reacting to the sight of them. A crooked, long bolt of lightning came racing out of the sky toward the two. Right as the lightning approached them, everything slowed down before me. It was like watching a movie in slow motion. I could see the lightning make its way slowly toward the ground with all of its jagged edges shooting off in different directions. The two disappeared back into the woods right as the lightning struck a tree near where they had been standing, shattering the tree, leaving only charred remains. I wanted to race into the woods after them to see who they were. But, my curiosity would have to wait because I had developed a sudden painful headache that made me dizzy. I crawled into bed to relax and recover, listening to the storm, wondering who they were. My head pounded.

ANGEL

CHAPTER SEVEN

The day of the scrimmage had arrived. I hurried and ate my lunch, which was of five-star restaurant quality.

"My scrimmage is at 1:00 p.m. at the high school," I reminded Cora, who was sitting with me at the table.

"I know. I'll be there," she said, not looking away from her newspaper propped up in front of her.

"I just want to make sure that you don't go to Moeller, because that's where JV is playing."

"I am well aware of where you are playing today." I could tell that Cora was still unhappy, but I wasn't going to worry about her because today was the day that I had been waiting for my whole life; I get to play in a football game just like my dad. He would have been so proud. His son was playing varsity.

"How are you getting to school?" Cora's voice interrupted my daydream.

"Eric is picking me up," I told her.

"Isn't he on the JV squad?"

"Yes, but he has to take the bus to Moeller from the high school."

"No, I meant is he old enough to have his license?"

"Yes, his birthday was in June."

Cora went on reading, seeming to be content with Eric taking me to football. "So where are you meeting him?"

Two loud thuds came from the front door. I had told him where we lived. I had forgotten another one of our rules: never tell anyone where we live. I jumped up quickly to get out the door before I was scolded.

"Before you go, finish your juice. It's hand-squeezed," Cora said to me, pointing at the cup of juice. I drank it and quickly ran to the door.

"Nicholas, please do not tell anyone else where we live, and no more breaking the rules. Do I make myself clear?"

"I won't. I'm sorry."

"You better not or we will move. We can't take any more risks."

"Okay. See ya, Cor—Mom!" I shouted as I opened the door.

"Let's go, Keller. I don't want to be late." Eric had on his green JV game jersey. I was wearing the gold game jersey that Coach Miller gave me.

"Nice jersey. I can't believe you are playing with varsity. Well, I better get the big star to his debut."

I opened the door to his old black VW Beetle, which was in mint condition. "I don't think I'm actually going to play. I'm probably a backup just in case someone gets hurt."

Eric smiled and turned up his car stereo. A new song came on the radio. "Keller is going to be a varsity rock star," he sang, replacing the words with his own. It would have been annoying, but Eric was funny.

I got dressed in the pitiful JV locker room down the hall from the varsity locker room. It was weird being the only one in a gold jersey in a sea of green. Eric wouldn't stop talking about me playing varsity.

"Dude, you are so lucky to be playing with varsity, and to think you are only a sophomore. No sophomore or freshman has ever played on varsity, not even Oliver. When Coach Miller started coaching he made the rule that no underclassman would play on varsity no matter what. It is going to piss off Oliver to see you playing varsity, which is awesome. You nailed him during tryouts, and now you are up on varsity. This can't get any better. The only thing that would be better is if I could see his face when you walk into their locker room."

I had noticed how much Eric liked to hear himself talk. I don't think he needed to actually have anyone around him to talk, but unfortunately he had half of the locker room listening to his every word.

"Listen, it's just a scrimmage," I said, hoping to shut him up. Was Eric right? Was I really the first underclassman to play varsity? No way! There had to have been someone else.

Coach Hoff walked into the locker room wearing his typical short grey coaching shorts and his green polo shirt with clipboard in hand. "Let's go, team, out to the bus. We leave in five."

Everyone stood up and filed out. Eric was the last one through the doors and yelled back to me, "Hit some Moeller varsity chumps for me, Keller! See ya, star!"

I got up and headed toward the varsity locker room down the hallway. Coach Miller was standing outside of the locker room. He looked at me walking slowly.

"Keller, if you don't hurry up, I am going to send your butt back to JV." I jogged to where he was standing and walked through the double doors.

The entire team was sitting in plush green and gold chairs, watching one of the coaches drawing up plays on the chalkboard in the front. I walked along the wall to the back of the room. All eyes were on me. I searched for an empty chair in the back. Oliver didn't look away until I was in the back and sat down. No one could stare at me all the way in the back, not even Oliver.

Looking around I realized that I had never been in the varsity locker room before. It was incredible. The school colors, green and gold, were everywhere. Each of the varsity players had his own polished green locker with his name engraved on a gold plaque above it. The lockers were big. I could stand in one easily with room to spare. The JV lockers were each the size of a small bread box. I could barely fit my clothes into them.

Instead of benches, each locker had its own green and gold chair. Throughout the locker room there were big flat screen TVs. I couldn't believe that this was a high school locker room; it had to be a pro-football team locker room. The

JV locker room looked like a janitor's closet compared to this mecca of football. Now I knew why Eric couldn't stop talking about me playing with varsity.

Coach Miller walked up to the front of the room. He talked about the defensive plan we were going to use against Moeller. Coach Miller had been the head coach for the last thirty years and had won seventeen division championships and eight state championships. Cora had given me the run down about the football program and Coach Miller after I made the team.

Coach Miller is a legend in Winsor and the whole state of Illinois. He was the only shining star on Winsor's team when he was in high school. He set a bunch of state records himself. He was offered dozens of scholarships to most of the college football powerhouses around the country to play linebacker, but he turned them all down. His dad wasn't well and his mom had died years earlier, so he decided to stay close to his dad. He worked at the local apple farm, and most importantly, he joined the volunteer fire department. Winsor only had a volunteer fire department because of how small the town was back then. While serving at the fire department, he saved dozens of people from fires. So not only is he a legend, but a true hero.

Coach Miller continued drawing elaborate defensive plays, which I didn't understand at all. JV taught me the basics and I barely understood those. After fifteen minutes of talking, Coach Miller abruptly went down on one knee and bowed his head, looking at the ground. The room went quiet and everyone bowed their heads, too. I watched him intently, not knowing what he was doing, but as quickly as he went down on one knee, he was back standing on his feet.

"This is our house. No one comes into our house without getting a black eye!" Then all of the players jumped up, yelling and screaming.

"Boys, five minutes, then out on the field to stretch," he said.

All of the coaches walked out of the locker room following Coach Miller. The locker room was still going nuts with excitement. Some players were head-butting each other; others were hitting each other's shoulder pads. I felt like a fish out of water. What was I supposed to do now? I should probably get out of here and go to the field before being spotted again. I slid along the wall toward the door to escape this madness.

"So look what we have here."

I turned and saw the only thing in this palatial locker room that could tarnish it, Oliver Rails. He walked down the middle of the locker room like he owned the place, talking to anyone who would listen.

"So there's a JV player in our locker room. Are you lost, little boy? The JV hole is at the end of the hall." Now all of the guys in the locker room were listening to him. I just stared at him, not sure what to do.

"So are you lost *and* deaf?" he sneered with a twisted laugh.

I was only ten feet from the door. I could make a break for it and hope for the best, or I could stand my ground. My heart started to pound. Then out of nowhere, I spoke. "I am supposed to be here. I am playing with varsity today." I said it loud enough for everyone to hear.

"No way. You can't play with us," yelled someone from the back of the locker room.

"I think you got it wrong, JV. No ninth or tenth grader has ever played on varsity, even during a scrimmage. Especially not a little punk like you," Oliver said with a big grin, and he poked me in the shoulder.

From all around the locker room there was laughter, and some of the guys were yelling things like, "Go get him, Oliver!" and "Show him who's boss."

"So the only way to be on varsity is to be a pretty boy up on a billboard?" The words left my mouth before I could stop them. The locker room fell silent. Oliver was now just inches away from my face. He was so close I could tell he was chewing some sort of mint gum. His face twisted in anger.

Someone yelled, "Hit him." The locker room started to chant "Hit him! Hit him!" He turned back to acknowledge the chant. Oliver was looking away from me, and with a jerk he swung both of his arms back around to push me up against the wall.

Then it happened. Everything slowed around me like it had on the night with the lightning and the two people watching me during the storm. Oliver was turning to hit me with both hands, but his movement was in slow motion. His entire body was blurred like I was looking at him under water, and his movement was causing a wake in the air. Everything became almost still. I moved off to the side of his arms to avoid being hit in the chest. Then time resumed.

Oliver went right past me, stumbling into the wall and falling back onto the floor. The room was quiet; you could hear the music from someone's headphones in the background. Oliver stood up and brushed his long golden hair out of his face.

"A slippery little shit, aren't you?" He brushed the rest of his hair out of his eyes. "Well, JV, whatever reason you're here, you aren't welcome." He pushed by me. He walked back toward his locker, throwing chairs out of his way and cursing under his breath.

I walked out of the locker room and took a deep breath of relief. I suddenly felt very sick. I grabbed my Tic Tacs that I had stashed in my pants and ate a couple.

Once outside, I walked to the stadium's main gate. Moeller's bus was already parked out front. I walked over the track, which was covered by plywood to protect it from our cleats. The rest of the team was on the field a few minutes after me. Coach Miller put me with the linebackers to stretch. Stretching went quickly and the scrimmage began. I stood in the back, hoping to avoid Oliver and any of the other players. I had no idea why I was here.

The second quarter started and we were losing 0 to 7. The huge scoreboard in the end zone was showing instant replays of the last play. I was mesmerized with how good the scoreboard screen looked. It had a clearer picture than our TV at home.

"Keller, Keller? Where are you?" Coach Miller was searching the crowd of players for me. "Keller, quit hiding and get your butt out there! Go in and play middle linebacker."

I put on my helmet and ran out onto the field. I ran by the dejected varsity player who just got replaced by me. I ran up to the huddle. The guys in the huddle stared at me like I was the water boy or the mascot who accidentally ran onto the field during the game.

"Listen up! They're killing us! This is embarrassing! Look at me! Forget about JV and do your damn job!" Chad, the defensive captain, was standing in front of the huddle, relaying the play the coaches were calling in from the sidelines. Chad was massive. He looked more like a pro-wrestler than a high school football player. "Fire 53, ready, break!" What was he talking about? I had no idea what "fire 53" meant. What was I supposed to do?

I ran up and stood where I normally did with JV. Chad was to my right. Maybe if I stayed close enough to him, it wouldn't show that I had no idea what I was doing.

"Red 18, red 18!" the opposing quarterback yelled in a steady cadence across from us.

"Liz, liz, liz," Chad yelled and the line shifted left. I didn't move; I was frozen solid, not really sure what I was doing.

"Hut, hike!"

It was a running play right up the middle. I was not in the right spot. A player from the other side lowered his head and hit me, knocking me to the ground. The running back breezed right by me and was taken down ten yards past me. The whistle blew and the play was over.

I looked over at the sideline and there he was. Oliver was pretending to be me again, acting like I was a tree or something rooted to the ground. A group of guys around him were laughing. Down the sideline from him, Coach Miller was yelling. I knew it was directed at me. I ran back to the huddle determined not to let that happen again.

"Come on guys! They are running all over us!" Chad said.

"If JV was in his right position, we would have stopped him. They should send Josh back out to take his spot," said one of the guys on the end of the huddle.

"Yeah, right. We haven't been able to stop them with Josh, so let's focus!" Chad looked to the sideline and got the play. "45 weak pass. On two, ready, break!"

Chad looked at me and mouthed the words, "Just hit someone." The team settled into their positions. I ignored everyone else and I walked up to the middle. Out of the corner of my eye I could still see Oliver making fun of me. My muscles tensed and the fire smoldered.

"Mark 85, mark 85, hut, hike!"

The other team's quarterback got the ball and dropped back to pass. I ran through the opposing team and hit the quarterback around the midsection right as he turned to throw the ball. I jumped up and ran back to our side. It felt good to get my frustration out. I was now eager to hear the quarterback yell hike again so I could hit someone else.

It was halftime. We ran across the track to the lockers that were below the home bleachers. I didn't talk to anyone. I just sat and listened to Coach Miller yell. I didn't pay much attention to what he was saying. My heart was racing, and I could feel the blood pumping through my veins. I also had that horrible bitter taste in my mouth. Was my anger the trigger to making me a better football player, or was it something else? If my dad was here, I bet he could tell me what was happening.

Toward the end of the fourth quarter, I hit the running back in mid-stride, forcing a fumble. Chad recovered the ball and I heard the crowd cheer. For the first time, I noticed that people were watching us. The stands were packed on both sides of the field. It was amazing how loudly they were cheering, and I was oblivious to all of it.

I jogged back to the sideline. I remembered that Cora was in the stands somewhere. I searched all around the outer part of the stands for her because that's where she would normally sit, but instead I saw something that nearly knocked me off my feet—an angel, the most beautiful creature I had ever seen. She took my breath away. The sight of her made me lightheaded. Her long black hair was radiant, framing her face in such a way that it would make the Mona Lisa jealous. I didn't know anything about her, but seeing her made me want to know everything about her. I felt peace for the first time in a long time just by looking at her, the type of peace you get from knowing everything was going to be all right. This angel instantly became everything to me. But how? It didn't matter to me; nothing else mattered but her.

The euphoric feeling I was experiencing was interrupted when I bumped into a player on the sideline. I lost my balance and knocked over a table of drinks. I had turned around for just thirty seconds, but when I turned back toward the stands, she was gone. I searched the entire stands frantically for her, but I didn't find her. Was she a dream or an illusion? Was she just something else that I couldn't explain?

I then spotted Cora off to the side of the home bleachers, but she was not by herself. She was talking to a well-dressed older couple, and whatever they were discussing looked serious. Cora never talked to anyone out in public for any length of time.

The horn sounded to signal the end of the game, and both teams walked across the field to shake hands. A couple of the opposing coaches told me how well I played, but my thoughts were consumed by the mystery girl.

I followed the team to the locker room. Coach Miller was upset. He was yelling before we all were seated. All I could make out was, "Offensively we were pathetic. We barely won the game 17 to 7. If it weren't for the defense scoring twice, we would have lost."

I waited a couple more minutes to see if he said anything to me. I slipped out of the locker room to go get changed. This time no one looked at me. I got my equipment off, put my clothes on, and sat on a bench with my face in my hands to relax for a minute. My head was spinning. So much had happened in such a short period of time: Oliver not being able to hit me, Cora's heated discussion. But the thing that I couldn't get out of my head was the girl in the stands, my angel. I only saw her face for a couple of seconds, but I knew every detail of it like I had known her all my life. Who was she?

"Keller."

Startled, I jumped up and swung around ready for a fight.

"Relax, son." Coach Miller was right behind me.

"I'm sorry, Coach, for slipping out during your talk."

"No problem, son. Sit down."

I turned around and sat back down on the bench facing him.

"Keller, you had a great game. I'm proud of you. Most players could not have done what you did today. You handled the pressure with such ease. Come to think of it, most people could not handle that kind of pressure. I know you don't know our defense yet, but you will. Keep it up!"

PARTY
CHAPTER EIGHT

A couple minutes after Coach Miller walked out, the JV team came in. The mood was solemn; no one was talking. They looked like someone had died. Eric saw me and his solemn expression changed to a big smile.

"So, Eric, how was the scrimmage?" I asked him first before he could quiz me about the game. I was expecting to hear they lost.

"We tied, can you believe it? We tied. Why keep score if tying is a possibility? You should have seen Coach Hoff. He acted like a mad man—it was classic. He stormed across the field yelling at Moeller's coaches, demanding overtime. Three of our assistant coaches had to pull him back to our side and get him on the bus. Coach was still yelling from the window of the bus as we pulled away. 'Someone has to win,' he yelled. 'That's why you keep score. I don't care if it was just a scrimmage. Ever heard of overtime, you twits?'"

"Then why is everyone looking so upset?" I asked.

"Well, Coach Hoff wasn't done. He yelled at us the whole way home."

"Why was he so upset with you? You guys weren't the reason it ended that way."

"Coach Hoff said that we should have never been tied with such an inferior team in the first place. We should have killed them. So I'm wearing my track shoes to our next practice because I'm expecting a lot of running." Eric's smile returned to his face. "So did you dominate today or what?"

"We won 17-7."

"Did you play?"

"I played for three quarters."

"No way! You're the man!" Eric, wearing just his game pants, jumped up on the bench and yelled, "Keller played three quarters today with varsity and kicked some serious butt."

He was pumping his arms up and down. The atmosphere in the locker room changed instantly. Everyone started yelling and carrying on like they were at a party. If Eric wasn't my ride home, I would have snuck out the back door.

"Keller, we have some celebrating to do. You are coming tonight, right?" Eric jumped off the bench, landing in front of me.

"Coming where?" I asked.

"Are you kidding? To the quarry party!"

"What's a quarry party?"

"Well, it's *the* party." He rolled his eyes.

"I know it's a party, but what's a *quarry* party?"

"Twice a year there's a party at the old abandoned Filler's Rock Quarry outside of town," Eric explained.

"Are we allowed to be there?" I asked.

"No, not exactly, but Filler's Quarry has been shut down for a long time. There are over 1,000 acres of quarry, so each year the varsity football captain picks where in the quarry the party will be held. This year Oliver has picked a part of the quarry where there is a cool man-made lake with a long dock. This place is great for the rite of passage." When Eric said "rite of passage" his eyes lit up.

"Eric, what's the rite of passage?"

Before I could finish the question he started talking. He was just dying for me to ask him. "The varsity captain also picks a player from the team to compete in some sort of challenge called the 'rite of passage.' Last year the varsity captain, David Jones, set up a cage. He filled it with water to make mud. Then he put a greased pig in it, and the first one to catch it won. At the first party he challenged his twin brother, John Jones, and at the second party he challenged Oliver.

"There are two of these parties?"

"Yeah, there are two; I already said that. Come on, Keller. Keep up. One in the summer and one in the spring. At the summer party he challenged his brother, like I said. It was more like a pro-wrestling match between the brothers. But, when Oliver was challenged at the spring quarry party, it was definitely a match to see who could win. Oliver was a sophomore and David was the outgoing senior captain. The spring party is when the senior captain challenges the next possible captain, or if he is a junior captain, he challenges the next strongest player to prove he is still worthy of being the captain."

I looked around. Everyone was hanging on his every word, and Eric loved every bit of it. Eric continued, "When David and Oliver started the challenge they both tried to corner the pig, but when David realized that Oliver was faster, he tried to wrestle Oliver away from the pig. But David wasn't able to catch Oliver; he was too fast for him. Finally, Oliver got past David and pinned the pig against the fence, catching it. I'm sure Oliver has something crazy in store for one of the varsity guys tonight. I think he challenged Chad."

Eric took a deep breath and looked back at me. "So what time do you want me to pick you up?"

Everyone was staring at me. Unfortunately, this time blending in with the crowd involved me going to a party. If not, it would definitely draw more unwanted attention.

"What time does it start?" I asked.

"9:00," Eric answered.

"Pick me up at 8:00."

"Great! We need to make sure we get there early enough to get front row seats for the night's festivities."

On the car ride home, I thought of how to convince Cora to let me go, that I *had* to go because it was the only way for me to blend in. To my surprise, Cora agreed with me with no arguing or convincing. She even threw in "Have fun at the party," and "You did great in the game today!" I thought about asking her who she had been talking with in the stands, but instead I ran upstairs quickly to get ready, not wanting to press my luck.

As much as I wasn't looking forward to going, a part of me was curious to see what this quarry party was all about. I had never been to a party before except for the one that Andy and I had crashed before I moved here. But, this time I was actually invited.

Cora prepared a sandwich and left it on the table with a note saying, "Have fun tonight. Don't stay out too late. Love, Cora." I ate the sandwich in my room and listened to music until Eric showed up.

Eric blew his car horn right at 8:00 p.m. I ran down the stairs and out the front door, just in case Cora had changed her mind. Eric was sitting in his Beetle with his music blaring. The base was thumping and rattling his little car. After five minutes in there, I couldn't take it anymore. I turned down the music.

"How do you still have your hearing after listening to music so loud?"

"Did you say something?" he asked, pretending like he couldn't hear me.

He turned the music back up again and started to head bang. He definitely had the right hair for it. His long brown hair danced around to the beat of the music. I wished he'd pay more attention to the road than the music.

We spent the drive listening to the deafening rock music. When we got to the first gravel road outside of town, right off the main street, Eric turned down the radio. There was a worn out wooden sign that read, "Filler's Quarry." Eric pulled out a piece of paper. On it were handwritten directions and a crudely drawn map.

"What's that?" I asked.

"Directions to the party."

"You need a map?"

"Yeah, there are over a hundred roads throughout the quarry and as many entrances. This makes it impossible for anyone like parents or cops to crash it without a map, even though almost everyone in town knows we're having the party tonight. These quarry parties have been going on since my dad played football. I think my dad was jealous. He would have come if I'd invited him or if he'd found the map. I had to hide it in my boxers. He's having a midlife crisis."

We drove up and down gravel roads that all looked the same for ten minutes. Never once did I see a sign of another car, but just when I thought we were completely lost, I saw the glow of lights up ahead. There were at least a hundred cars parked all around a lake. Eric turned up his music again and we rattled into a parking spot. I got out quickly.

A group of JV football players were standing next to an old wooden dock that reached to the middle of the lake. This was no average lake that you would find out in the woods. It had been dug out and filled with water over time. The lake was enormous. There were a couple hundred people surrounding the lake next to the parked cars. There were several large lights on poles around the lake and some stretched over the water. The water was grey and murky. There were piles of rocks all around the lake, blocking all of the other possible entrances. There was only one way in and out.

Eric and I walked up to the group of JV guys at the end of the dock. Eric blurted out, "So what's the rite of passage and who did he challenge?"

A guy I barely recognized from the team spoke up.

"Oliver challenged Chad, and you will never believe what they have to do! Oliver got an old car and they are going to drive down the dock. The last one to jump out before the car hits the water wins!"

"No way!" Eric said. "The dock will barely fit a car. Where are they supposed to land when they jump?"

"They are going to jump into the water."

"No way!" Eric said again, even more excited. "Where did he get the car?"

"He bought the car from the junk car dealer in Alexandria. You know, the one with the big chicken out front."

In an even louder voice, Eric shouted, "This is going to be the best rite of passage challenge ever!"

By the time it was 9:00, it looked like most of the school had shown up. I stayed with the pack of JV guys who were standing close to the dock, so I wouldn't be noticed in the crowd. All of the varsity squad was standing where the dock connected to the gravel road. It was incredible that this many people were here.

"Eric, what do we do now? Are we just supposed to stand around and wait for this challenge thing?" I asked.

He looked at me shocked. "Of course and . . . we look for hot girls!" He brushed his hair out of his eyes like he was in a shampoo commercial.

There was a loud sound from behind us. I swung around, and at the entrance to the lake was a late model primer grey car with one of the headlights out. The car revved its engine and backfired. Thick black smoke plumed out of the tail pipe. The guys around the dock scattered. The crowd began to cheer.

The car's wheels began to spin, shooting rocks backward. For so much revving and spinning of its wheels, it didn't go very fast.

As soon as the car hit the dock, both car doors flew open. The car looked like a plane going down the runway. The car was quickly running out of dock to drive on. A group of varsity players raced behind the car. With about half of the dock left, the passenger in the car jumped and landed feet first into the water with a big splash. The driver was still inside. Half of the guys chasing the car stopped to help Chad up onto the dock. Then, with barely any dock left before the car plunged into the water, Oliver dove out of the car head first, entering the water in a perfect dive. The car went off the edge of the dock and hit the water with a large splash. The car's engine gurgled and sputtered, then died. The car sank into the depths of the lake in a matter of seconds.

The crowd roared to life. The rest of the varsity team pulled Oliver out of the water. He threw both arms up in the air, and the crowd cheered even louder like he was their king who was about to address his loyal subjects.

Oliver was eating up the attention. I thought I could actually see his head getting bigger. I looked around the lake at the cheering crowd. I noticed one person who wasn't cheering in the middle of a group of girls. She was very noticeable, sitting on the hood of a blue sports car with her arms folded. I moved through the crowd of cheering JV guys to get a better look at the one other person who didn't buy into the Oliver hype. Maybe she could be an ally or a friend. To my surprise, it was the girl from the stands, my angel, and she was no illusion.

She looked mad, arms crossed, but still as beautiful as she was earlier at the football game. Even with such an obvious disapproval for what was going on, she still was a bright light in these dark surroundings. Eric hit me on the arm.

"Dude that was incredible, wasn't it?"

"She sure is," I said under my breath.

"Oliver is definitely the big man on campus now! There is no doubt about it!"

THE DEAL
CHAPTER NINE

The beginning of my first day at school went by quickly, but now I was trapped in fourth period biology with two of Eric's friends. The two girls, whose names I didn't catch, couldn't believe I was playing varsity. I tried to diffuse them by emphasizing that I had only played in a scrimmage, but it didn't work. All they wanted to do was talk about it. Mrs. Bellhorn, our teacher, had to be over a hundred years old and completely deaf. They talked straight through her entire "Welcome to Science" speech without her giving any reaction to the talking. The bell finally rang, setting me free. I hurried out of the classroom and lost them in the crowd of people in the halls.

My first day of school was almost over, but still no angel. I recognized some of the guys from the football team. It still amazed me how many people went to this school. I wondered why Cora hadn't picked a large school like this before. It was so easy to blend in and get lost in the crowd.

"Excuse me. Excuse me. Can I have your attention, you busy little bees?" I recognized that person's voice; it was my counselor, Joy Lemmins. She was being broadcast throughout the entire school using hundreds of small TVs mounted in the halls. She was wearing a flashy pink-plaid jacket. Her glasses were pulled down to read the announcements that were in front of her on a table.

"If everyone could report to their homeroomies," she laughed at her little joke. "I know you were just there this morning, but we need to have our annual 10-10 Earthquake drill. Earthquakes are serious, so please listen to your teacher carefully so that we can keep you safe. Please go there now."

She smiled at the camera for a second. A voice from outside of the viewing area said, "Cut," but she was still on the TVs. She stood up and got her large jacket button caught on the table. She tugged so hard to free herself that she broke the button, and the force sent her falling backwards into the backdrop. She landed on her back, feet straight up in the air. She started to scream a high-pitched squeal. Then the screen went blank. The students all around me were laughing at her.

I didn't feel like laughing; I wanted to escape this horror. I didn't want to take part in this earthquake drill. The thought of it made me sick to my stomach. I swallowed almost an entire pack of Tic Tacs on my way to homeroom, but I still felt sick. I sat down in Mr. Nickel's class. He was a very tall man who looked like an eagle with his pronounced nose and little hair. He showed no emotion, so when he spoke it sounded robotic like he was reading a speech for the first time. He proceeded to talk about why earthquake safety was important, and coming from him it sounded even worse. I tried to block out everything he was saying. I didn't want to hear it; it hurt too much. It hurt too much to remember. After his speech, he instructed us on how to protect ourselves from an earthquake.

"If we have another earthquake like the one on 10-10, the safest place is under your desk. So do it now and put your hands over your head until the bell rings. When the bell rings, you can go to your fifth bell class," he squawked.

I curled up in a ball under my desk with my hands over my head, and I tried to fight the voices from the past coming back to haunt me, reminding me of everything I was trying to forget.

**

"Jim, I got back as soon as I could."

"Is he okay?"

"He'll be fine."

"Dave, what's going on out there? It's been too quiet here."

"The quake leveled the city like we thought it did, and most of the neighboring towns, too. Most of the buildings in town are destroyed or are on fire. There are people searching frantically for friends and family in what is left of the town. Some of the firefighters are trying to fight the fire. I saw Jacob, Mason, and Lear from the department, but that was it. Isn't the boy's dad a firefighter?"

"I think he is, but I'm not positive."

"Oh yeah, the National Guard has arrived. They have set up several temporary hospitals to get any survivors with critical injuries stable enough for transport."

"Did you find your parents when you were in town?"

"No, I wasn't able to find them at what was left of the post office, and I couldn't get them on the phone. Whenever I call, I get the same message over and over. 'I'm sorry. All circuits are busy. Please try back later.' I'm pretty sure they are with my aunt on her farm. At least that is where they were heading this morning. This was their day off. That's where I'm heading next. Did you get a hold of your folks?"

"One of my parents' neighbors was here and said my mom was okay, but my dad punctured his lung and broke a couple ribs. They have taken him to Christ Hospital in Cincinnati. I guess they weren't hit too hard by the quake, so that's where people have been instructed to go if they can get there."

"So what are you going to do with the boy? You should leave him with someone."

"I'm friends with his aunt. She will be here any time. When I talked to her earlier, I told her I would wait with him here until she arrives."

"You should have sent him with the rest of the kids so you could be with your dad in Cincinnati."

"No, I need to stay with him and watch after him, especially after everything he's done."

"What has he done?"

"He has given us hope."

**

The bell rang three times, snapping me out of my trance and ending the nightmare. I walked through the hall half-dazed, trying to block out any more of my memories of the earthquake. I found my fifth bell class, math. I was taking Advanced Geometry, which was normally an eleventh grade class. Cora always made sure that each new school I attended challenged me.

I sat in the front row, farthest away from the door. I could avoid eye contact with anyone that came in by sitting in this spot. Plus, I didn't feel like talking with anyone.

My teacher was Coach Hoff, which was good because I was sure he would recognize me and not put me through the new student routine. The bell rang and everyone sat down. Coach Hoff walked in and started reading the attendance sheet, which he had on a clipboard.

"Hoffman."

"Here."

"Kramer."

"Here."

He missed me altogether. This was far worse than saying I was new because now I would have to raise my hand and get up in front of the class.

Then I heard a name that I did not want to hear. "Mr. Oliver Rails."

"Yes, present," said the smug voice from behind me.

"Finally, Ms. Yelling, are you here?" Coach Hoff called.

"Here."

I slowly began to raise my hand. "Oh, Mr. Nicholas Keller, are you here?"

"Here," I mumbled, lowering my hand quickly.

"Sorry about that. New students are at the end of the list and ..." He continued to talk, but I didn't hear him. His words ran together like gibberish. He said "new student" a couple more times and said something about football. I could feel the stares of the entire class boring holes into the back of my head. Why couldn't he have just called my name? Oliver being in the class would be hard enough, and this was not helping things either.

It seemed like Coach Hoff talked about me for hours. Finally, he stopped. "Okay, class, we go to lunch at 11:20. You have twenty-five minutes to eat and get your butts back in the seats, ready to learn. See you back here soon."

I was farthest away from the door, so I pretended to lean down to get stuff out of my backpack, hoping that most of the class would be gone by the time I got up.

"So, Keller is in our class. Aren't we lucky?" I looked up to see Oliver with one of his buddies from the team standing just a few feet away from me, blocking the door.

"Hey, Oliver," I said, pretending like we were friends.

"So how did a little tenth grader get into Advanced Geometry?"

"I took geometry at my last school."

"Oh, a smarty," his friend laughed. I tried to walk around them. Oliver stepped in front of me, blocking my escape.

"Where do you think you're going?"

My muscles started to tighten and the fire began to burn.

"Keller, you need to be respectful to your superiors, in here and on the field."

I looked up at Oliver ready for a fight.

"Oliver, leave him alone," a female voice rang out from behind him. He looked back at her and that was my chance.

I walked by him out of the class. I walked down the busy hall quickly, hoping she could buy me enough time to duck into the bathroom to hide. I walked into the first bathroom I could find, locking the stall door. My muscles began to relax as time passed. I grabbed my Tic Tacs from my pocket and popped some into my mouth. The cool taste calmed my stomach. At this rate I would eat a pack a day here.

What was happening to me? The sickness I usually experienced in the mornings was now happening all the time. I never felt this bad when I was younger, and those days were a lot more stressful. I came out of the stall carefully, making sure to see if the coast was clear. I was alone. I stared at my pale face in the mirror and splashed water on it to gain some composure before going back out.

I walked to the cafeteria watching out for Oliver and his buddy. There were hundreds of kids everywhere eating their lunches. Still, I knew that Oliver would not have a hard time finding me if he wanted to. I would have to hide.

A group of students was in front of me. I hurried up to walk with them to get food. When we got to the food court, I was stunned. They had everything you could ever want to eat and more. It was like a bunch of restaurants all put together right in the middle of the cafeteria. There were at least twenty people working the different lunch lines. They were all dressed in long white coats and hair nets. They looked like they should be in labs, not fixing food. All of the food was prepared for you while you waited. No soggy old food; everything was fresh. They had the basics like hamburgers, pizza, sandwiches, salads, and snack food. In addition to those items, they had Mexican food, Chinese food, and a whole buffet line of different hot dishes. It took me five minutes just to decide on the pizza and fries. With everything that had happened before lunch, I only had five minutes left to eat and get back to class.

I sat down at one of the empty tables off to the side of the enormous lunchroom and began to eat quickly.

"What's your hurry?"

I turned and looked up with a mouth full of pizza. It was her, my angel.

"Now, don't choke," she smiled. "You don't need to hurry so much. Mr. Hoff always comes back from lunch at least ten minutes late."

I slowly started to chew my food again, unable to look away from her beautiful blue eyes. She batted them at me and turned and walked away. Her voice was unmistakable. The beautiful girl from the stands and the party was the same one who just defended me. I couldn't believe it. Maybe my luck was changing.

"Hey, Keller! You on this lunch too?" Eric was walking toward me with what looked like half of the buffet items on his tray. Matt, another guy who I kind of knew from the JV team, was right behind him with a bunch of french fries hanging out of his mouth.

"No, I have to be back in a minute."

Eric flipped the chair around and sat on it backwards. Matt copied him. "Who do you have this period?" Eric asked.

"I have Coach Hoff."

"You're lucky," Matt said with a mouth full of food. "I heard he sometimes doesn't even come back from lunch. Most of the varsity team has him for math. At least that's one class they all pass."

"Well, Keller, it looks like we will have the same lunch after all," Eric said.

I was done eating my food a few minutes after they sat down. I started to get up. I didn't want to take the chance that Coach Hoff was going to be on time this year or risk possibly meeting Oliver in the hall.

"See you guys later at football practice!"

When I got back to class there were only a couple of people sitting in their seats. I guess everyone knew Coach Hoff was notoriously late getting back to class after lunch. Some people were eating at their desks, while others lounged in their seats, talking to each other. I sat down and got out my grammar book to do the assignment that Mrs. Wolfe had given us during third period.

I glanced up to see her, my angel, walk into the class. I looked down, afraid I would be caught staring. She had two friends with her. They all sat down right behind me. Her friends were talking about shopping at the mall and what they wanted to do over the weekend. It was painful to listen to them. They sounded like two chipmunks carrying on a conversation. But when she spoke, her voice was different. It wasn't like a chipmunk; it was more like an instrument, a harp. She didn't speak as much as her friends. I didn't think it was humanly possible to talk as much as they did. She talked in short sentences only to get her point across, not like the other two who just wanted to hear themselves talk. Her voice was soothing. I drifted off, totally relaxed listening to her.

Her voice lingered in my head like clouds on a cool autumn day. I had never heard anything that made me feel the way she did. Her voice affected me the same way seeing her did. I felt at peace. For a minute, I forgot all about the earthquake drill and Oliver.

"Okay, class, sorry I'm late. Let's get down to it." Coach Hoff walked into class with a half-eaten sandwich in one hand and a clipboard in the other. Geometry went quickly. I tried to pay attention to Coach Hoff, but it was useless knowing she was right behind me. The bell rang and the class emptied. I turned to see if she was still in the classroom, but she was gone.

The rest of the day went as fast as the morning. Football practice was shortened. It was raining so hard that we stopped about halfway through, and Coach Miller made us watch tapes of our season opener opponent. I was able to avoid Oliver the whole practice. Eric was not as lucky as I was because Coach Hoff was still upset over their tie and had JV practice the entire time out in the pouring rain. Eric didn't talk much on the ride home, probably upset that I was so dry.

He dropped me off at the top of my driveway. I ran down the driveway, avoiding the big puddles. Cora was waiting for me at the door with a big plate of chocolate chip cookies.

"So how was your first day?" she asked.

"It was okay." I took a cookie off the glass platter, dropping my football bag and book bag on the floor.

"What happened?" Cora asked, shutting the door and looking concerned.

"We had an earthquake drill."

"Oh, Nicholas, I'm so sorry." She put the plate of cookies down on the small table next to the coat closet. "I didn't think they would do that here. If I had known, I would have let you skip today for sure. I am sorry you had to relive that day." Cora gave me a big hug, holding on to me tightly.

When Cora stepped back, I looked at her. "Cora, it's okay. Really, I'll be fine."

"So how was the rest of your day?"

"You know Oliver Rails from football?"

"You mean that bully?"

"Yes. He's in my geometry class."

"Did he cause you any trouble?"

"Well, he started to cause some trouble, but . . . it worked itself out."

"Well, that's good. So you don't think he will cause you any more trouble?"

"No, I think everything will be fine."

She was giving me the "I'll go switch your class" face.

"Cora, seriously, everything is fine."

I grabbed my bags, dropped them off in my room, and then headed to the kitchen. Cora was cooking one of her gourmet meals that took hours to make. She had on a light-blue apron that had no spills on it, of course. She had the table set with some rolls in the middle. I grabbed one from the basket and sat down. They were warm and smelled like honey. I put some butter on it and took a bite. The roll melted in my mouth.

"Cora, these rolls are incredible."

"I'm glad you like them; it's a new recipe." She carried over a covered platter to the table and set it down. "Nicholas,

I know you haven't had a good day, but there's no easy way to say this: you have to quit the football team."

"What? Are you kidding? We have already been through this. Why?" I demanded.

"You are drawing too much attention to yourself. We have done well so far over the past five years, but we can't afford to slip up now."

"At least let me finish the season, and then I will never play football again!"

"No, by the time you are done, you will have set a bunch of school records, and a tenth grader doing it will draw even more attention. Plus, colleges will start scouting you and digging into your past."

"But I need to go to college."

"Not on a football scholarship. You don't need a scholarship; you need to fly under the radar. You know this."

"That was just a scrimmage. Please, just let me play in the first couple of games, and if I am drawing too much attention, I will stop playing."

Cora stood in silence.

"Remember, it was just a scrimmage, and the other team was not that good," I said, hoping to persuade her.

Cora took off her apron. She laid it on the counter and leaned against it. "Okay, it's a deal. I will let you play, but remember—"

"I know. I'll quit."

ELLE
CHAPTER TEN

The next morning was unusually cold for late August. The rain had coated the grass and all of the leaves. The sun was beginning to rise, making the grass and leaves look like they were covered with tiny diamonds. I was already sitting outside on the porch, waiting for Cora.

I wasn't able to sleep at all because of the deal I had made with Cora. Why would I make that deal with her? The only reason I was playing varsity was because of how well I was doing. If I was going to stay on the team, I would have to become an average player and that would be a one-way ticket back to the JV team or, worse, the bench. I have sacrificed so much over the years, and what has she given up? Absolutely nothing. Well, maybe some shopping sprees at the mall, but as soon as I go to college, she will have her old life back again, just as she left it.

The cold morning and my Tic Tacs were helping calm my sick stomach. I had already eaten a pack overnight and was well into my second. I was glad Cora wasn't up yet, partly because I didn't want to hear her say that she was sorry for the deal she was forcing me to make, but mainly because I didn't want to smell her coffee.

My first three classes flew by just like my first day. I was invisible to almost everyone in my classes and in the hall. The guys on the JV football team were the only ones who paid any attention to me. I was like a hero to them. Every chance they had to talk to me, they would. I guess they thought if they talked to me that somehow they would be part of varsity too. But as much as the JV players talked to me, the varsity guys wanted nothing to do with me. I was sure Oliver had something to do with it.

I was hoping that the two girls in biology would either leave me alone or be sick. But there they were, and they had somehow positioned themselves to the left and right of my assigned seat. How did they get Mrs. Bellhorn to switch their seats? It was bad enough when they were two rows behind me. Now it was going to be torture. I still had no idea what their names were, and to be honest, I didn't care.

When I got to my desk, I smiled at them, pretending to look in my bag for some elusive pen or folder. They both said, "Hi," and that was it. They didn't speak to me throughout the whole class, which was a relief because I was pretty nervous about seeing my angel in my next class. I had a serious case of the butterflies.

The bell rang. The two girls said in unison, "Nicholas, we'll see you tomorrow," and they both walked out together, ponytails bouncing back and forth.

I walked slowly down the hall, looking to see if Oliver was around. Luckily enough, he wasn't. I walked into class with my head down just in case he was already seated. I sat quickly, and my sudden movement sent an intoxicating breeze into the air. It was perfume from somewhere. There were faint hints of vanilla, mint and some other tropical fruit or sweet flower that I had never smelled before. It was heavenly. If I could swim in it, I would leap from my desk.

"Hi."

She was talking to me! I turned around in my seat.

"My name is Elle."

Her name was just as beautiful as she was. How could someone be this incredible? Maybe it was my hormones making me feel this way. Hormones or not, I loved the feeling.

"You're Nicholas, right?"

I couldn't speak, so I smiled. She was even more beautiful close up. Her flawless skin looked as smooth as rose petals. I couldn't believe that the same girl I had admired from afar was now sitting behind me and talking to me. I wanted to reach out and brush her cheek with the back of my hand to feel how soft her skin must be. Her eyes were hypnotic. I was instantly and hopelessly under her spell.

"So how do you like Winsor?" she asked.

I realized that I was just staring at her. "Oh, I like it all right."

"So where did you move from?"

"I moved from a small town in upstate Ohio," I replied.

"Did you like it there? . . . Well?" she said.

"Well, I'm not sure." The words stumbled clumsily out of my mouth.

"What are you not sure about?" she asked. "You either liked it or you didn't!" A half-crooked smile that could melt an iceberg appeared on her face.

Coach Hoff walked in. I turned back around quickly, happy to be saved from her question. Such a simple question, so why couldn't I answer it?

She leaned forward and whispered in my ear, "You can let me know your answer later."

All of the hairs on the back of my neck stood straight up. Coach Hoff started talking about some project we were going to work on over the quarter. My mind was still numb from Elle. She had me all flustered. I thought I was prepared for absolutely everything, but the way I was feeling now was something Cora had never prepared me for. I was lost.

"Okay, class, see you after lunch." Coach Hoff was the first one out the door. I got up with everyone else in the class and walked down the hall with them. Elle brushed by me, and the smell of her perfume sent electricity through me. I had to walk slower to put more distance between us.

I replayed the way she said her name and smiled over and over in my head. I found myself in the lunch line, oblivious to everything around me.

"Do you want fries with that?"

I cleared my vision. Standing in front of me was a woman the size of a tree, wearing a large white lab coat.

"Kid, do you want fries or not?"

"Uh, yes," I answered. I could hear Cora's voice warning, *Pay attention to what you are doing at all times.*

97

I paid the cashier and walked down one of the long aisles in the middle of the lunchroom. I found an empty table near the back of the room. I was pretty confident that Oliver would not be back here because most of the kids surrounding me had their books out and were studying. I was sure this was not where the cool kids sat.

I started to eat the salad that I had gotten by accident with my fries. I glanced up to see Elle walking toward me with a small group of people. What was I going to do? I couldn't get up and run—that would definitely be too weird. Okay, I would just have to play it cool. What did I know about playing anything cool? I was more like the people around me.

"Everyone, this is Nicholas." Elle was standing with her two girlfriends from class and a boy that I had never seen before. "Can we sit with you?" Elle asked. Before I could answer, she sat down. Her friends all sat down like sheep following their shepherd.

"So, Nicholas, this is Jennifer and Julie." If she had not introduced them, I would have sworn they were both different versions of Malibu Barbie. They had perfect tans, blonde hair, and designer clothes. "And this is John."

"Hey! What's up, dude?" John said, reaching across the table to shake my hand. I offered my hand, and instead of a handshake, he slapped it.

"So you are the tenth grader that made varsity?" John asked.

"Well, I—"

"Sweet, dude!"

John reminded me of a surfer from California with his blond hair and beach attire.

"John's my boyfriend and captain of the water polo team," Jennifer or Julie said.

"So that's how I am labeled now? 'Boyfriend'?"

"Oh, Johnny!" she said, and both the Barbie twins giggled.

"So what brings you to Winsor?" he asked.

"Well, my mom got transferred here."

"Cool," John said.

It was odd because Elle didn't fit in with these people. Elle's beauty was different. It was the type that would inspire great works of art or cause someone to go to war. Not any of this fashion model stuff. She was inspirational.

The entire lunchroom was staring at our table. Worst of all, they were staring at me. People walked by the table, making sure to say hello to Elle, and she would always respond with "Hello," or "How are you?" Who was this girl? Why did everyone want to talk to her, and why was she here with me? I had to get up to escape this. It was way too much attention.

I got up. "Nice to meet you all," I said leaving the table. I looked back at Elle and she caught me. She gave me a small smile and waved. I almost walked into a concrete column. I dumped the garbage off my tray and walked back to class.

HENRY J. THEASING
CHAPTER ELEVEN

For the next three days, I ate my lunch down one of the long hallways in the art area. I was pretty sure Oliver didn't know where it was, and Elle was never around when I went back there to eat, so it was a safe place for now. Elle didn't try to talk to me in class, and Oliver left me alone the rest of the week.

On Friday, I was wearing my green tie that Cora had set out for me to wear like the other varsity players. Coach Miller made varsity wear ties for home games. Coach Hoff was finishing the last problem on the chalkboard. The bell rang.

"Okay, class! See you tonight at the game," he said.

"Hey, Nicholas, good luck tonight." Elle was at the side of my desk. I looked up to see her blinding smile. This was the first time I had really looked at her since I ran away from her and her friends at the lunch table.

"Thank you," I said. "Are you going?"

"Well, of course. I think I have been to every game since I was a baby."

"Okay, great. Then I will see you there."

"I'll be in the bottom row in the student section. If you see me, wave, but make sure Coach Miller doesn't catch you," she said with a mischievous wink.

"Okay, great!" I repeated with my voice cracking in the middle of great.

Game time came quickly. I sat in the back of the varsity locker room listening to music. I now had a locker in the back. My name hung over my locker on a gold plate. I sat staring at it, unsure if this would be my last day sitting in here with the team.

The team still didn't accept me, but now they at least didn't try to kick me out, and that was good enough for me. Everyone was dressed for the game when Coach Miller and the rest of the coaching staff walked in. He called to us to come over and take a knee.

Everyone bowed their heads, including the coaches. No one made a sound. After a few minutes, Coach Miller said a loud, "Amen."

We stood up and Coach Miller continued, "Now listen up, team. Everyone knows how important it is to put this game out of their reach early. They are a wounded animal, and they are begging for us to put them out of their misery. We need to punish them when they have the ball, and when it's our turn, we need to score." Coach Miller paused. "Do you know what time it is?"

The team responded in a thunderous, unified voice, "It's game time!"

We followed the coaches down the hall and out the doors. There was a sea of cars separating us from the stadium. Grills and tents were littered around the parking lot. People were tailgating before a high school football game—unbelievable. There was a green and gold bus with the Winsor Cougar painted on it. Cougar flags were flying everywhere.

We went around the outside of the parking lot toward the stadium. It was glowing a bright, warm yellow. It was alive. Above the glow, towering over the stadium was a lit sign that read "Henry J. Theasing Stadium." I was surprised that I had never noticed it before because it seemed impossible to miss. Maybe I noticed now because it was lit up like the Rockefeller Center Christmas tree. You could see that sign from everywhere, even if you were driving on the nearby interstate. Whoever he was, Henry J. Theasing must have been pretty important or have given a lot of money to the school.

We began to jog toward the stadium, but instead of going toward the front gate, we ran toward a door in the side of the stadium. It was just a plain green door. It looked more like a storage closet than an entrance. When I got up to the door, I saw stairs that led down. I funneled into the narrow passage with the rest of the team. All along the wall were names painted in green and gold lettering. At the bottom I saw my name freshly painted in gold, Nicholas Keller. My chest swelled with pride. I knew my dad would have been proud.

The dimly lit corridor widened. I could see a light up ahead in the tunnel. It was like what I have pictured will happen when I die. The coaches stopped and moved to the side. A booming voice roared in front of us from where the light was.

"And now for your Winsor Cougars!"

I ran with the team up a ramp toward the light and through a banner. It was amazing how the lights blinded me coming out of the tunnel. The roar of the crowd was deafening. The 10,000-seat stadium was packed mostly with people dressed in green and gold. We ran over to our sideline to cheers of the crowd. It was incredible that this many people would attend a high school game. It was like we were gladiators in Rome about to fight for Caesar. Our band was in the end zone playing the Winsor fight song, and the cheerleaders were performing routines to get the crowd into even more of a frenzy.

The PA announcer said, "If you would now stand for our national anthem. Please welcome our hometown girl, a Winsor Cougar, a world-famous recording artist. Please welcome Chanin Anne."

A woman with light-brown skin wearing all white except for a green and gold boa walked out from behind the stands. Thousands of pictures were being taken of this woman. I had never heard of her, but judging by the horde of police around her, she had to be famous.

We lined up, took off our helmets, and laid them at our feet, facemasks facing out. We put our hands over our hearts and followed with our eyes the large American flag that a color guard was parading down the center of the field. Coach Miller had us practice a couple of times how to stand for the singing of our national anthem.

Coach Miller didn't often speak much about other things besides football, but I still remember what he said word for word about the national anthem. "Listen up, men. A lot of people have died for that flag, and it is our duty to show them respect and to respect the greatest country in the world."

After she was done singing the most incredible national anthem I had ever heard, the refs called both team captains to the center of the field. Oliver and Chad ran out and shook hands with the refs and the other team captains. We won the coin toss and the fans roared so loudly it shook my insides. Oliver came running back, high-fiving everyone near him. I stood at the back toward the bench and put my helmet on, trying to make sure I didn't give Cora any more reasons to make me quit.

The Mason Comets lined up and kicked the ball to us. Oliver and the offense went out onto the field, carried by the cheers of the crowd. The fans loved to see their golden boy, the face of the team, run out. A part of me was jealous of him. I always had to blend in and be nothing special. Oliver was expected to stand out, to be more than average. Oliver and I were opposites.

"Keller, Keller." Coach Miller was standing in front of me. "Snap out of it, boy. I know it's not like the scrimmage. Don't worry about the crowd, the lights, or anything else. Just worry about playing football. You are starting tonight."

I followed Coach Miller up to the sideline. The crowd grew quiet. Oliver was getting killed out there. Every time he touched the ball, the other team would swarm around him. He wasn't sticking with the plays the coaches were calling; he was trying to do it all himself. Instead of throwing the ball or handing the ball off, he would tuck the ball and keep it himself, trying to make a play. How selfish could he be?

"Okay, defense, let's go!" Coach Miller yelled. Oliver and the offense jogged off the field. Oliver jogged right toward me. It was unavoidable that he was going to pass me. Right when he passed me he said, "Just because you are starting doesn't mean you're anything important. You are nothing special!"

I followed the defense onto the field. What Oliver said began to eat at me. I was tired of being nothing special. I didn't hear what play Chad called. The fire that had been dormant awoke, filling me with rage. I was focused on only one thing, the quarterback. He shouted, "Blue 52, blue 52, set, hike." My muscles tensed and the fire propelled me forward. I ran past everyone and jumped over the lone blocker. I hit the quarterback ferociously, knocking him to the ground.

"I hurt him," I said. None of the guys around me heard what I had said, but I wasn't saying it for them. I was saying it to myself in disbelief. He was sitting up, but he was holding his arm. The trainers motioned to the emergency personnel on the sideline. I couldn't see what they were doing when they got to him.

"Huddle up," Chad shouted at me.

We all stood and watched them put a sling on his arm and load him onto a cart. They took him off the field. He waved with his uninjured arm, and the crowd applauded.

The promise I made to Cora and my regret for hurting the quarterback dominated my thoughts for the rest of the game. I played hard, but did very little to stand out. With their quarterback out of the game, we went on to beat them 10-3.

I jogged with the team. A crowd had formed at the main gate, waiting for us to come off the field. Oliver was in front, pumping his fist, playing it up for the crowd. I was so preoccupied that I didn't even look for Elle. Hopefully she would understand.

I didn't take off my helmet so that no one could see my face. In crowds, Cora always made me wear a hat. About halfway out of the stadium, I heard a familiar voice in the crowd yell, "Good game, Nicholas!" I knew who it was because her voice gave me butterflies. I looked up to see Elle smiling at me. I smiled back.

I changed quickly to meet Cora outside. I moved silently through the team. I made it to the door and heard Oliver yelling, "We are the Cougars, the mighty, mighty Cougars!"

The locker room responded to him with, "We are the Cougars . . ."

Coach Miller came in just as Oliver started the chant again. The rest of the coaches, all looking like we had lost the game, followed behind him.

"Do you think we have something to cheer about? Do you?" Coach Miller asked in a very calm voice, which was scarier than his shouting. "The only ones who should be celebrating are the defense because they won the game for us. They even saved us when Oliver fumbled the ball on our own 10-yard line." The locker room was as quiet as I had ever heard it. Coach Miller had everyone's full attention.

"Chad and Nicholas, good job tonight. I want to see more of the same effort from you two and the rest of the defense. Great job," Coach Miller said with a smile. I noticed for the first time that the entire defense was on the same side of the locker room.

"Defense, get dressed and get out of here."

I was halfway out the door when Coach Miller began to shout at the offense about how poorly they had played and that maybe the JV offense should start next week. I knew he wasn't yelling at me, but it was still hard to listen to.

I walked out the back door by the JV locker room, where Cora was leaning against our truck, waiting. She saw me and smiled. I climbed into the passenger seat. She merged into the line of cars trying to get out. Crowds of people were celebrating in the parking lot, which forced all of the cars down to one lane to exit.

"So, you had a good game," Cora said.

I couldn't tell if it was a question or a statement. "Thanks."

I looked out the window, and a group of students were staring right at me. One of the boys in the crowd with his face painted green and wearing a large gold chef's hat pointed at me and said something to the rest of the group. The group started to clap and chant, "Keller, Keller, Keller!" Then the chant erupted among the other fans around our truck.

The next ten minutes waiting for our turn to get out of the parking lot were the longest of my life. Cora pretended like nothing was going on and I did too. I could only sink down so far in my seat. Any lower, I would be laying on the floor.

"We need to talk, Nicholas."

"I know what you're going to say. We are moving or I have to quit."

"Is that what you want me to say?" Cora asked.

"Well, no, but isn't that what you were going to say?" I asked.

"No, I was going to talk about how proud I was of you during the game."

"Proud? What part are you proud of? The part when I broke the guy's arm because I was angry?"

"No, not that part. But after that you faded into the background. You never stood out again. Sure, your name was announced for a tackle or two, but—"

"Wait, they announced our names?" I asked.

"Sure, they said your name, but you never made a spectacular play again after the first one. Believe me, after the first play, I wanted to grab you and run out of there, but you showed me that you learned from your mistake. I'm proud of you."

My face felt like it was on fire from embarrassment.

"Since you are already embarrassed, I might as well ask who the girl is."

"What girl?"

"You know, the girl that waited for you after the game to tell you good game."

"You were watching?"

"Well, it was hard not to notice. I happened to be standing next to her, trying to get your attention. You didn't even know I was there when I yelled to you, but she sure got your attention with barely any effort."

"She's a friend from school."

Cora didn't say anything.

A DATE
CHAPTER TWELVE

Nothing could have prepared me for school on Monday. When I got off the bus, Eric was waiting for me with what had to be half of the school. They were all cheering my name, "Nicholas, Nicholas, Nicholas." The chant burrowed into me like a hot poker, making me instantly uncomfortable with nowhere to run.

Eric pulled me off the bus and pushed me to the center of the mob. He raised his hand and they all quieted. He then belted out, "Nicholas Keller is the students' pick for MVP of Friday's game against the Mason Comets."

Everyone cheered after Eric's announcement. Eric pulled out a large beaded necklace with footballs on it and forced it over my head. The necklace looked like it was thrown from a Mardi Gras float. Eric yelled again, "This is the first time that an underclassman has gotten the MVP necklace, and it makes me proud to call him my friend."

Eric walked me around to different groups of people. It was like he was showing off his shining, new toy that everyone wanted to play with. I finally escaped Eric and the crowd, but it wasn't any better inside the school. Everyone in the school knew me now. "Keller, great game," "MVP," and "Nice hit," came from everywhere. Even teachers got in on the action. I became nauseated.

I was planning to eat in the hallway again, but now I could see that wouldn't work. Everywhere I went, people were coming up to me. I took off the football necklace and shoved it into my bag. I hoped to break it in the process, just in case Eric saw me without it, so I could use that as an excuse for why I wasn't wearing it.

I barely made it through biology. The two girls began talking to me again with new vigor. They wanted to go over every play of the game. They talked about how awesome it was that I took out the other team's quarterback. The bell rang and I bolted out of the classroom and into the hallway to get away from them. I arrived at Coach Hoff's class completely rattled. This was more attention than I had ever received in the last five years combined.

Coach Hoff was already in the classroom, sitting at his desk with his feet up, reading the morning paper. The bell rang and all of the students rushed to their seats, shocked that he was there already. He never moved; he just continued reading his paper while the class settled down.

"Well, class, before I let you go to lunch, we should give a round of applause to our football team for leading us to our first win against our cross-town rivals, the Comets!" The class started to applaud.

"Wait! Wait! I would like to congratulate Mr. Nicholas Keller for being the first underclassman to play and start on varsity. He did it with real style, knocking out the Comet's quarterback during his first play of the game!" The class exploded into louder celebration. I sank down in my seat. I turned around, hoping that if I smiled, their cheers would end, but instead I caught a glimpse of an angry Oliver.

"Okay, class, go to lunch."

I knew that Oliver was going to be waiting for me for sure after all of that. I was right. Oliver and his buddy were slow to get out of their seats when we were dismissed. I tried to hurry up and get out, but Oliver was right there.

"Mr. Keller, may I have a word? Rails, you and Chester get going," Coach Hoff said to them. Oliver walked out of the class dejected.

"Keller, you are one hell of a football player. It's exciting to see you play. To be honest, I haven't seen anyone play football like that since Coach Miller played back in the day.

"But that's not the reason why I wanted to talk to you. You need to stand up for yourself. Don't let Oliver or anyone else make you do something you don't want to do. Don't let them pick on you, okay? Bullies are only bullies if they have someone to bully. Do you understand?"

"Yes, sir," I responded.

"Okay then, off to lunch."

I grabbed my lunch, but I wasn't sure where to eat. I needed to escape from all of this madness. I wandered through the empty halls. I couldn't eat in the lunchroom or the hall now, so where could I go?

Up ahead a door opened. I waited for the person who had opened it to vanish, and then I went in. It was the staircase to the second story, and under the stairs was what looked like a perfect place to escape. It was a small place where I could sit and no one could see me. This could be my sanctuary, my safe spot.

I slid down the brick wall onto the thinly carpeted floor. I unpacked my lunch and began to eat. Was Coach Hoff right about standing up to Oliver? But how would I do that without drawing more attention? Was Oliver making me do things that I didn't want to do? Looking around, I realized he was, because I was hiding and eating under the stairs. He wasn't the only reason I was hiding, but he was part of it. I started to see Coach Hoff's point.

The twenty minutes under the stairs were good for me. I was able to relax and regain some of my composure. Back in class, Oliver and Chester were not interested in me. That was a relief because as much as Coach Hoff might be right about standing up to them, saying it is one thing and doing it is another.

Coach Hoff gave us several problems to work on with a partner. Elle leaned forward and asked, "Do you want to be partners?"

"Sure," I said without turning my head. I fumbled with some papers on my desk to buy some time to calm down. I turned my desk around, slowly facing her.

I didn't say anything; I just kept my eyes on the paper. The problems were so easy that I finished in a couple of minutes. I looked up to see if Elle was done. Her paper was blank. She hadn't worked any of them. She was just staring at me.

"Is everything okay?" I asked.

"Yes."

"Why haven't you worked on your problems yet?"

"I was waiting to see how long it would take for you to look at me."

"What's that supposed to mean?"

"Now don't get upset, Nicholas. I was curious to see if your avoidance of me also applied to looking at me in class. Have I done something to make you upset with me?" she asked.

"No, you haven't."

"Then what is it? You don't have to answer me now, but give me a chance to be your friend at least. Tomorrow at lunch let me eat with you. I will get my food and meet you under the stairs." Her angelic face looked innocent. Blood started to rush to my face.

"Please don't be upset with me," she continued. "I came back to see if you were okay today and saw you go into the stairwell. I went in there to find you, and I heard you under the stairs. I didn't say anything to you because I was afraid that you would think I was stalking you."

I was speechless.

"Well, I will assume from your silence that it's okay to eat with you." She began to work on her problems, breezing through them just as I had. I watched her work on her problems. Her fluid, artistic writing was just another thing that made her perfect in my eyes. The bell rang.

The next day in class Elle didn't say anything to me, but she had a big smile on her face. Every time we made eye contact, the butterflies in my stomach exploded.

"Breathe," I whispered to myself. It didn't help.

I sprang to my feet when we were dismissed for lunch and was the first one out the door. I took a different path to my hiding spot. There seemed to be a bigger crowd in the halls and around the entrance to the stairs than last time. After a couple of minutes, I slipped through the door and slid back behind the stairs. Sitting under the stairs was not relaxing at all. It was more like sitting in a dentist chair, waiting for the drill. I propped myself up against the wall, waiting for her. Each time the door opened, I held my breath. Maybe she forgot.

"Nicholas, it's me," Elle called under the stairs like she was waiting for me to open a secret door to let her in. She peeked her head in. She looked around at the small space like she was sizing it up. I hadn't really seen her yet today. She looked stunning as usual. She was a bright ray of sunshine in this dark, poorly lit place under the stairs. She always dressed very simply, but it made her look even more beautiful and breathtaking. Her beauty was indescribable. She didn't have to wear all the fancy clothes or jewelry that the other kids wore.

"Is this seat taken?" she asked. "Oh, a smile. Careful, I might think you want to be friends." If only she knew what I thought about her.

"So what are you eating, Nicholas? Anything good?"

I showed her the gourmet sandwich and pasta salad that Cora had made me.

"Wow! Did you get that here?" She had a tossed salad, french fries, and a grape pop that she had gotten from the cafeteria. It looked pretty standard.

"No, my mom made it. She's kind of like a chef. Well, not quite, but she loves to cook."

"Well, no wonder you don't eat the cafeteria food all the time. If my mom packed lunches like that, I would avoid the cafeteria too!" It wasn't one of Cora's fancier lunches, but the bread was homemade and the turkey had a cranberry dressing on it. I guess the sandwich next to the tri-color pasta salad looked pretty fancy.

I took a bite of my sandwich. She began to eat her salad, croutons first, dipping them into her dressing. When they were gone, she stabbed one piece of lettuce at a time, dipping them the same way she did her croutons. In between her bites of salad, she would take one of the fries and dip it into her ranch dressing too. She was absolutely adorable.

"So why are you eating under here?"

I didn't have to think hard about this one. Cora had prepared me to answer this question a million times. "I like my privacy."

She thought for a moment in between ranch-covered fries. "I can leave if you'd like."

I cut her off. "No, no, that's fine." My lack of control amused her, making her grin from ear to ear.

"Good. I wasn't going to leave anyway. I am determined to be your friend. You're stuck with me, Mr. Nicholas Keller." I loved the way my name rolled off her tongue. It made me feel important, like someone special.

"So what's forcing you under the stairs? Being private is one thing, but this is . . ." She shrugged her shoulders as if to tell me I was mental.

"Well, I just don't like all the attention, you know, with all the football stuff."

"What did you expect? You are the first underclassman to start varsity—heck, to be on varsity. Not to mention you're a great player!"

I looked down hoping she didn't see my red cheeks. "I didn't know that I was good before I came here. Well, actually, I never thought I would play."

"Why? You must have been the star player at your last school."

"Elle, I had never played in an actual game before, not even a scrimmage. I only played football because my dad did."

"What does your dad think now with you being the big time varsity star?"

I didn't look up to answer. "My dad died some time ago."

"Oh, Nicholas, I'm so sorry." She took my hand and her warmth flowed through my body, making me feel comforted. Elle looked horrified that she had asked such a hurtful question, but how could she have known?

"Elle, it's okay. He's been gone for a while now."

Her eyes watered up.

"Please, Elle, it's okay." I grabbed her other hand to comfort her. I couldn't bear to see her sad.

"I really stuck my foot in my mouth, and here you are trying to make me feel better about it. I was right, you are something special, Nicholas."

I let go of her hands and sat back.

"Nicholas, do you mind if I eat with you tomorrow?"

I smiled. "I would like that very much."

"Well, great! It's a date! We better get going."

We walked back to class together. It was the first time I had walked through the halls without looking over my shoulder. With her around, all my worries vanished.

THE VISIT
CHAPTER THIRTEEN

The rest of the week was peaceful. With Elle at my side, the occasional uncomfortable situations were muted. She was very calming. I ate lunch with Elle everyday. I don't know what she said to her friends about why she was gone at lunch, but I didn't care, just as long as she was with me. Friday was no different than the last couple of days, but it was game day so I did get a little more attention than normal with people wishing me good game and such.

I was going to make a couple of key plays just to keep us from losing. That was my game plan from now on. I figured if I just did that, I would still be able to start but not bring attention to myself so I could stay on the team.

I walked home from the bus stop. Cora was in the kitchen.

"Hey, Nicholas, what do you want to eat before tonight's big game?"

I walked into the kitchen. Cora was wearing a green and gold jersey that had a white "32" on the back, my number.

"Cora, where did you get that?"

"Well, I wanted to show support. The moms of the varsity team got these made, so I threw caution to the wind and bought one to support the Boosters. Do you like it?"

"Of course! It just caught me off guard."

By Cora doing this, she would bring attention to herself and inevitably to me. With her playing the part of my mom, I was sure people in the stands would treat her the same way I was treated at school—like a celebrity.

"So what do you want for dinner before the game?"

"I will take a mushroom burger."

"Okay, coming right up."

Just then the doorbell rang.

"Nicholas, are you expecting someone?" She didn't look too concerned.

"It's probably Eric seeing if I need a ride to the game tonight. I didn't get to talk to him today."

"Okay, then will you get the door?" Her hands were already covered in raw meat. I walked to the door and opened it. A man and a woman stood outside the door. They were dressed like most of the wealthy older couples that lived around here. He was wearing loafers with pressed khaki shorts and a green polo shirt. She was wearing matching shorts, a gold shirt, and a large white derby hat.

The lady spoke, "Is Cora home?" I stood there. Something about her made me feel uneasy. I wanted to slam the door on the two of them. "Nick, is Cora home?" the lady asked again. Cora was suddenly standing next to me.

"Hello, Cora," the lady said.

Cora stood frozen, staring at the pair of them. Her mouth was wide open. Something was wrong. I glanced outside to see if they were driving the sea green truck.

"You aren't the people who have been following me, are you?" I blurted out.

The couple looked at me and then looked back at Cora. My paranoia was getting the best of me.

"What do you want? I told you I had nothing more to say to you at the scrimmage," Cora said.

"I would like to have a word with you in private, dear."

"Do we have to do this now? We are getting ready for the game tonight."

"Yes, I know you are, but this can't wait," the lady responded firmly. Cora looked concerned. She was trying to tell me something, but I didn't know what it was. Cora's look went from concerned to scared, but that had to be a mistake because Cora was never scared of anything, especially not an old woman in some crazy, big hat.

"Now, now, dear. There is no reason to fret. Mr. Theasing can talk to Nick while you and I talk."

Cora snapped at her, "His name is Nicholas."

"Oh, yes indeed, I am so sorry dear. Cora, just a word, please. It will only take a moment."

The couple walked in the front door without waiting to be invited. Cora did nothing to stop them. My muscles began to tense up. I could feel my heart starting to pound and the fire erupting. I was ready for whatever happened next. Cora grabbed my arm, sensing I was getting ready for a fight.

"Nicholas," she looked into my eyes, "Ester and I are going to talk in the kitchen. Show Mr. Theasing to the family room. Talk about football." She spoke very slowly in a calm tone.

"Oh yes, Henry loves his Winsor Cougar football," Mrs. Theasing responded.

Mr. Theasing followed me into the family room. He sat down opposite me. I avoided making eye contact, trying to listen to Cora and Mrs. Theasing in the kitchen, making sure Cora was okay.

"So, Nicholas, you had one hell of a game last week."

I didn't look his way, hoping this would convince him to stop talking to me.

"Nicholas, you are the best player out there, even better than Oliver Rails."

"Thank you."

"Are you ready for tonight's game against the Millville Eagles? They have a soft defense, so Oliver should play better."

Cora's conversation was growing louder. Something was wrong. I looked over at Mr. Theasing. He too was staring at the kitchen door, concerned or scared; it was hard to make out which. He began to look as white as a ghost. From the look of his reaction, he must not have known what his wife was planning to talk to Cora about. He caught me looking at him. He coughed, clearing his throat loudly enough that they could hear him in the kitchen. The heated debate silenced.

He turned his attention back to me. "You've been playing football for a while?"

"Well, sort of."

"What? You had to have been a star before, right?"

"Well, I've been on teams for the past four years, but never played."

"Surely you've played in some games before this year."

"No, this is my first year of getting into games."

He looked like someone had just punched him in the stomach, winding him. "Woo, a player of your caliber is a rare find. We are sure lucky to get you. You are the first underclassman—"

"I know," I interrupted, "the first underclassman to play varsity. I know."

Cora walked through the swinging kitchen doors completely expressionless. "Well, thanks for stopping by," she said to Mrs. Theasing, sounding completely composed.

I got up and Mr. Theasing walked over to his wife, who was wearing a fake smile.

"Cora, thank you for your time, and good luck tonight in the game, Nick." She smiled like she had made a joke. "Nicholas, I mean. We will be watching you with great anticipation."

Cora's solemn face didn't change after she shut the door.

"So what was that all about? How do they know you? Were they the same people that you were talking to during my scrimmage?"

Cora turned toward me and said, "Nicholas, I will tell you everything, but not now. You have to do something for me, no questions asked." Cora never kept anything from me so this must be serious.

"Okay, whatever you want," I told her. I was looking into her brown eyes. She looked like a little lost kid not sure what was going to happen next.

"Quit football now," she said.

"What?"

"Listen, you did a good job, but if you don't quit, we will have to move or something worse may happen."

"Okay, I will tonight."

"You have to Nicholas," she said.

"I will tonight, but I will do it my way."

HOPE

CHAPTER FOURTEEN

I concentrated on Elle while in the tunnel waiting to run onto the field. The fireworks went off. We ran up the tunnel and through the banner, splitting the cheerleaders.

I couldn't quit football. Who would want to be friends with a quitter? Not Elle. I couldn't do that. I had to fake an injury. That was the only reasonable way to stop playing and not look like I was abandoning the team.

"Okay, men! Get out there and stop them. Nobody will score on us tonight," Coach Miller roared over the cheers of the crowd.

Oliver continued to struggle horribly. Every chance we had to score, he either messed it up or missed out on the opportunity.

"Set, hike."

I ran past everyone right to the quarterback, knocking him back several yards.

"Keller, keep it up," Chad said, hitting me on the helmet. "Without you, Oliver would have already lost this game for us." With every play I made, I felt the pressure of not wanting to let my team down with a fake injury.

Time after time, Oliver could do nothing on the field. After Coach Miller's screaming at halftime, I figured Oliver would wake up, but the second half was the same.

"Set, blue 44, hike," Oliver yelled. He went to throw the ball and threw it right to the other team for an interception.

The score was 0-0 with 45 seconds left now. The crowd was eerily silent. Thanks to Oliver, the Eagles only needed five more yards, and they would be in field goal range.

Coach Miller was yelling at me, "Let's go, Keller! We need a big play!"

The Eagles' quarterback hiked the ball and dropped back like he was going to throw it. Chad and I hit him right when he scrambled out of bounds to stop the clock. He had gained a yard. There were only 38 seconds left on the clock. Back in the huddle no one was talking. Everyone was panting, out of breath. We had been out on the field most of the game.

"33 fire. Nicholas, just go get whoever has the ball," Chad barked.

"Set, hike!"

The quarterback ran the ball away from me toward the sideline. It was like the coach on the other side told him to get the ball and run away from me and try to get a yard or two. I caught him and pushed him out of bounds after he gained a couple more yards. There were only 30 seconds left. Their kicker was warming up on the sideline. They were close enough to send him in to attempt a field goal.

The quarterback ran up and hiked the ball quickly. We were not ready, and he ran toward the sideline, but without as much speed as before. This time he was purposely not going out of bounds. He was taking time off the clock. Right before a group of us hit him, he went out of bounds. Ten seconds were taken off the clock, which now read "20" in bright neon yellow numbers that seemed to taunt us with every second that went by.

"Time out!" Coach Miller ran out to us in the middle of the field. "Listen, they have taken Keller out of the game these last couple of plays. We need to block this kick so we can give Oliver and the offense a chance to at least win it in overtime."

I glanced into the stands, which were motionless. I saw Elle in the crowd standing in the front row. She had her hands folded like she was praying. She was praying for a miracle. I would have to be that miracle.

My muscles on cue began to pulse and tighten. My heart began to pound. My surroundings slowed as the Eagles set up to kick the game-winning field goal. I was focused on Elle, who started to cheer. I could see her face and how alive and radiant she looked, full of hope. She was triggering something inside of me; the fire that normally was ignited by rage was now being unleashed.

I turned from Elle and focused on the kicker. The ball was snapped back to the holder. I ran around the grasp of the other team's players with ease just as the ball went hurtling toward the holder, who was waiting to put the ball down for the kicker. He caught the ball, and I dove in front of them to block the kick. In midair, I focused harder and everything slowed even more. The kicker's leg was blurred from his forward motion to kick the ball. His leg created a wake behind it. I couldn't just block the ball, because it would give Oliver the chance to be the hero. I would have to do something that would guarantee a win right now for Elle. Not by Oliver's doing, but by mine.

The kicker's leg went forward, connecting with the ball. The ball hit right into my midsection. In midair, with my left hand, I caught the ball and threw it to the only player from our team that was close enough to catch it, Chad. To everyone else it would look like it deflected into his arms off of my block. When I hit the ground I saw him catch the ball and run. No one was near him as he sprinted down the field. A couple of the big linemen from the other team had stumbled back onto me. I couldn't see if he scored, but then the crowd roared. The horn sounded that the game was over. Chad had scored the winning touchdown.

The crowd's cheering was deafening. Fireworks were going off. I closed my eyes and realized this was my only chance to end everything my way. I closed my eyes and lay perfectly still. I could feel the players all around me getting up. I didn't want to give any indication that I was conscious, so I continued to lay motionless.

"Keller! Hey, Keller! Can you hear me?" One of our guys was yelling at me. Then he yelled to the sideline, "Coach, Keller is hurt!"

The chain of events that followed went so fast. The trainers were trying to wake me up. They used smelling salts, but right when they put it under my nose I held my breath so I wouldn't react.

The coaches were also trying to get me to open my eyes. "Keller, can you hear us?"

I had to make this a serious injury so I wouldn't be allowed to play again. They must have summoned the paramedics because I was being strapped to a board and loaded onto a gurney. The crowd's cheers had gone quiet. I was being rushed across the field. The paramedics were taking my vitals and then I heard Cora's voice.

"Is he okay? Please, Lord, let him be okay. Is he okay? Can someone answer me?" Cora sounded so scared. I wanted to reach out to her and grab her hand to tell her I was okay. Instead I opened my eyes. "His eyes are open! Nicholas, can you hear me?" she said with her eyes full of tears.

A bunch of unfamiliar faces surrounded me. The trainers were replaced with paramedics and some other people in plain street clothes. I guessed they were doctors who had been in the stands, because the paramedics were listening to them. Then Cora pushed into the crowd of faces around me.

"Nicholas, can you hear me?" she asked me again.

"Yes," I whispered.

Immediately everyone around me quieted. One of the doctors said, "Do you know where you are?"

"At the football stadium, I think. Did we win?" I said. Relief passed over the faces around me, but Cora still looked upset.

"Nicholas, can you move your feet and arms?"

I wiggled all of them one at a time. I had to do it slowly to keep up the charade.

"He should be all right," someone yelled from out of view. The paramedics continued to talk to me, asking me all types of questions.

Then, over the stadium intercom, I heard, "Nicholas Keller is going to be all right." The crowd erupted with loud cheers.

"Let's get him into the ambulance," said the paramedic closest to Cora. Cora began to talk to him while they loaded me into the ambulance, and right next to her Elle was listening. Her back was turned to me, but her black hair was all I needed to see to know it was her.

"Keller, you okay?" Coach Miller was in the ambulance with me.

"Yes, sir. Did we win?"

"Yes, we did, son, thanks to you." He patted me on the arm and got out.

The trip in the ambulance was extremely bumpy. Cora continued to talk to the paramedics about me. I was grateful it was a short trip because with all of those bumps I might have ended up actually being hurt. The short trip meant we had arrived at Bethesda South, the closest hospital to the school. Then I thought of something that I hadn't thought of before. They were going to run tests on me that would show that nothing was wrong. They would say I had a slight concussion or something, and that would be it. They would clear me to play again in a couple of weeks. Then I would have to quit for sure. This plan seemed better when I was lying on the ground. But even though I hadn't planned on this, it still felt like the right thing to do.

They unloaded me. Several doctors were waiting for me. The paramedics and doctors were talking about me as I was being rushed inside. I couldn't hear what they were saying. They rushed me into a room. The room was buzzing. Nurses and doctors were hurrying in and out. They began to ask me all of the same questions I had been asked previously on the way here. They slowly removed my helmet, and I could feel them cutting through my jersey and removing my pads. Luckily enough, I had on a t-shirt and boxers.

"Excuse me, excuse me. Who is the doctor in charge?" Cora was not anxious or scared anymore, but now sounded like her normal, determined self.

"I am. I'm Dr. Jeffrey Flemming, head of the ER. Are you Nicholas' mother?"

"Yes, my name is Cora Keller. I would like for you to wait for our family doctor to get here before you proceed with any tests."

"My staff is more than qualified to handle this. We are top in the nation for any brain or spinal injuries. We need to run tests now to make sure your son doesn't have serious injuries. We don't have time to wait, Ms. Keller; we will get your family doctor up to speed when we are done with our tests."

"Our family doctor, Dr. Chase Letterby, will be here any minute."

"Did you say Chase Letterby?"

"Yes, I did. Do you know him?"

"You mean *the* Dr. Chase Letterby?"

"Is there another?" There was a long pause.

"Ms. Keller, there is no way he will get here in time."

"Actually, when Nicholas didn't get up off the field I called him immediately. Luckily, he was on his private jet about to land in Chicago, coming home from England. He should have landed nearby ten minutes ago," Cora said like she was name-dropping. It was so snobby and rude; I had never heard her be that way before. It was disgusting. She sounded more like that old hag Ester Theasing than Cora.

"Yes, Ms. Keller. We will wait for a little bit, but then we have to start the tests. Even Dr. Letterby would agree that we can't wait too long." The doctor was defeated. I guess the way she was name-dropping, making Dr. Chase Letterby sound like a celebrity, was effective. Slimy, but effective.

"Thank you, Dr. Flemming."

The room cleared out, including Cora. There were still two nurses in the room making sure everything was fully stocked and ready. I closed my eyes when they looked over.

"Can you believe they know Dr. Chase Letterby?" one of them whispered.

"Isn't he the top doctor in the country, and wasn't he operating on a member of the Royal Family just last week? That's why he was in England."

"He's the doctor to the stars, you know, and is drop-dead gorgeous. He is tall, dark, and hunky."

The two nurses continued to gossip about his good looks and what of theirs they wanted him to examine. I tuned them out. I drifted off thinking of Elle. She was the only one moving in my thoughts; everyone else was like still cardboard cut-outs. Then the black swirling clouds blocked my view of her and closed in on me.

"Nicholas, Nicholas." I opened my eyes. I thought I had died because the silhouette of an angel was over me. My eyes focused. It was Elle. I couldn't tell if I was asleep or awake until I tried to move and found I was still strapped to the table.

"Are you okay? Do you want me to get a doctor?" she asked, looking very worried. I ignored her question; I was more interested in why she was at the hospital.

"What are you doing here?"

She took my hand. "You got hurt, so I had to come see if you were all right."

"Why?"

"What kind of question is that? We are friends, aren't we?" she asked with a smile.

"Yes, of course we are, Elle, and to answer your first question, I feel fine. No need to get a doctor."

"I'm glad. You had me worried. I couldn't get much information about how you were at the stadium, so I came here right away to find out for myself. Plus, I had to see you in person."

There was a lot of commotion out in the hall. I couldn't turn to see what it was. Elle never looked away from me to see what all the excitement was about. Her eyes were just staring into mine. I wanted to tell her everything because I didn't want to lie to her. After years of lying to people about pretty much everything, I just wanted to be honest with her. I could hear voices getting louder and louder outside the room. Even with them talking right outside the door, Elle still stared into my eyes. I hoped whoever it was would leave me and Elle alone just for a couple minutes longer. Right then the doors opened.

"Excuse me, miss, you will have to wait outside," a deep voiced boomed. Elle squeezed my hand and disappeared out of sight.

"Hello, Nicholas, I'm Dr. Letterby." He was towering over the top of me, blocking out the bright light like an eclipse. He was wearing a black suit with a pink button-up shirt and a matching pink tie. His jet-black hair was messed up, but it looked intentional. His face looked like it was carved out of granite, not a flaw anywhere. His smiled revealed perfectly aligned teeth that sparkled like diamonds.

"So, Nicholas, I hear that you were hurt winning a football game."

"Yes, sir," I said.

"Does it still hurt anywhere?"

"Well, kind of," I said, not really sure what else to say.

Dr. Letterby left my sight, and I felt him starting to examine me.

"Why was this boy left on the ambulance gurney and not transported to a proper bed for examination?" His deep booming voice echoed in the room.

Dr. Fleming answered, "Ms. Keller told us to wait until you got here."

Dr. Letterby turned back to me so only I could see his face. He gave me a wink and then said again very loudly and seriously, "What kind of operation are you running here? You should at least have moved him. I guess this will have to do for now."

He turned around to face the crowd. The room had to be filled with every doctor and nurse from the hospital. I was sure

Cora was in the room among the sea of people all gathered to see Dr. Chase Letterby.

"Dr. Flemming, you and your staff have done enough for now. I need to run a couple of tests, but before that I need to talk to Ms. Keller and Nicholas alone. Do you mind?"

"Yes, of course," Dr. Flemming's voice cracked. "Okay, everyone, let's give them a minute." Dr. Flemming and his staff left the room. Dr. Letterby's request was a question, but from the response, it was taken as a command. The doors closed behind them.

"So, Cora, it's been some time. Did you miss me?" Dr. Letterby's large arms engulfed Cora in a bear hug over the top of me.

"It has been a while, Chase," she said, prying herself out of his large arms.

"Nicholas, you've changed a lot. You look like your mom with just a hint of your dad, which is a good thing because not everyone is blessed with good looks like some of us. Speaking of beauty, Cora, you are still as breathtaking as ever." I couldn't see Cora's expression. Was she blushing or was she stone-faced?

"Chase, enough. We need your help cleaning up a mess."

"Well, of course, that's why I'm here."

"Nicholas has drawn some unwanted attention to himself, as you can see, and instead of just quitting like he was supposed to, he faked this injury, which ended up drawing a lot more attention to us."

"Come on, Cora. Give him a break. You have both been hiding for a long time. A little slip-up is to be expected."

"We can't afford slip-ups; it only takes one time to be recognized, and then it's all over."

I needed to apologize to Cora, but I was still strapped to the gurney, unable to get up to look at her. "Cora, I'm sorry. I just didn't want to look like a quitter."

"Yeah, and he's got to look good in front of his girl. You know, the one that was in here—"

Cora interrupted, "I know who the girl is, Chase, but we can't afford luxuries like relationships." She turned and looked at me. "Even with a cute junior girl."

Chase hadn't heard anything Cora had said. He just continued to talk like he was trying to figure out a puzzle. "No, the girl wasn't it. Maybe he's trying to play football like his dad, and who could blame him for trying to take after his old man? I'm sure if he were still here, he would have forced him to play ball."

I tried to break free from the straps holding me down. I wanted to jump up and mess up that pretty face of his for bringing my dad into this. He wasn't like that; he would have never forced me to do anything. I started to yell, but Cora's face was over mine. She whispered, "Ignore him. It will be okay."

I fought back my anger.

She lifted her head and spoke in a commanding voice, the same sort of voice Chase used on the doctors and nurses. "Okay, Chase, it's time. You know what to do?"

"Of course I do. I will run some tests and make sure my medical opinion is that he can't play football again."

"Thanks, Chase. I owe you."

"A date then, maybe?"

"Sorry, Chase, I will never owe you that much."

Chase leaned over me. I was still angry. I didn't want to look at him, but I didn't have a choice.

"Nicholas, do me a favor. Please say that you have some tingling in your arms and legs whenever I ask. Can you do that?"

I nodded, still too angry to speak.

The next several hours consisted of lots of tests and big crowds. Everywhere Chase went, a big crowd followed. He was like a rock star. When different test results came in, he would just say, "Interesting, interesting." From time to time, he would ask me if anything hurt, and I would say that I felt tingling in my arms and legs.

At one point, he leaned down and pretended to examine my neck. "I just want you to know that your lady friend has been here the whole time," he whispered, "but Cora sent her home a little while ago. I tried to get Cora to let her stay, but I lost that battle."

I was still angry, but the fact that he tried to get Cora to let Elle stay helped me to see past his stupid comment about my dad. It was close to midnight when I was finally wheeled into a room on the third floor, room 322. There was a police officer stationed by my door. He stared at me hard like he knew who I was. He just nodded.

Cora was already sitting in the room. Dr. Flemming and Chase followed me into the room with a smaller entourage than usual.

"Dr. Flemming, I would like to stay to observe him overnight. I will need an office so I can go over the test results. Do you have any?"

"Of course, Dr. Letterby, you can use my office." Just like before, his question was taken as a command.

"We need to let Mr. Keller get some sleep," Chase said.

"Dr. Letterby, before we do that, can his visitors see him?" a nurse standing at the door said, blushing and looking down at the floor. Her actions didn't faze Chase. I guess he was used to women acting that way around him.

"Well, that's up to Ms. Keller."

"That will be fine, but not too long."

"Nurse Jones, tell Officer Weaver to let the visitors in and then he can go," Dr. Flemming said.

I heard a sound like a stampede coming down the hall. All of the JV team and most of varsity entered my small room. Coach Miller was standing at the foot of my bed, holding a football.

"On behalf of the team, we want to give you the game ball. Without your plays in the last two games, we would not have won. Your hard work and determination are an inspiration to all of us." Coach Miller set the ball, which was filled with signatures, at the end of my bed. "Get better, son."

Then one by one, each player walked up and touched my bed. Some said, "Get better," or "Get well." The last two players were Eric and Chad.

"Nicholas, I just wanted to say thanks."

"For what?" I asked Chad.

"Well, for putting up with all the crap we gave you. We will make sure to play as hard as you did while you're out. We won't let you down." Then Chad also patted the bed and walked out.

As soon as Chad left, Eric turned to me and said, "I can't believe Chad Reiger was just in your room telling you he wouldn't let you down. You are the luckiest guy alive." He looked at me in the bed and said, "Well you know what I mean by lucky."

"Don't worry, Eric, I know what you meant."

"I heard that Elle was here to check on you. You are so luck—"

Cora spoke up, "Eric, I'm sorry, Nicholas needs his sleep. You can see him later."

"Okay. Sorry, Ms. Keller." He leaned in close to me so only I could hear. "Tonight a legend was born." He turned and bounced out of the room.

VANDERBILT

CHAPTER FIFTEEN

"Cora, go home. I'll be fine. You have to be tired," I said. She was awkwardly trying to sleep in one of those horrible hospital chairs.

"I can take care of Nicholas. Cora, go ahead. I promise to watch over him. Remember, he's not really hurt," Chase whispered with his hands around his mouth like he was playing a game of telephone.

Cora got up from the chair and sat down next to me, patting me on my head. "Nicholas, sleep well, and next time, make sure I'm in on the plan."

No sooner had she left than I fell asleep listening to the sounds of my hospital room. I drifted into unconsciousness, and I was immediately surrounded by the familiar darkness. Off in the distance I heard Elle screaming for help, but I couldn't move. The black swirling darkness was holding me still, paralyzing me. My muscles started to push against it, but Elle's screaming broke my concentration. The darkness seeped into my lungs; I tried to breathe, but I couldn't. I began to choke, just like before. Elle's screams were horrifying. I had to fight to get to her. She needed me. The fire inside erupted and then I pushed back the putrid darkness with all of my might.

I awoke suddenly to find Chase standing over the top of me with a look of concern and intrigue twisted into his face.

"Nicholas, you okay? You were shaking pretty hard."

"I just feel sick," I whispered.

"You feel sick? How?" he asked.

"Before we talk, could I get some Tic Tacs? They make the sickness not as bad."

Chase pressed the call button on my bed. Two nurses answered at the same time and in unison, "Can I help you, Dr. Letterby?"

"Yes, could one of you please bring me some Tic Tacs?"

"Yes, of course, Dr. Letterby, but what kind?" one of the nurses asked. He looked at me.

"White, please," I said, fighting back the nausea.

"I will need white Tic Tacs, and could one of you dears bring me a cup of tea?" A few minutes passed and a smiling nurse entered the room holding ten different types of Tic Tacs.

"I didn't know which ones you wanted, so I got one of each." The nurse was out of breath, and her hair was falling down out of her bun. She looked like she had just run a 40-yard dash.

"Didn't you hear that I only needed the white ones?" Chase asked. Her cheeks turned a scarlet red that matched her hair.

"Well, as soon as you said you wanted Tic Tacs, I ran down and got them."

The other nurse came hurrying into the room with white Tic Tacs clenched in her teeth and one cup of tea in each hand, one iced and one hot. Different colored packs of sweeteners were balanced on her arm. She didn't say anything; she just set the cups of tea down on the little table next to the bed. Both of the nurses just stood there.

"Well, ladies, you two have been incredibly prompt and very thorough. Make sure, before you get off your shift, to both give me your names and contact information because I am always looking for good nurses to assist me." Before Chase had even finished his sentence, both of them were writing their information on whatever paper they could find in the room.

"Again, prompt. Thank you. That will be all."

They both grabbed each other's hands and left the room like two schoolgirls who had just been asked to the prom. I leaned forward, grabbed the white Tic Tacs, and popped them into my mouth.

"So how do you feel now, Nicholas?"

"I feel better. Thanks, Chase."

"Tell me about your sickness."

"Well, it feels like morning sickness. At least, that's what I think it feels like."

He shifted his weight in his chair and was now leaning closer to me, making sure not to miss anything. "How long has it been this way?"

"It all began when I started having these dreams about the darkness."

He looked perplexed. "Interesting. Have you experienced anything else?"

"Besides my morning sickness and dreams?" I asked.

"Yes, like aching muscles, acid backing up into your throat, stomach feeling like it's in knots, tightening of muscles?" He looked eager, anticipating my answer.

"No, I don't have any of those things," I lied. "Why?"

"Oh." Disappointment washed over his face, and he sat back in his chair. He took one of the cups of tea and began to sip it. His interest died instantly. "Well, it's probably low blood sugar. That's why the Tic Tacs help," Chase said. "You should really get some sleep now, Nicholas."

"Before I sleep, could I ask you some questions, Chase?" He looked apprehensive. "I just wanted to know how you became such a successful doctor."

Chase thought very hard, rubbing his chin. "I guess it couldn't hurt anything if I told you how I became a great and successful doctor. Well, Nicholas, the whole doctor thing came really easy to me. I graduated early from Vanderbilt Medical School and did my residency at New York General. That's where I became the doctor I am today." He stopped talking. He was smiling, staring off into space. He was admiring something from his past, most likely himself. This was going to take all night if he kept stopping.

"But, Chase, how did you become a doctor to the stars?"

His face lit up; he could barely contain his smile. "Well that's a funny story, Nicholas. It was my final year of residency, and I still didn't know what I wanted to do. I could do pretty much anything in medicine because I was that good. I felt like I was waiting for something to help me make my decision. I picked up a late shift for a colleague on New Year's Eve in the ER. It was an extremely cold December 31. It was about ten degrees below zero, and we had gotten four inches of fresh, powdery snow that day." He stood up and started to act out the story.

"It was a very slow night. There had only been a couple of patients, and most of them had come in earlier before my shift started. I was attending to some paperwork when we received a call that there had been a head-on collision. A woman in her late teens with life threatening injuries was on her way in. As soon as I got up, the doors to the ER flew open. The paramedics were wheeling in the bloodied girl." Chase was really getting into it now. He was not even looking at me; he was looking at the door. The two nurses who had gotten the Tic Tacs and tea were standing in the doorway, engulfed in Chase's story. Seeing the nurses motivated him to really play it up now. It reminded me a lot of Eric.

"I took her into the exam room. She had lost a lot of blood. She was AB-negative, the rarest of blood types. I started to work on her broken body, which lay motionless on the table. Her vitals began to fade. I was losing her. Her heartbeat began to slow. The nurse in attendance came running into the room. She told me that we were out of blood, and, due to the weather, it would take twenty minutes to get a backup supply. I knew my O-negative blood, which is the universal donor type, would buy the girl some precious time. I ripped off my coat and pulled up my sleeve, and I set up a transfusion from my arm to hers. While we were connected, I continued to work on her. I couldn't let her die."

Both of the nurses, who were now in the room, were hanging on every word Chase said. Was it even possible to give someone a transfusion straight from one person to another? It was his story and he was on a roll. I couldn't stop him if I wanted to get answers.

"My blood bought the girl desperately needed time. I worked fast trying to put her back together. Finally, after four hours of surgery, I was finished. She was going to be okay.

"Right when I sat down to relax, still with the transfusion going, a nurse came in. 'Dr. Letterby, someone is here to see her. Is it okay if they come back?'

"'Yes, nurse, that will be fine,' I said while unhooking the transfusion.

"A man and woman dressed in formalwear came into the room. They were surrounded by men in dark suits carrying guns. I stood up as the woman, who was wearing a beautiful, beaded lilac gown, floated to the side of the girl and began to weep. She looked like she had come straight from a New Year's Eve party. The man was in a black tuxedo and was right by the woman's side, comforting her.

"After a minute, he turned to me. 'Will she be okay, young man?'

"'I do believe she will be fine, sir,' I replied to the man in the tuxedo. The men, who I guessed were secret service, blocked the doors so no one could enter or see in.

"The man in the tuxedo spoke again. 'You are the physician who saved her life?'

"'Yes, sir, but my team was—'

"He held up his hand. 'Son there is no need to be modest. The nurses told us how there was no blood for her and you gave her your blood so she wouldn't bleed to death. And you did this while you were saving her life. You are an incredible doctor and a hero.'"

I tried not to laugh at Chase; I had to turn my head and pretend to cough so he couldn't tell. The two nurses, who had started out in the hall, had now managed to inch themselves into the room and were almost sitting on my bed, mouths wide-open in complete awe of Chase.

"Nicholas, do you know who that girl was that I saved in the ER on that cold New Year's night?" Chase asked.

Before I could answer, the red-headed nurse said, "It was Princess Katherine."

Chase smiled. "Yes, it was Princess Katherine. After that night, I became very close with the Royal Family, and that is how I found my calling of helping celebrity clientele. But I don't just operate on the rich; I also operate on common folk like you." He was looking right at the two nurses, and they started to applaud him like he was standing on stage after finishing a performance of Hamlet. I couldn't believe he called them common and they still applauded.

This was my chance to find out his connection with Cora. "Chase, that was amazing, but how did you get to know my au—my mom so well?"

He smiled, still in storytelling mode. "Well, I met her at Vanderbilt, and we were really close friends. I helped her when—" He stopped abruptly. He looked at the nurses and said, "Thank you, ladies. You have been a great help. That will be all for tonight."

They both looked disappointed, but they left nonetheless. I hoped he was having them leave so he could finish his thought.

"Nicholas, it's time for bed."

He turned the lights off before I could try to question him more. I lay there in the darkness even more curious about their relationship. The questions of the day consumed me, but once again, Elle melted away those thoughts.

ANNIVERSARY
CHAPTER SIXTEEN

When they came in to tell me the diagnosis, I acted like I was devastated. Cora even cried and comforted me. Chase convinced the staff at Bethesda South that I had a hairline fracture in a vertebra and that I shouldn't play football again. No one there dared to challenge him. He kept me in the hospital for another week. It was horrible. Cora must have made a rule that I could have no more visitors because, after the first night, there was no sign of anyone coming to visit. Flowers, cards, and notes would show up, but nobody was attached to them except a candy striper or Cora.

After I was released, Chase left on his million-dollar jet, which was as big as a regular commercial liner. Chase tried again for the hundredth time to convince Cora to get on the plane with him, but the answer was still no.

Once home, I had to stay there for the next two weeks to keep up the charade of being severely injured. Being away from Elle for three weeks wasn't part of my plan. Maybe just quitting would have been better. I kept waiting for Cora to lecture me, but again, like several times before, nothing. I kept busy by listening to music and watching TV.

The two weeks of confinement were finally coming to an end. I was able to keep up with my homework, thanks to Cora going to school to get my assignments from my counselor. After the first time she got my homework from Joy Lemmins, she came home swearing that we were going to move just so she wouldn't have to talk to "that stupid nitwit" again. She was one of those people that Cora didn't like to be around. I couldn't blame her.

"Nicholas." Cora walked into the family room where I was watching TV. She looked upset. Her normally precise mascara had run a little. Her nose was a tint of red. Before I was able to ask what was wrong, she said, "We are going to take a trip tomorrow before you go back to school." She took a tissue and wiped her nose.

Take a trip? We never left our city limits unless we were moving, and we weren't moving because she hadn't done any packing.

"Cora, where are we going?"

"Nicholas, do you know what today's date is?"

"I have no idea. It's September something."

"No, tomorrow's the tenth of October."

The grief that Cora had been experiencing covered me like a wet blanket. How could I not know the date? How? Tomorrow would be the five-year anniversary of my parents' death. I put my face into my hands, feeling ashamed. The memories of that day started to flood back. Luckily, Cora sat down next to me and rubbed my back, keeping me in the present.

"I want to take you to see your parents' graves."

"Do you think it's safe to go?"

"We have been gone too long, Nicholas. If we are careful, we should be fine."

"*Should* be fine? Don't you think it's too big of a risk?"

"It is a big risk, and one that I don't think we should take, but it has been too long." She pulled out another tissue, tucked it in her sleeve, and wiped away some more tears. "It's time we go home."

**

It was surreal driving back to our hometown. The trees' amber leaves fluttered in the cool autumn breeze. The sky was full of grey, low-lying clouds covering the sky. I didn't sleep at all the night before, and from the look of it, Cora hadn't either. I hadn't thought that I would ever see my home again, or at least not this soon. I was hoping Cora would talk about something to distract me like she normally did, but today she was not interested in talking. All I could focus on was the question, the single question that worried me: what was I going to say to my parents?

I wondered how the place would look. Had the past five years changed things, making them unrecognizable? The more I thought about it, the more questions came to mind. As we got closer, the sun managed to push through the clouds, making the rays look like thousands of tiny slides coming down from heaven. My mom used to say that those were slides for angels to ride down to earth.

Around the sun, the sky was blood red. The clouds farthest away from the sun were vibrant orange. The beautiful sky was a slight distraction, but the agony that was eating away at my soul needed more distraction. Thoughts of Elle were the only thing that made me feel like I could handle what was ahead of me.

The truck rumbled down the road. It seemed to remember every bump and dip, effortlessly driving on the winding road. It seemed like only yesterday I was riding on this very road, fleeing with Cora. The road straightened out, and my heart quickened with anticipation. We were getting close to home.

The road took us through a small wooded area on the outside of town. In the distance I could see a clearing with a large sign, which was new. When we got closer to the clearing, I could see that it was a city sign that read, "Mt. Vernon." There were hundreds of flower bouquets and wreaths surrounding the large wooden sign. The flowers blocked out the rest of the writing below the city name. Among the flowers were pictures of people, memorials.

When our truck passed the sign, we were out of the woods and in a clearing. What we saw next was shocking. The city cemetery, which once was on a small plot of land right next to the town, now stretched on for miles. There were buildings off in the distance, but they were far away like a backdrop in a theater production. The once small Mt. Vernon Cemetery was now enormous.

Cora drove us to where the old entrance to the cemetery used to be. It had been widened, and the entrance now had a large wrought-iron gate surrounding it. In large letters over the entrance it said, "We will never forget how you were taken 10-10." We drove through the large gate slowly. I stared out over the cemetery in disbelief.

There were people carrying large bundles of small American flags, which they were putting on every grave and monument. Cora's eyes were red and watering. She was holding the steering wheel so tight that her knuckles had turned white. I wanted to comfort her, but there was a lump in my throat making it impossible for me to talk. Cora slowed the truck and then I saw it—the oak tree on a small hill where we had buried my parents. The small tree had grown a lot in five years, but I knew that we had arrived.

We sat in silence just staring at the tree. I remembered the last time Cora and I sat in this place. It was when she told me we would have to disappear and leave everything we knew behind. It's hard to believe that it had been five years; it seemed like yesterday.

"Nicholas," Cora said in a raspy, almost inaudible voice, "we can't stay long. You must ignore all the people around you. That's very important."

I looked around the cemetery. There were hundreds of people scattered throughout.

She continued with her instructions, "I will stay in the truck with the engine running just in case anyone recognizes you. If you notice anyone staring or if you feel uneasy about anything, get back here right away."

I was not looking at her. I couldn't stop staring at the tree. "Nicholas, did you hear me?"

I was still unable to talk, so I nodded and got out of the truck. I walked directly to the tree, trying to keep my head down as much as possible to avoid eye contact with any of the people nearby.

Every headstone I passed had something horribly in common: the date of death. There were whole families that had all died together. I was jealous that I was not another grave marker here along with the rest of my family. My mom and dad's headstones were right in front of the tree, just like I remembered. My parents' graves were covered by flowers, more than any others around. Someone had placed a hand-carved stone bench at the end of their graves.

On my mom's headstone were inscribed the words, "I am here. All you have to do is close your eyes." When asked what I wanted on it, that phrase was all I could think of. The night before she died I was having trouble sleeping, and she said those very words to me. "Nicholas, don't worry. I am here. All you have to do is close your eyes."

My dad's headstone only had the word "love" inscribed on it because that's what my dad was, love. He didn't say much, but he loved my mom and me. He took such good care of us, always making sure that he was everything a father and a husband should be. So when asked what I wanted on his headstone, "love" had to be it.

"Hi, Mom. Hi, Dad. I'm sorry it's been so long since I've visited. Aunt Cora thought it would be better if we stayed away for a while. I'm not sure why we came now, but I am glad we did. As you know, we have been moving a lot. This time I'm actually at a school where I am not just a number. Dad, I made the varsity football team this year and played in a couple of games. You would be proud."

I rambled on about school and football, and then I ended with telling them about Elle. I couldn't control my emotions any longer. I fell to my knees and began to sob uncontrollably. "Why didn't I die too? Then we all could be together now. Mom, Dad, I miss you so much." My tears watered the ground in front of me.

I became sick. I felt like I was being turned inside out, like I would never be okay again. I got up off my knees to get my pack of Tic Tacs out of my pocket. I took a deep breath and wiped my face. Suddenly, I felt like something was wrong. The fire inside me lit, and instinctively I snapped around and began to walk briskly toward the truck. A small group of people had been watching my every move and was now moving toward me. A voice inside me said, "Run!" I broke into a sprint, weaving in and out of the headstones. The fire burned hotter and my surroundings blurred.

When I got into the truck, Cora was still looking straight ahead. "Where did you come from?"

"Cora, we have to go now." Cora didn't take time to look out the windows or question me further. She put the truck into drive and whipped us around with the wheels squealing loudly on the pavement.

We were out on the main road passing the Mt. Vernon sign when she asked, "What happened? Did someone approach you?"

"No, but I felt like something was wrong, and when I turned around to walk to the truck there was a group of people moving toward me from every direction, so I ran."

"Nicholas what do you mean you felt something was wrong?" she asked calmly. The panic that had just been in her voice was now gone.

"I don't know, I had just finished talking with Mom and Dad when I felt it. I don't know why, I just felt like I was in trouble."

Cora listened but didn't say anything.

COURT
CHAPTER SEVENTEEN

After our trip, I was finally allowed to go back to school. I no longer felt the need to hide or blend in once I went back. My secret was still hidden, but Nicholas Keller could finally be a part of something. For some reason, I felt safe here at school. I had confidence. This was a different feeling for me because I usually only felt this way when Cora was around. Maybe it was because I had talked to Elle the night before, and she was excited that I was coming back. She said that she couldn't wait to eat with me under the stairs.

Apparently for the last couple of weeks, Eric had been talking to everyone in the school about me. He was like a campaign manager trying to get me elected for something I wasn't running for. Eric had made it his personal mission to make sure they erected a statue to me for my heroics. With everyone knowing me now, it made me wonder if all the cloak and dagger, moving around and hiding, had been a mistake by Cora. Even Oliver stopped picking on me, probably because I was off the team, which is what he wanted all along. He was now completely ignoring me. I didn't have to hide any longer. That burden was lifted off my shoulders.

The Homecoming Dance was coming up soon. Over the last week I had become determined that I was going to ask Elle. Normally, any dance or social event was off limits, but Cora had asked me if I was going, so I figured I could go if I wanted to. Even more surprising than being allowed to go was that I was nominated to Winsor's Homecoming Court, which was incredible because Elle was too. It seemed like the stars were aligning. Maybe it was destiny for us to go to the dance together. I was pretty sure that she had been asked already, which was understandable because the dance was only a couple of weeks away, but I was hoping she had been waiting for me to ask her.

On my way to meet Elle under the stairs to eat, I stopped by my locker to get some books. That's when I heard the familiar chipmunk voices. It was Jennifer and Julie, Elle's friends from math class. They were standing by the water fountain, talking in their usual loud way for all to hear.

"I can't believe she was nominated for court and we weren't."

"I know. How long do we have to keep being nice to her?"

"This was supposed to be *our* year. We are seniors. She's a lowly junior."

They walked by me. They didn't even notice I was there.

**

"So, Elle, are you excited about being on the Homecoming Court?" I asked, propping myself up with my backpack against the wall, finally under the stairs with her.

"No, not really."

"Why not?"

"Homecoming Court is just some stupid popularity contest," Elle said, not looking up from her salad and grape pop.

"What's wrong with that?" I asked.

Elle looked up. She looked angry.

"Elle, are you okay? I'm sorry if I made you mad."

She gave a half-hearted laugh and said, "Nicholas, you didn't make me mad. It's just that no one paid attention to me last year or the year before, and now I'm on the Homecoming Court after being invisible for two years. I never fit in with the popular crowd because I never gossiped, had the right clothes, or had the right zip code . . . and I was okay with that. But everything changed when I got contacts, began to wear some make-up, and had a certain football player begin to like me. I know what you're thinking—why did I do all of that if I didn't want to be noticed? I'm not shallow, Nicholas. I just wanted to be happy with what I saw in the mirror." Tears welled up in her stormy eyes.

"Nicholas, I didn't care about what anyone else thought, but now people want to be my best friend and be around me. On the inside, I'm still the same Elle that they never noticed." Elle was shredding her napkin in her lap. She took a deep breath, looking angry.

"Elle, I would still like you, even if you wore glasses and no make-up. You could never be invisible to me."

She laughed, wiping away a couple of tears that rolled down her cheek. "Well, of course you would, Nicholas. You are different. You are such a good friend." She smiled.

"Elle, would you go to Homecoming with me?"

"Nicholas, I can't go with you. I'm going with someone else. . . . I'm going with Oliver."

The fire burned in me, consuming my soul. "Who?" I said.

"Oliver," she repeated, but in a whisper like it was some terrible secret.

"So are you dating?" I asked.

"No way, we are going as friends. I would never date him. Our parents have been friends for a long time, and Oliver was that football player who I said liked me."

"What does that have to do with you going with him to the dance? I thought you hated the fact you've become popular."

"Oliver asked me after the first football game, and I had to say yes. Nicholas, if it makes you feel any better, I would rather go with you. You are the only person I would like to share that night with. We have become such great friends."

**

After my first day back to school, Elle and I continued to eat under the stairs, but now we did it in silence. Eating there together was once comfortable and cozy, but now it had become tiny and claustrophobic, putting us uncomfortably close.

"So, Nicholas, are you going to the game?" Elle's question sounded awkward. She was not eating much of a lunch today. Just a cookie and her grape pop.

"Yes, I stand on the—"

She interrupted, "I know, you stand on the sidelines with the team. Sorry, I forgot."

The team still wanted me to be on the sidelines even though I was injured. They all insisted that they needed me to be there. I was like a rabbit's foot or a lucky penny.

"Nicholas, I want to know something. Are you going to the dance?"

"I haven't given it much thought. I don't have a date," I said. I looked up, meeting Elle's penetrating eyes. She took my hand.

"Nicholas, please come to the dance."

"Okay, I'll go," I said like a mindless zombie.

She let go of my hand and I snapped out of it just long enough to realize that I didn't have anyone to go with or a suit to wear. Why was I going? Better yet, why did she want me to go? I was upset with her, but I decided I would at least try to go anyway. This might be my only chance to go to a dance during high school.

After school, I saw Eric hanging out near my locker. "Hey, Eric," I shouted.

He spun around like he was in a Western, about to draw his guns. "Hey, Nicholas. How's my star?"

"Good. I have a question. Who are you going with to Homecoming?"

"Hey, it's a little late to be asking me to Homecoming," Eric joked. "Plus, I'm not Ms. Popular Elle, who you are infatuated with."

"Very funny. Seriously, who are you going with?"

Eric was now batting his eyes at me and making kissy faces. I pushed him up against the lockers. The force of my shove made his long, brown hair fall over his face. He pushed the hair back out of his face.

"Ouch, Keller, I'm just playing around. I'm going with a big group of people. We rented three limos and are going to eat at McDonald's. Then we are off to the dance. Why? Do you want to come with us?"

I didn't hesitate. "That would be great, if you have room."

"But why the change of mind? When I asked you yesterday, you weren't remotely interested."

"Well I want to go now, okay?"

"Of course, we always have room for the star of the tenth-grade class."

"Eric, don't start that again because next time I won't be so gentle. I'll push you through the locker."

He laughed at me. "See you tonight, star." He ran by me to avoid getting pushed again. He yelled to me as he ran down the hall, "Don't run after me. I don't want you to hurt another vertebra."

When I got home, Cora was washing the truck. She was on the other side rinsing off the soap when a stream of water came shooting over the truck, drenching me. She looked around the truck, laughing at me. I ran to the front porch just out of reach of getting squirted again.

Cora walked up to the porch. She looked like she had been swimming, not washing a car. She was drenched from her head to her toes. It was warm for October, but not warm enough for getting soaked.

"You know the water goes on the truck, right?"

She smiled. "So are you ready for the big game tonight, Nicholas?"

"Well, I guess, but I don't know what I should be ready for. I don't play, remember?"

"Yes, I remember that. I'm talking about before the game and halftime. Homecoming Court? Remember, you ride in the parade before the game. Then at halftime you walk out and wave to the crowd. They will announce the Freshman and Sophomore Prince and Princess, the Junior Duke and Duchess, and the Senior King and Queen. At least, that's what the paper said that I got from Joy Lemmins."

She was right. I had totally forgotten about all the Homecoming Court stuff. The different classes had all been working on building floats for the Best Float Contest, and everyone was talking about the parade and the court. This past week, Joy Lemmins was on the announcements each morning, reminding everyone all about it.

"I forgot," I told Cora.

"I knew you had, especially with all of the stuff with Elle. Nicholas, I knew you were going to ask her, but when you didn't say you needed a suit or anything, I figured she said no or you decided not to ask."

"I did ask and she said no."

"I'm sorry, Nicholas. Who is she going with?"

"She's going with Oliver Rails."

Cora's expression didn't change when I said his name. She just stared at me. I wasn't sure what she was waiting for. I couldn't take it. I had to break the silence.

"So what am I supposed to do tonight for the parade and stuff?"

Cora's face lit up again. "You are supposed to wear a suit and meet at the school at 5:00 p.m. to ride on the sophomore Homecoming float with the other nominees. Then during halftime, they will announce who was selected for the Homecoming Court." The more she described it, the more animated she became. "Once the court is selected, they will represent their different classes at the dance."

"Cora, how do we *represent* our classes?"

"Oh, you will be announced and walk down a carpet of some kind. Then the winners will dance to a couple of songs."

"But Cora, I don't have a suit."

Her smile got even larger. She grabbed me, dragging me into the house. There, hanging on the coat closet door, was a garment bag with two red griffons on it and the name "Oxford Clothes" in large fancy writing. Cora quickly took out the suit. It was something royalty would wear. It was a navy pinstriped suit with silver buttons. There was a green tie with a white dress shirt inside the suit. It didn't look like it was made from fabric. It moved like it was made out of water.

"Cora, where and when did you get it?"

"The *where* is a long story, but the *when* was when Joy Lemmins told me you were nominated. I was hoping that you would wear it to the actual dance, but the Homecoming festivities during the game will have to do."

"Cora, I'm going to the Homecoming Dance with Eric and his friends."

Cora's eyes lit up even more. She nearly knocked me over hugging me. "Nicholas, that's great. I'm so happy for you, and it's for the best that you're not going with Elle."

I knew she was right. Going with Elle would have made leaving that much harder. Maybe it was good that she was going with Oliver; it would definitely make things easier. Leaving a friend was something I could do, but leaving a girlfriend would be a new pain I wasn't eager to discover.

Who was I kidding? I longed to have the chance to feel that.

**

It was amazing how well the suit fit. I looked like a celebrity ready to walk the red carpet for a big movie premiere.

"Nicholas, you look handsome." Cora had walked into my room. She was wearing a pair of faded jeans with a gold Winsor hooded sweatshirt. She had her hair up in a ponytail with green and yellow ribbons coming down from it.

"So how do I look?" She spun around like she was modeling for a high school fashion show.

"You look like a Winsor High School model," I chuckled.

"Well, that was the look I was going for, but I don't want to upstage you!" She turned quickly and bounced down the stairs. "Hurry, you don't want to be late."

We got to the school right on time. The parade was already lined up in the school parking lot and ready to go. I saw the sophomore float near the front of the line. From a distance, our float looked like a large brown egg that had a little yellow chicken sticking out of it.

"Good luck, Nicholas. I will see you tonight," Cora said, throwing me a pack of Tic Tacs.

Joy Lemmins was standing right in front of my class float, which turned out to be a football with a yellow football player coming out of it, not a chicken. I tried to walk by Joy Lemmins without her noticing me, but it didn't work.

"Well, goodness gracious, bless my stars. There he is, the star of the tenth grade, Mr. Nicholas Keller," she said in a high-pitched voice. She grabbed me and pulled me right next to her with her arm around my waist. "I'm telling you, if I knew then what I know now, I would have given you a king hat with your class schedule that day you were in my office. And to think I was worried about you," she said, giggling. *Did she really just say that?*, I thought.

"I'm here to get on the tenth grade float for the Homecoming Court."

Joy started to laugh in a larger-than-life belly laugh.

"Don't be ridiculous! You are riding with the rest of the tenth grade Homecoming Court nominees in a nice red convertible—" She stopped mid-sentence, looking down at my suit. "Oh my! Is that an Oxford suit?"

I nodded yes, which was a mistake because she began to feel the suit and turn me around, looking me up and down saying, "Oh my goodness," over and over again. It was like I was a kid trying on clothing in a fitting room for my mother.

"That suit is gorgeous! Each Oxford suit is handmade with the finest fabrics and by the finest craftsmen. Where did you get it?"

"It's a long story."

She smiled and pointed at the red convertible in front of the tenth grade float. Two girls and a boy were already sitting in the car. I recognized the girl sitting by herself from homeroom but didn't know her name. She was sitting up on the trunk with her feet resting on the back seat.

"Nicholas, you get to sit up here with me," she said.

I got in and sat next to the petite blonde, who was wearing a pale yellow dress with a large white bow on the back. She looked like a southern belle; all she was missing was a large parasol and fan.

"Hi! My name is Amber King," she said to me.

I turned and stuck out my hand and said, "Nice to meet you. I'm Nicholas Keller."

She laughed and shook my hand. "Nicholas, everyone knows who you are." She linked her arm around mine and the car started to roll forward.

It was perfect weather for the parade. The temperature was in the mid 60s with a light breeze. The fall sun was beginning to set with a harvest moon high in the sky.

The parade lasted forty-five minutes. We wound in and out of busy streets, led by a pair of police cars. The whole time, while waving to the people along the route, I thought about what Amber said—*everyone knows you*. Yet, my secret was still safe, which again made me question why I had been hiding this whole time.

Going down the last street back toward the school, it dawned on me that Elle was somewhere behind me, which made my heart race. But my image of her beauty faded quickly, tarnished by the thought of Oliver sitting right next to her.

The parade stopped. Amber gave me a big hug. "See you at halftime."

I got out of the car and headed to the locker room, where the team would be waiting to go into the tunnel. I sat down in front of my locker, where my equipment hung untouched. My jersey, which had been sewn back together after being cut off of me, was now framed and hanging in my locker. The frame had an engraved inscription that read, "Winning is not the most important thing—teammates are." How ironic that that was what they put on it, especially since every billboard I had seen said, "Winning isn't everything—it's the only thing." Everyone on the JV and varsity teams had signed it, including the coaches, but with only one obvious exception: Oliver.

Coach Miller called everyone over to do his pre-game talk. Everyone was restless today. During Coach Miller's speech the guys were still talking. Normally Coach Miller didn't put up with that, but today he didn't acknowledge that they were talking, understanding that Homecoming had something to do with their restlessness.

"Excuse me," he spoke up in a louder voice and waited for the room to quiet. "Tonight we have three guys on the team who are part of the Homecoming Court. Please stand," he said.

Oliver stood up and Chad stood up. I waited to see if someone else stood; I hoped another person would stand.

"Nicholas, stand up," Coach Miller said, motioning to me. I stood up in the back.

He pointed to each one of us in order. "Chad, if you are chosen to be Junior Duke, or if Oliver is selected to be Junior Duke, or if, Nicholas, you are selected to be Sophomore Prince, I hope you remember that it's an honor, and you are representing the football program and your school. So be on your best behavior."

He motioned for us to sit. He continued his talk about how every win from now on is important because it gets us one step closer to our goal of winning a state championship. He went to one knee and bowed his head. A minute later he rose to his feet and yelled, "Let's go!" and the team jumped up.

I walked behind the team to the tunnel with the student trainers. The team ran onto the field through fireworks and cheers from the crowd. I walked over to the sideline. The stadium seemed to be even more crowded and louder than at other games.

With five minutes left in the half, Joy Lemmins appeared about ten feet from me. Seeing her nearly gave me a heart attack. She waved me over to where she was standing. I reluctantly walked toward her, still remembering the last time she saw me. I was hoping she wouldn't grab me again and feel my suit. That would be a lot more embarrassing in front of ten thousand people.

"Nicholas, you need to go to the south end zone where the scoreboard is. All of the Homecoming Court is down there waiting for you."

I looked down at the far end zone, and there was a group of people congregating, all dressed up in suits and dresses.

I walked along the track toward the end zone. The closer I got, the more nervous I felt. Amber spotted me right before I made it to them. She ran up to me and gave me a big hug.

"So glad to see you again, partner! Are you nervous? I'm a wreck!" she exclaimed, pulling me over to the other waiting nominees.

"No, I don't get nervous," I lied.

Then out of nowhere, I was grabbed from behind and spun around. It was Joy Lemmins.

"Okay, now, everyone line up. When you hear your name over the PA, you and your partner will walk to the center of the field and face the home stands and wait. They will first announce the Freshman Prince and Princess, Sophomore Prince and Princess, Junior Duke and Duchess and then Senior King and Queen. If you are so lucky as to win, step toward me, and you will get your crown or tiara. Then we will have a group photo taken for the paper."

Right then the halftime buzzer went off, and both teams ran to their locker rooms. Chad and Oliver ran over to us and got in line behind me. Elle was somewhere behind us, maybe right behind me. *Nicholas*, I told myself, *you need to forget about her. It's going to be hard enough to move feeling the way you feel now. Plus, she is going with Oliver to the dance.* The nervous feeling subsided, but my jealousy bubbled back to the surface.

I hadn't noticed that they had already announced all of the freshmen and the one other sophomore couple. Then over the loud speaker I heard, "Amber King escorted by Nicholas Keller." Amber pulled me across the field to the middle, right next to the other sophomore couple.

The next names were announced, "Elle Canan escorted by Chad Reiger." I turned and looked at them. There she was. She was more stunning than I had ever dreamt her to be. Her black hair had big thick curls that bounced as she walked. Her eyes sparkled, reflecting the light from the stadium, making them look like bright blue stars. She was wearing a long brown flowing dress with yellow accents that made her look like she was floating on air. She looked right into my eyes the entire way. I couldn't break away from her gaze. She had me, again, under her spell. Then she gave me a smile and turned with Chad, facing the crowd. The rest of the Court followed.

The announcer thanked everyone on the Homecoming Court and Joy Lemmins, who did a very awkward curtsey in front of the home crowd, almost tipping over. Then the announcer said, "And now, for your 2012 Homecoming Court: The Freshman Prince and Princess are Joe McDonald and Lisa James; your Sophomore Prince and Princess are Nicholas Keller and Amber King; your Junior Duke and Duchess are Elle Canan and Chad Reiger."

I looked back to watch Elle walk up. Behind her I saw Oliver looking angrier than I had ever seen him. He didn't win; Chad did. The most popular guy in the school didn't win Homecoming Duke. How was this possible? The captain of the football team always wins. Then the announcer said who the Senior King and Queen were, but I wasn't paying attention. I was obsessing over why Oliver hadn't won.

I felt a warm, soft hand grab mine. I looked over and Elle was right next to me with a big smile. She squeezed my hand and let it go. The warmth from her hand spread through my entire body. Right then, I knew that I loved her.

That night I sat on my bed, staring at my suit and trying to remember every detail of the last couple hours. The crown I had won was on my desk. The fact that Elle was still going with Oliver to the dance didn't crush my excitement completely. The moment we shared on the field was one I would remember for the rest of my life, even after I moved away.

My excitement was nothing compared to Cora's. I had to get away from her. During the whole ride home, she talked about me winning. The way she talked made me think that she must have won something herself. She was also impressed that when they took the winners' photograph for the newspaper, I turned my head so it wouldn't be a clear photo of me.

Finally, I was alone in my room. I put my head down on my pillow and fell into a dreamless sleep.

DANCE
CHAPTER EIGHTEEN

A light, cool rain was falling the next morning. The excitement I had felt the night before had washed away with the rain. Whatever effect Elle had on me was all but gone. I searched my room for my Tic Tacs, but all I found were empty boxes like little skeletons littering my floor.

"Cora!" I yelled.

"Yes, Nicholas?" she called from downstairs.

"Do you know where any Tic Tacs are?"

"There are some in my purse. I'll get them."

I heard the comforting rattling sound as she walked up the stairs. She tossed them to me. I quickly put three of them in my mouth.

"Nicholas, you shouldn't get so worried about tonight. You are going to have a wonderful time with your friends. Plus, you are going to look sharp. You will have to beat the girls off."

"I thought that I was supposed to avoid relationships?" I said.

Cora rolled her eyes at me. "You know what I mean."

"Maybe I shouldn't go."

"No, you have to go; you will have a great time. Plus, you are the Sophomore Prince. In the three months since we've been here, Nicholas, you haven't exactly flown under the radar. The one thing it has shown me is that maybe I've been too strict with you. Now that you're older and you've made all the right decisions, I should trust you more."

I shook my head in disagreement.

"I may have done things differently, but you have not been recognized and you have been able to lead a normal life—well, somewhat normal. So there is no way I'm going to let you miss Homecoming, Mr. Sophomore Prince."

**

We pulled into Eric's subdivision, Cleave Lakes. All the houses were identical, large two-story brick homes with small yards. The only way to tell them apart was by the numbers on the mailboxes. Up ahead, I saw Eric's house. There were two white limos and one purple one in front of it. There were cars parked up and down the street.

"Wow, there sure are a lot of kids going with you." Cora pulled in behind a black BMW SUV. Our Ford truck definitely showed its age behind such an expensive new car. The light rain from earlier had disappeared, leaving behind a partly cloudy sky.

Cora got into her handbag and handed me some money. "Okay, here is $160 for your dinner, picture, and whatever else."

"Cora, we're going to McDonald's and then to the dance. I doubt the pictures are going to be $155."

"Just take it, Nicholas. You never know." She shoved the folded money into my hand and got out of the truck. She was carrying a black bag with her purse. We walked up to the group.

"Nicholas is here," someone yelled. The crowd turned and they surrounded me. I knew most of them. Some of them I had class with; others were on the JV football team. I spotted Eric right in the middle. He was wearing a black suit, his hair was slicked back into a ponytail, and he was wearing a bright pink tie.

"Whose funeral?" I said to him.

He laughed and said so only I could hear him, "All the other guys, because they don't have a chance with the ladies. But don't worry, Keller, you can be my wingman and have my leftovers." Then he shouted, "Okay, now everyone get together for pictures!"

I couldn't believe my ears or eyes. Cora was orchestrating the pictures for the groups of moms next to us. Cora pulled a professional-looking camera out of the black bag. She kept directing us to move around while all of the other moms took pictures.

"Okay, that's enough pictures. Let's go!" Eric said. "Nicholas, Matt, Erin, Melissa and Livi, in the purple limo with me. The rest of you divide up into the white limos."

I knew Eric had his eye on Livi, because when she went to get into the limo, he opened the door for her and offered his hand to help her in. The rest of the girls followed with no help from Eric. Then Matt got in, leaving Eric and I outside.

"So Eric, is Livi your girl?"

He looked at me with a grin that would shame the Cheshire Cat. "She is, but she just doesn't know it yet." I followed him into the limo.

We rolled down the window to wave to the moms. Cora gave me a wink. Livi was tall and slender with brown hair and pale skin. She had three classes with me, and from what I could tell, she was brilliant. She always knew all of the answers. I was a little stunned that Eric liked her. I always pictured his dream girl being a not-so-bright blonde and very mature for her age. Wasn't Livi too smart for Eric? Maybe he was trying something new.

Melissa and Erin looked pretty much identical to each other—small, brownish-blonde hair. The only difference was their hairstyles. Erin had big curly hair and Melissa's was long and straight. These two were the same ones in biology class that wouldn't leave me alone the first couple of weeks. I had become good at blocking out their continuous chatter.

The inside of the limo was like something out of a movie. Everything was covered in leather or gold. Eric was talking to Livi, ignoring the rest of us. I was sitting next to Melissa, who also was admiring the limo.

"So, Nicholas, were you excited to win Prince? You know, being a new student and all," Melissa asked. Matt, Erin, and Melissa all stared at me, waiting for my answer.

"Yes, it was a surprise."

"After Keller hit Oliver during tryouts, I knew he would represent the Sophomore Class well," Matt said.

"I don't know much about football, but the way you inspired the varsity team after your injury, you had to win it for sure. If a sophomore could win King, you would have," Erin said, winking at me.

Eric and Livi were still engrossed in their own conversation, which was a relief because Eric would have made what they were saying into some huge story, probably including a damsel in a tower and a dragon with Oliver's head on it and me saving everyone.

I started to get hot. I cracked the window to cool down. The limo was beginning to feel really small. I was not used to people talking about me, especially people I barely knew. I didn't like it. Melissa and Erin went on about how awesome the football team had been playing.

Matt chimed in, "Yeah, it's incredible that they're still winning. Oliver can't seem to score any points. If it weren't for the defense, we would have probably lost half of those games."

Then Livi joined the conversation, "Wasn't Oliver supposed to be good?"

Eric answered, "He was good on JV, but for some reason he couldn't take it to the next level."

Then the limo stopped abruptly. Erin pretended to fall into me.

"Excuse me," she said, batting her eyes at me.

I felt uneasy being around these girls.

The driver rolled down the tinted window that separated us from him. "We have arrived at McDonald's, sir."

"Very good," Eric replied. I was relieved to have a chance to escape Erin's gaze.

Eating at McDonald's was fun. We pretty much took over the entire restaurant. Melissa and Erin followed me around

175

like lost puppies and made sure they sat by me, just like in biology class, but a lot closer. I made sure not to give either one of them the wrong impression because I was sure they were waiting for some sign of interest.

**

When Cora and I had first arrived at the school for registration in August, I had been stunned by how elaborate the school looked. But now, I would have sworn we were somewhere else if I hadn't seen the Winsor High School sign out front. Our school had been decorated with millions of tiny white lights. They were on every tree, bush, and flower, and even the statue in the middle of the parking lot. The moonless night made the lights shine even brighter.

The three limos pulled up in front of the school behind some of the other limos letting off groups of people. I put a couple of Tic Tacs in my mouth just to calm my nerves. The ramp to the school's entrance had a red carpet down the middle. There were old-fashioned lampposts lining both sides of the carpet. In between the posts were incredible flower arrangements, made up mostly of white roses on large concrete pedestals. We walked down the red carpet, but I lingered a couple of feet behind everyone. I marveled at how beautiful everything looked. The rest of our group didn't seem to notice anything. Maybe they had just come to expect this sort of thing, and the elaborate decorations were nothing new. The school never cut any corners; they always did everything first class.

The decorations outside were nothing compared to the ones inside. The long hall that led to the lunchroom had vanished. The lockers on both sides had disappeared too. There was now a cobblestone path that weaved in and out of a rolling sea of multi-colored roses. Along the path were the same lamps from outside, lighting the path with flickering candlelight. Underneath each lamp was a sitting area, each with unique wooden benches. The roses looked so inviting. I wanted to jump into them and swim in the rolling sea. The girls in our group oohed and aahed at the decor while we walked through the enchanted setting. Both Erin and Melissa were right next to me.

Up ahead was the lunchroom; well, at least that's what it used to be. The ceiling was filled with long, white flowing silk that shone iridescently. In the center was a hanging chandelier covered by millions of tiny crystals. I wouldn't be surprised if they were actual diamonds.

"Okay, crew." Eric turned around to address the group. "The dance ends at 11:00 p.m. and the limos will be out front at 10:45. We will leave at 11:15. If you aren't there by then, you'll have to find your own ride home." After Eric finished talking, the group split up.

"Let's go get our pictures taken, and then we can dance and get some grub," Matt said. I'm sure Matt was more interested in the food. He was one of the bigger guys on the JV team. At McDonald's he ate double the amount I did.

We followed him over to the gym. It still looked like a gym, but it was set up with a couple of spots to get your picture taken.

"So how do you want to do the pictures? Together or by couple?" Livi asked.

Before anyone could speak, Eric answered, "Let's divide up by couples so we can make our parents happy."

I hid my smile because I knew this was part of his plan to be with Livi. He was making his move.

"Livi and I will go first."

Eric and Livi left us and walked up to the first picture station, which was also decorated with roses. Both Erin and Melissa grabbed my arm at the same time. The girls stared at each other, trying to get the other to let go. I felt like the rope in a game of tug-of-war. I looked at Matt and his face looked shocked, obviously because he wasn't picked.

"Okay, I'll get my picture taken with Matt," I said, hoping to break the tension. Both the girls laughed and so did Matt.

Melissa walked over to Matt and grabbed his arm. They walked to an open photographer. Erin put her arm under mine, triumphantly hooking us together. Erin was much shorter than me, and her brown, curly hair kept getting in my face every time she turned her head, which she did a lot. It was like her head was on a swivel, scanning everyone around her to see who was staring at us. The photographer that took Eric's picture called, "Who's next?"

We walked over and I gave him $40, paying for both of our pictures.

"Why thank you, Nicholas. You're such a gentleman," Erin said, leaning in closer to me. I was already regretting paying for her pictures.

The photographer positioned us in the sea of flowers. Erin had repositioned herself almost entirely in front of me, not at my side like the photographer had put us. Right before he took the picture, I saw Elle pass behind the camera. My heart stopped. Oliver was right there with her. Poof, the flash went off, blinding me. I blinked a couple of times. I can't imagine how I must have looked for the photo.

Erin asked, "Are you okay?"

"Yes, I'm fine," I told her.

She gave me a big hug. "Well, good. I don't want my date not feeling well," she said loudly enough for everyone to hear.

We walked by one of the large light stands, where our group was waiting for us to finish. Elle and Oliver were next in line. Elle was staring at the ground, and didn't look up. I was unable to see her face, but I could tell something was wrong.

We walked back into the transformed lunchroom. I was sure that when I saw Elle and Oliver together, it would ruin the entire evening, which it probably would have if I hadn't seen that Elle was upset. My concern for her well-being suppressed any jealousy.

Erin dragged me out onto the dance floor, following Eric and Livi. Thank God my parents made me dance with them, because it turned out to be very useful. I didn't recognize the music that was playing, but it had a good beat that I could dance to. Eric, Livi, Erin and I danced for what seemed like forever. Matt and Melissa danced to a few songs but then disappeared. I looked for Elle in the sea of dancers, but I never found her.

"Hey guys, do you want to go get something to eat?" I asked, speaking over the loud, thumping music.

"Eric, let's go get some food," Livi said.

"Okay, I can go for some food."

The food area was set up on the opposite side of the lunchroom across from the gym, but all I could see was a long, tall wooden fence covered with ivy. There was a short line of people waiting to get into the small opening at the end of the fence, where a small podium stood with a glass lamp on it. At the top of the fence there were white pin lights illuminating the area where we were standing in line.

"So, Nicholas, how does this compare to your last school?" Livi asked.

"I don't know. I didn't go to Homecoming last year."

Livi, Erin and Melissa gasped. Matt and Melissa had rejoined our group and were standing right behind us in line.

"Nicholas, I can't believe it. Why not?" Erin asked.

"Well, I didn't have anyone to go with," I said.

Livi responded first, "I find that hard to believe. I know at least ten girls who would have killed to come to Homecoming with you tonight." Livi looked over at Erin and Melissa.

We were just two groups away from the hostess, when Jennifer and Julie, Elle's so-called friends, came walking out of the food area. They were both wearing identical short, skintight pink dresses. Both of them had their hair all done up in an elaborate style with diamonds pinned throughout. They were followed by their dates, and then right behind them was Oliver. He looked upset. I stood closer to the fence, hoping he wouldn't see me standing there. Elle trailed a couple of feet behind him. He looked back at her, shook his head, and walked away quickly to catch up with Jennifer and Julie and their dates. I could only see Elle from behind.

"How many in your group?" The hostess was older, probably in her twenties. She was dressed in a black suit and a bow tie. She looked like she belonged behind a bar at a wedding reception.

Matt responded, "There are six of us."

The woman looked at her clipboard and said, "Just a moment."

I watched her disappear into the fenced area, which was still invisible to our group. Eric walked up to the entrance and I followed him, curious to see what was hidden behind the fence. It wasn't just a bunch of tables with cookies and punch. There were black leather booths everywhere. Some of them were raised off the ground and others were floor level. Once again, surrounding everything was a sea of roses, but this time the roses had fountains in between shooting water from one area to another. Connecting the booths together were cobblestone paths similar to those we had seen at the entrance. Each table had an oil lamp as lighting. The lamp was only producing enough light for the people sitting there to see each other. From the outside, you couldn't tell who was sitting at each booth. There were more people in tuxedos and black bow ties buzzing from table to table, taking orders and delivering food. This was as nice, if not nicer, than any restaurant I had ever been in.

The music stopped. "Excuse me, excuse me. Could all of the Homecoming Court make their way to the DJ's table?"

The voice over the microphone was easily identifiable as Joy Lemmins'.

"We can come back to eat after your Homecoming Court stuff," Livi said. Eric agreed.

I looked behind us and the line was now the length of the lunchroom. "No, you guys go in. I'll be done with the Court stuff soon, and I'll come in and join you," I said.

"Are you sure?" Erin said, linking her arm with mine.

"Seriously, it will be really quick. Go on in. Plus, look at that line." Erin looked disappointed when I took back my arm. I walked off mouthing to the group, "It's okay. I'll be right back."

I turned around and walked toward the DJ's booth in the front of the room. There was a small opening in the crowd of dancers, and through it I saw the yellow in Elle's dress. I squeezed through the crowd; Elle was right in front of me. I then became aware of the butterflies dancing around in my stomach. Her face was blank, expressionless, just staring into space.

"Elle."

She looked at me and gave me a faint smile. She looked different. Her beauty was still there, but something else was wrong. I moved closer to talk to her. Then the music stopped abruptly and two large white spotlights appeared on us.

Joy Lemmins was standing behind the DJ's booth. She was wearing a rhinestone-covered, dark green dress. With all of those rhinestones, she could have been used as the chandelier for the dance. All of the tiny stones sent a sea of green and white light around the room.

"Before we start the Homecoming Court thingy, I would like to thank everyone again who helped out with putting together another wonderful Homecoming."

The audience's sparse clapping was drowned out by Joy's loud clapping, which was magnified over the microphone. I stood right next to Elle, hoping for her to grab my hand like last night, but nothing. I felt so distant from her.

Joy continued, "And now, for our Homecoming Court's dance. Let's have our couples go out onto the floor."

The crowd backed up, making a large circle in the middle of the dance floor. An arm interlocked with mine on the opposite side of Elle. It was Amber. We walked out on the dance floor along with the other couples. My back was to Elle and Chad. The music began. At first I couldn't hear the music. My mind was focused on Elle. I felt Amber start swaying back and forth, which forced me out of my trance, and I followed her lead. I recognized the song instantly. It was one of Cora's favorite songs, "Faithfully" by Journey. I picked up the beat, and Amber was now following my lead. My back was still facing Elle. I tried my best to turn us, but Amber didn't budge at all. The more that I listened to the music, the more I wanted Elle, not just to see her but to dance with her myself. I wanted to feel her warm arms around me, to feel her body against mine.

I felt a tap on my shoulder. It was Chad. "May I cut in, Keller? I don't like how close you are dancing with my girl," he said with a smile. He leaned in and whispered, "Plus, I know *she* would rather dance with you." He motioned back toward Elle, who was standing alone, looking at us and waiting.

I let go of Amber and walked up to Elle. "May I have this dance?"

She nodded.

I took her hand and put my other hand on her waist. She did the same. Her touch radiated through my body, once again filling me with warmth.

She spoke first. "Don't worry, the song will be over soon and then you can get back to your date."

"What are you talking about? I don't have a date. I'm only here because you asked me to come. Remember?"

"I saw you getting pictures with Erin. She has told a bunch of people that you are her date."

"She's not my date, and plus, aren't *you* here with a date? Why should you care who I'm here with?" I said, putting more distance between us.

She moved closer. "Because I made a mistake," she whispered.

"What mistake?"

"I should have said no to Oliver. It just seemed like I was supposed to say yes at the time. Then you came into my life. We became close, and all I wanted to do was come with you, share this night with you, but I couldn't do that to Oliver. So I decided to come to the dance with him and hopefully get to spend some time with you in the process. That's why I asked you to come." Her breathing quickened. A single tear rolled down her cheek. I wiped it away.

"The whole night, Oliver has been complaining about you, saying you're the reason why he's having a bad football season," she continued. "He also blames you for him not winning Junior Duke. I didn't say anything to him because I didn't want to make him angrier than he is already. I didn't want him to come after you to pick a fight. He's so mad and is acting more irrational than normal. He also thinks that I'm in a bad mood because I'm not with you, which I guess is true," she laughed.

The song ended and another song started. I let go. Elle pulled me close and said, "Please, one more. Chad would rather dance with his girlfriend."

"Who, Amber?"

"Chad and Amber have been dating since the beginning of last year."

"Well then, I would love to have another dance."

We swayed to the music, while I tried to process what she had just said. "You know, Elle, you're too good," I said. She looked up at me puzzled. "What I mean is, you went to a dance with someone you didn't like just because he asked first. You took into consideration his feelings and not yours when, clearly, he didn't deserve it." She laid her head on my shoulder.

A moment later someone put a hand on my shoulder and wrenched me around. I felt a stinging sensation under my right eye. It made my head whip to the side. The stinging sensation began to burn. Oliver was recoiling back from hitting me. He looked scared. The fire filled every part of my body. I was ready to take him on. But why did he look so scared? He was the one who had just hit me. Thoughts raced around in my head. Then, from the stunned looks on the surrounding faces, I realized why. He just hit me with everything he had, and it didn't even phase me.

Elle stepped in front of me. She started to scream at him, "You coward! Get away from us."

Chad stepped in front of both of us, blocking our view of him. "Oliver, what do you think you're doing?"

Oliver yelled, "Chad, get out of my way. He needs to pay for taking the captain of the football team's date."

"Are you blind? Can't you see that she only came with you because she's nice? And she doesn't care about you being captain of the football team. Come to think of it, Nicholas has acted more like the captain this year than you have. You're no captain of mine."

"We'll see if he's captain material," Oliver said, staggering back into the crowd. Chad had fifty pounds on him and was double his size. There was no way Oliver would try anything else with Chad separating us. Oliver pointed his finger at me. "Nicholas, you will pay for . . ." but before he finished, he walked away.

Coach Hoff emerged, being pulled by Joy Lemmins. She must have gone to get him as soon as Oliver hit me. Both of them looked around. Joy said something to him and he spoke immediately.

"Keller, Reiger, what's going on here?"

Before Chad could answer I spoke up. "Nothing, Coach. Everything is fine." The answer was enough for him. He turned and walked away. Joy Lemmins stood there in shock.

Elle turned her attention to me. "Nicholas, are you okay?"

Amber and Elle were both looking at my cheek.

Chad patted me on the back. "Keller, you are one of the toughest guys I know. I don't think many of us could have taken Oliver's punch and still be standing. Plus, not telling Coach makes you captain material," Chad said. He smiled and took Amber in his arms. "Come on, babe. He's in good hands now."

"Come on, Nicholas. Let's go sit down," Elle said, putting her arm around me, holding me up like a crutch. I took her arm and put it down at her side, holding onto her hand. We walked over to the entrance of the café. The line was still long. I led Elle past the hostess and down the cobblestone path. I searched for Eric.

I saw him up ahead in one of the large round booths a foot off the ground, sitting with Livi, Matt, Melissa, and Erin. The booth they were sitting in was filled to capacity. Eric and Livi were sharing a large ice cream sundae, and Matt, Melissa, and Erin were all eating their own desserts. We walked up to the booth. I had Elle's hand still in mine. Scanning their faces, I got two reactions: Eric, Livi, Matt and Melissa looked happy to see me, but Erin didn't look pleased to see me holding hands with Elle.

"So how was the Court stuff?" Eric asked.

"It was fine," I responded.

Before I could say anything else, Elle said, "It wasn't fine. Oliver hit Nicholas."

Both Eric and Matt stood up in the booth.

"Sit down guys. I'm fine. It's over."

The girls in the booth looked as concerned as Elle did.

"What happened?" Erin asked. Elle explained what had happened detail by detail. When she was done, no one said anything except for Eric, of course.

"Nicholas, you are a machine. He blindsided you, and you didn't get knocked down or out. Incredible! You. Are. The. Man." He put his hand up for a high five.

Before I could respond, Elle said, "Your booth looks crowded. We are going to sit over there." She dragged me over to an empty booth that was in the very back of the area. The booth was small—only big enough for two, maybe three people. It was the highest booth there, up five stairs. Sitting in this booth was like being in a romantic tree house. Elle leaned in really close to look at my eye.

"What are you doing?" I asked.

She said, "I'm making sure you're okay. I don't see any bruising, and there's no swelling."

"Elle, I'm fine, and by the way, he hit me on the other side of my face."

She laughed.

A waiter walked up and said, "Hello, my name is David. Welcome to Winsor Café. Have you had a chance to look at the menu?" We both looked at each other.

"We don't have any menus," I said.

He glanced down at the empty table then produced two from his apron. "I'll give you some time to look. I will be back in a few minutes."

Sitting there with Elle was like a peaceful dream. If I had to get hit one hundred more times just so I could be with her, it would be worth it.

"Nicholas, can I ask you a question?"

"Sure, what is it?"

She paused and looked down. "Do you hate me?"

"Elle, why would you ask that? I don't hate you."

"Nicholas, sometimes I hurt the people I care about because I am trying to do the right things. Jennifer and Julie have no problem with hurting others because they only think about themselves."

I put my arm around her. "Elle, listen. You are so thoughtful and caring. You have such a big heart and that can never change. You are nothing like Jennifer and Julie."

She smiled.

DINNER
CHAPTER NINETEEN

"**N**icholas, are you going to eat this?" Elle had my apple already in her mouth.

"I guess I'm not now."

She laughed, spitting part of the apple out.

"Elle, you might as well eat it now." Elle was lying on her stomach with my apple in her hand. Her legs were bent up and moving back and forth making small circles. She was so cute.

"Nicholas, ever since Homecoming, my parents have been wanting to meet you. What do you think?"

"Why do they want to meet me?" I asked.

"Well, I'm not sure. Oh, never mind," she said pouting, sticking her bottom lip out like she was five. She was adorable.

"No, I would love to meet them. It sounds great!"

"It does? Well, okay then. How about dinner this Friday?"

"Okay, Friday it is."

**

That Friday was the first one in a long time that I didn't have football. It had been a long season. The varsity team marched right through the playoffs and won State easily. There was an incredible ticker-tape parade in downtown Winsor. During the parade I sat with Chad in the car right behind the coaches, second in line. The team voted on who should sit with Chad, the MVP of the playoffs and the championship game. They picked me, not Oliver. I felt guilty sitting in the lead car with Chad, but Cora reassured me that I had helped the team win State. I was an inspiration, she said, even if I had faked an injury. But I still thought Oliver should have been up there in the spotlight, not me. He was the golden boy, the chosen one—and I stole that from him.

The December temperature had quickly dropped into the low 20s, which was colder than usual for this time of year. We had already seen an inch of snow, but that was okay by me because I loved snow.

I got home from school on Friday excited to go to Elle's house for the first time, but really nervous to meet her parents. I didn't know what to expect.

"Nicholas, the phone is for you!"

I had fallen asleep waiting to get ready to leave, so I didn't hear the phone ring. I sprang out of my bed and grabbed the phone, still half asleep. "Hello?"

"Hey, Nicholas. Instead of coming over at 7:00, could you be here at 6:30? My dad would like to meet you before he leaves for his meeting."

"I can do that. Do you need me to bring anything for dinner?" I asked.

"No, just bring yourself."

"Okay, see you soon." Her angelic voice was soothing, but then I realized what she had just said. *My dad would like to meet you.* I was supposed to meet both of her parents together. So if he was unable to be there, why did I have to come over earlier? Did her dad have to meet all of her friends? It seemed so strange.

"So what time do you have to go over tonight?" Cora asked, standing in my door.

"I have to be there at 6:30 now." I rubbed my eyes trying to wake up.

"You better get a move on; it's 5:30," she said, walking out of my room.

"Cora," I called to her, "do you think it's odd that her dad wants to meet me?"

Cora walked back into my room and said, "No, that's normal," and walked back out.

I was still groggy from the nap. I had totally forgotten about the fight I had with Cora earlier about going over to meet Elle's parents. She didn't want me to get too close to her and her family because it would already be hard enough to move away at the end of the year. She didn't want me to experience a "broken heart" as she put it. Also she was concerned about the questions they would ask. Cora didn't like for me to be questioned without her, and I didn't care for it either. But as much as I hated the questions, if I chose not to go, the pain of not seeing Elle would be far worse.

I glanced at the clock; it was 5:40. My heart started to race. I didn't want to be late. The shower had not warmed up yet, and I was already halfway done. I quickly shaved, only cutting myself once. I got out still soaking wet. I ran down the hall to my room, drying off on the way. I put on my favorite pair of jeans and a nice red button-up that Cora had bought for me last Christmas. I fixed my hair and glanced at the clock. 5:55. I slipped my shoes on and hurried down the stairs.

"You're looking sharp, Nicholas."

"Thanks, Cora. What's that?"

She was holding a small potted plant with a ribbon around it. The brown pot had three green sticks coming out of it, each supporting a vine that had several deep pink flowers on it. For such a frail looking thing, the flowers were radiant, full of life.

"It's a Phalaenopsis Hybrid Orchid."

"No, not what *is* it. What's it for?"

"It's a gift that you are going to give to Elle's mom for her house."

"Why? Elle told me not to bring anything."

"If you want to make a good impression, then you need to bring a gift."

"I am just going over there for dinner, probably pizza or something."

"I doubt that very much," Cora said. "Here, take it and make sure you say 'Thank you,' and 'Yes, sir. No, ma'am.'"

"I always do."

She pushed the plant into my hands, walked me to the front door, and opened it.

"Can I at least have a jacket?" I asked.

The lightly powdered snow on the ground was whipping up in the wind, making it feel much colder than the actual temperature. She took the plant out of my hands and grabbed my winter jacket from the closet. I put it on and she gave me back the potted plant. "Go, already. You don't want to be late. The truck has the keys in it."

This was the first time I was able to drive after getting my license. My birthday, November 23, had come and gone with little excitement. Just how I liked it—no fuss. I kept my birthday a secret from Elle. As much as I was now getting used to everyone knowing me, I still didn't like the attention. So the only thing that I did was go get my license.

Driving to the house took no time at all. Even with the snow, I arrived five minutes early. I got out of the truck with the small pink flowers swaying back and forth in the snowy wind.

Elle's house was not like any of the other kids' houses that I had seen. Hers was more modest and a lot older, but kept up very nicely. I walked up to the door, which was adorned by a large bell-covered wreath. I rang the doorbell. Elle opened the door before the ringing had stopped. She looked more beautiful than usual. Her hair was pulled back, exposing her neck. Her cheeks were full of color and her lips shined. She had on a white blouse with lace around the neck. I had an overwhelming urge to lean in and press my lips to her neck and feel her warm skin. When she opened the door farther, it allowed her perfume to surround me, making me dizzy. I stood frozen to the front step.

"Hi, Nicholas."

It took a second for me to answer. "Hi, Elle. You look stunning this evening."

She blushed and smiled, opening the door and motioning for me to enter.

"Well, this must be Nicholas."

"Good evening, Mrs. Canan." Mrs. Canan was standing at the top of a short flight of steps that led up to their family room. She was also pretty. I could see where Elle got her blue eyes and beautiful hair.

"Please, Nicholas, come on in and take off your jacket."

"This is for you." I handed the plant to Mrs. Canan.

Her eyes met mine, and she said in the most sincere way, "Thank you so much for the flower, Nicholas. That was very thoughtful. I know the exact spot for it."

Then she said, "Please, sit down."

"Thank you very much. You have a beautiful home."

Elle took my jacket and hung it on a coat rack that looked like a Christmas tree. Their house had dark wood floors. The walls were painted a rich brown color and covered by art and pictures. All of the furniture was dark wood with a lot of colorful accents. The couch was leather. I could tell that Mrs. Canan took great pride in her home. Everything was perfect. The entire house had been decorated for Christmas. From the large Christmas tree with a train around the bottom to the Santa Claus doorknob covers, it was one of the most festive houses I had ever seen. Cora was more into the modern Christmas decorations. This house felt so warm and cozy.

"Would you like something to drink, Nicholas?" Elle asked, but her angelic voice was not as calm as it usually was; she sounded nervous.

"No, I am fine, thank you."

"No really, please have some warm spiced apple cider. We made it fresh today."

I looked at Elle and she gave me that adorable smile. "Well then, I would love to have a glass, Elle. Thank you."

"So, Nicholas, Elle tells me that you just moved here this year. Where did you move from?"

"I moved here from a small town in upper Ohio. My mom got transferred because of her job."

"What does she do?"

"Mom, don't ask him twenty questions," Elle said, walking back into the room with three mugs on a Christmas tree platter.

"I was just trying to get to know him, dear."

"Here is your apple cider." Elle handed me a glass, and then gave one to her mom. She sat down next to where I was standing. I had been waiting for Elle to sit down before I did. My father always waited for my mom to sit, and he also used to open every door for her.

Mrs. Canan sounded as if she was choking on her drink. I turned and looked at her, and she was smiling at Elle. Elle was giving her an evil look. I was missing something.

"Nicholas, are you hungry?" asked Mrs. Canan.

"Yes, ma'am," I told her.

"Well, let's eat then."

I followed them into the small but elegant dining room, which was also decorated for Christmas.

"Nicholas, you can sit here next to Elle."

I pulled out Elle's chair and she sat down. I waited for Mrs. Canan to be seated and then I sat. Again the two of them were talking with their eyes. I felt like asking them if they wanted me to leave so they could talk. The table was definitely not set up for pizza. It was set with fancy place settings.

"Mr. Canan will be down in a minute. We should start dinner without him. He will eat at his meeting," said Mrs. Canan.

The table was set for four people, so his meeting must have been a last minute change. We passed around the roasted chicken and three different vegetables, which were all prepared differently. They bowed their heads and I did too. Then Mrs. Canan said a very short prayer. Mrs. Canan and Elle began to eat and so did I. The food was incredible. I usually didn't like other people's food because I was used to the gourmet dishes Cora made, but Mrs. Canan's food was what I considered a good home-cooked meal.

"Mrs. Canan, this food is incredible."

"Well, I'm glad you like it, but you should tell that to the cook," she said, glancing at Elle.

"Elle, the food is delicious."

"Elle is our personal chef. If I was going to cook, we'd be having pizza tonight." We all laughed. It was funnier to me because that's what I thought we would be eating.

"Honey, is he here yet?" Mr. Canan said in a booming voice, walking down the stairs.

"Yes, dear. We are in the dining room."

Mr. Canan walked around the corner. I stood up. Mr. Canan stood about a foot away from me. I felt like he was surveying me, making sure he could identify me in a police lineup if he had to.

"Well, this must be Mr. Keller, who I've heard so much about and watched on the football field." He extended his hand and I grasped it.

"Nice to meet you, Mr. Canan."

"Please, sit down, Nicholas. Don't feel like you have to stop eating on my account." This seemed like a test, so I continued to stand.

"Sit down, Nicholas," Elle said to me.

I sat down slowly, and Mr. Canan sat across from me at the table. It was like we were about to arm wrestle or play a game of chess. I slowly began to eat my food, feeling Mr. Canan staring at me.

"So, Nick, is it okay if I call you Nick?"

"Yes, sir," I said immediately.

"What are your intentions toward my little girl?"

I was not expecting that question, and with a mouth full of food, I nearly spit it out all over the table.

"Dad, what are you doing? I told you that we are just friends," Elle said.

"Well, I wanted to hear what he thought about you for myself," Mr. Canan said to Elle, while looking at me.

I cleared my throat. "Well, sir, your daughter was one of the few people who befriended me when I first moved here. I feel blessed to have such a wonderful friend in my life."

Mr. Canan stood quickly. "Okay. Well, it was nice to meet you, Nick." He walked over and kissed the top of Mrs. Canan's head. "See you, honey," he said and then winked at Elle. He smiled, grabbed his jacket, and disappeared down the flight of steps.

The rest of dinner was not as eventful as the beginning. Mrs. Canan continued to ask me question after question about Cora and me. She also apologized several times for how abruptly Mr. Canan left. I think Elle was trying to eat fast so that she could take me away from her mom's questions. When dinner was finished I helped clean the table and thanked Mrs. Canan for having me over.

"Mom, we are going downstairs to watch some TV."

"Okay, dear. Nicholas, if I don't see you again tonight, it was a pleasure to meet you."

Elle dragged me downstairs away from her mom. Right when we got to the bottom of the stairs, she turned to me.

"I'm sorry, Nicholas. That was so embarrassing."

"What do you mean?"

"Well, my mother asking you all of those questions."

"Don't worry about it; the questions weren't that bad."

"Also, sorry about my dad."

"I have to admit that was uncomfortable."

"I told him that we are just friends over and over."

"It's okay. When I'm a dad, I think I'll be the same way."

She smiled and took my hand. "Thank you for all those nice things you said about me." Her smile paralyzed me. I couldn't say anything. She turned the lights on, illuminating the basement.

"So what do you want to do?" she asked.

"Not sure," I sputtered.

"Well, do you want to watch a movie?"

"That sounds fine. Whatever you want to do. But can I ask you a question? What were you and your mom talking about?"

She looked at me with a confused expression.

"You know, when you were both using your eyes to talk."

She smiled. "My mom is not too subtle. She was happy to see you were such a gentleman."

She turned away from me and walked over to one of the two big black leather couches forming a massive L. She grabbed the remote and turned on the large widescreen TV. She walked over and turned the lights back off. The TV was now the only light in the room. She sat down right next to me. My pulse quickened; I had never been this close and completely alone with her. My nervousness made me cold and numb.

She grabbed a blanket that was draped over the couch and threw it on her legs. "Are you cold?" she asked.

I was ice cold, but even if I had been on fire, I would have still told her I was cold just to share the blanket with her. She scooted closer so the blanket would cover both of us. The room had a couple more blankets in it, but she chose to share with me. Is this what friends do—share blankets? She scrolled through the movie guide. She rattled off several movies and asked if I liked any of them. I was so nervous I nodded at every movie she said. Finally, she turned on a movie that I had never heard of and probably would never have picked out for myself. It was about women from the early 1900s.

The movie didn't hold my attention, but still, it was the fastest two hours of my life. I didn't want it to end. I had just managed to get my hand close to hers right when it ended.

"Thanks for coming over, Nicholas," she said as we walked to the door. I had already put on my jacket.

"It was my pleasure, Elle. Can we do this again?" I asked, hoping she would say "Yes, how about tomorrow?"

"Well, of course!" She unlocked the door. I walked out and turned around.

"Goodnight, Elle."

"Goodnight, Nicholas."

My feet didn't want to move; they demanded I stay longer. I couldn't turn away. She smiled and started to shut the door. I reluctantly walked to the truck. The bitterly cold air was a shock to my body, allowing me to fully regain all of my senses for my drive home. After I got in the truck, I sat in the driveway for a moment. The light post flickered off and on. I flashed my headlights to say goodbye back.

Cora was waiting for me in the family room, wrapped up in one of her large down comforters.

"So how was your night?"

"It was fine. We ate dinner and watched a movie."

"Did they ask you a bunch of questions?"

"Well, of course they did. They were trying to get to know me." Anger flared into my voice.

"I told you this would happen. You need to avoid those types of situations, Nicholas."

"What are you talking about? They just asked me a couple of questions; they didn't fingerprint me."

"Nicholas, you don't understand."

"No, obviously I don't. You need to make me understand. One moment you are okay with breaking the rules, and now you are upset with me for breaking the same rules. I'm tired of all this lying. I love her and I don't want to move again."

"If you love her, it's even more important not to be around her anymore, because it will only break her heart!" Cora started to tear up. I didn't understand what she was talking about. I didn't want to argue with her. I had just had a great night.

"Cora, I am sorry. I know you are trying to protect me."

Cora took a deep breath, collecting herself. She got up and walked over and hugged me.

"Sorry, honey, let's talk about this later." The conversation was over. She walked upstairs to her room, leaving me standing alone.

The phone rang and I answered it so quickly that I almost knocked over the lamp on the coffee table.

"Hello, Nicholas. It's me, Elle."

The nervousness from earlier welled up inside me once again. "Hey! Is everything okay?" I asked.

"Yes, I just wanted to thank you for coming over. And I wanted to know if you would like to come over," she whispered.

"That sounds great!"

"Well, how about now?" she said.

"Are you kidding?"

"No, seriously, can you come over? I would like to spend more time with you."

"Of course. I'll be right over." What was I saying? Cora would kill me, and I am pretty sure Elle's parents would not want me to visit so late. It was already 11:00 p.m.

"Okay, Nicholas. Make sure you park on the street a couple houses down. Then come around to the back of the house. You will have to come down through my window. See you soon!"

The dial tone rang in my ear. How was I going to ask Cora about going over to Elle's house again when she was so upset with me about everything that had to do with Elle?

I walked up the stairs to Cora's room. The door was shut. The TV was on.

"Cora, I have to go out for a bit." I waited for a minute for a response.

Cora opened the door and said, "Please don't be late." Her face was red and damp with tears. Before I could tell her that I was sorry again, she put her hand on my cheek and said, "Have fun," and closed the door.

I got back into the truck. I couldn't think about Cora anymore; I was on my way to see Elle.

I parked five houses down from Elle's and made my way to the back of her house. I looked at the two window wells and saw one with the light on. I crept over to the window and looked down in it. Staring up at me was Elle, which nearly gave me a heart attack.

"You scared me to death," I whispered. My breath was sending out a cloud of smoke from the cold air.

"Come on," she said, stepping away from the window. I maneuvered down through the tiny window into her room.

"Wouldn't it be easier if I came in the front door or even the back door?"

"It would be if you were allowed to be here. This is too late for a visit in my parents' eyes. Also boys aren't allowed in my room."

"Aren't you afraid we might get caught?"

"Well, I have locked my door and there are plenty of places to hide." She smiled mischievously. "Nicholas," she walked up to me, "I want to spend more time with you. You make me feel wonderful and the way you treat me . . . I love it. Is it okay with you if we spend a lot more time together?"

"Of course."

"I want to get to know you better. Without any time limit and nobody listening in."

"So you want to know where I used to live? Things like that?"

"No silly, I know you don't like those questions. My questions will be easy, more about you. I want to know what makes you tick—like what's your favorite color, your favorite flower, and stuff like that. I want to get to know you." She placed her hand on my chest. "And if you want, you can ask me questions too." I nodded.

"Come, sit over here." She sat down in a chair that looked like a huge round disk that at least four people could sit in. I took my seat next to her. The curve of the chair forced us together. I had taken off my jacket and laid it next to the window just in case I had to make a quick escape.

"So what is your favorite color, Nicholas? We will start with an easy one."

"It's greyish-blue. Orange used to be my favorite color, but now it's changed." That was the color of her eyes, which were holding me captive, allowing her to get what she wants from me helplessly for eternity.

"So what's your favorite color, Elle?" I asked quickly, hoping that she wouldn't make the connection.

"Well, I like red." Her room was decorated with red stuff everywhere. Her furniture was covered in red quilts and pillows. Her bed was covered with red stuffed animals. It fit her.

She then started asking me more questions. Starting with my favorite flower, then favorite food. Question after question. My fear of being asked questions had subsided because these were all questions that I did not have to lie about. These were all about me. I asked a couple of the same questions back, but I could tell she was on a mission to find out everything she could about me.

This went on for an hour. She started to slow down, only asking a question every couple of minutes. She started to close her eyes between them. She asked if I minded if she rested. I didn't care. I was in heaven there with her. Her legs had gradually moved on top of mine, which made it very difficult for me to concentrate during some of the questions. I wanted to reach out my hands and put them on top of her legs, but I didn't.

After a question about my favorite candle scent, she fell asleep. She lay curled up, motionless. I sat there for a while just staring at her, wondering how I was this lucky to be here with her.

After a while, I reached down, scooped her up off me, and put her in bed. I covered her up and turned out the light next to her bed. In the darkness, small stars and planets illuminated the ceiling. She was full of these little surprises. I smiled as I climbed back out of the window.

SNOWFLAKE
CHAPTER TWENTY

After that night with Elle, we began to spend all of our time together. I was still not sure how she felt toward me, if she wanted more, but I didn't care. I was happy. For the first time in a long time, happy. My sickness and those horrible dreams had almost disappeared completely.

We spent all of winter break together. Cora and I went with Elle and her family to Christmas Eve service. I also spent Christmas with her. Cora and I celebrated the way we always did that morning. We exchanged presents while we watched *It's a Wonderful Life*. Cora got me a bunch of new clothing. All of it, of course, matched the latest trends but still fit with my more conservative style. She also bought me the most incredible watch. It was engraved with a saying on the back: "Time is what you make of it. Love, Cora."

I gave Cora her presents. I had bought her a silver platter that she had been eyeing for some time and a patchwork blanket that was like one we had a couple years ago that had been left behind in one of our many moves. The blanket had been given to her by someone close to her, but I never knew who. When she opened the blanket, she nearly cried.

"Thank you, Nicholas. This was so thoughtful."

We ate a light brunch that Cora had been preparing for hours. Then I got ready to go to Elle's. If Cora had any reservations about me going, she didn't voice them.

The small Christmas that I was used to was exactly the opposite of Elle's Christmas. Her entire extended family was all there. They were dressed in Christmas clothing. Elle and I didn't get to spend much time together alone, but it was fine because this family Christmas was something I would cherish for the rest of my life.

Winter, like Christmas, went by fast; spring was on the doorstep. Right when Winsor seemed ready to thaw out, it was covered by ten inches of wet, heavy snow. The whole town was shut down and put on a Level 3 Snow Emergency. Only emergency personnel were allowed in the street. School was cancelled that very night.

"Nicholas, pick up the phone. It's for you," Cora yelled from the kitchen.

"Hello?"

"Hey, what's up?"

"Eric, I figured you would be on your way to Livi's by now for some quality time."

"Nah, she wants me to stay home because 'it's too dangerous,'" he said just like he thought Livi would have sounded. "She threatened that if I came over, we would be done. So I wanted to see if you were up for doing something."

"Eric, you know that it's 9:00 and the snow is still coming down. I think we are going to get another couple of inches before morning."

"You sound like a weather man. Of course I know we are getting more snow, which makes it even better for extreme tubing."

I wanted to keep my options open because I hadn't talked to Elle since school had been cancelled.

"Eric, I'm not sure if I can go out."

"Give me a break, Keller. Just call Elle and get permission to hang out with your buddies, and call me back." He was right. I wanted to spend as much time with Elle as possible.

Like Livi, Elle thought it was too dangerous for me to come over, but she told me to come over tomorrow morning after the plows had a chance to catch up. Then we would spend the day together. I really wanted to see her, but the promise of spending the whole day with her tomorrow would have to do. I called Eric and told him I was in for sledding. I got dressed in the thermal snow gear that Cora had bought me from one of the online ski shops. She always made sure we had appropriate clothing for any climate.

"Cora, I'm going out with Eric."

She was putting some elaborate decorations on a cake that she had been working on most of the day. "Okay, but I don't want you out too late."

I walked outside and wandered over to the tree line to wait for Eric. I stared up at the snow-filled sky. The large trees around the yard were covered by snow. I began to drift off, thinking about Elle and our future together. The trees creaked as they swayed in the wind, but then there was a cracking sound that interrupted my daydream. One of the large trees was falling at me from out of the darkness. Time slowed and I moved easily out of the way of the trunk, but one of the larger limbs caught me and pinned me to the ground momentarily. I broke the branch with ease and popped up.

Two familiar silhouettes were standing up by the road. My heart stopped because beyond them was the sea green truck. A large SUV barreled down the road from the other direction. I moved toward them, but they were already in the truck, leaving. I examined the base of the tree; it had clearly been cut. They were trying to kill me.

Eric pulled into my driveway, but he wasn't driving his Beetle. "Where's your car?" I asked, still in shock of nearly being killed.

"It's at home. Mom made my older brother let me borrow his truck. He's home from the Marines, so I got to take out his baby," he said with a big smile. On cue he revved the thunderous engine.

The truck was in between a monster truck and the truck Cora and I had. It was painted pumpkin orange, and it had so much polished chrome on it that headlights weren't necessary.

"So what kind of truck is this?"

"It's a Hummer—one they actually used in the military. Not like the ones that you can now buy. This came straight from the base. My brother spent a couple of years restoring it."

"So where are we sledding, Eric?"

"You mean extreme tubing? Sledding is for kids. We are going over to Matt's house. His backyard is perfect. He has an insane backyard for tubing." In the back of the Hummer were three large inflatable tubes like the ones you use for water.

For the next couple of hours, we tubed in Matt's backyard, which was actually part of a golf course. It was far better than any sledding I had ever done. The extreme part was dodging the large pine trees that littered the slope. We stopped and were just sitting on the tubes at the bottom of the hill. The snow had tapered off. The glow of freshly fallen snow lit up everything around us.

"So, Nicholas, are you dating Elle or what?" Matt asked.

"We are just friends," I said.

"Are you kidding? You are attached at the hip. I even heard Oliver talking about you guys the other day at football conditioning."

Eric joined the conversation. "Who cares what he thinks? He's nothing now—just a complete and utter loser."

"So, Matt, what was he saying?" I asked.

"Who cares what he said? Nicholas, he's a loser," Eric insisted, but Matt ignored him.

"He said that he had *made* Elle and that he was 'done with that trash, anyway.' You can have his leftovers."

Elle was not that type of girl, and I wouldn't let anyone talk about her that way. I became outraged. My body started to become tense. I felt the steam coming off me. My body was on fire. I was ready to fight Oliver *and* those two people who tried to kill me.

"Easy, Nicholas, he's not worth it," Eric said. "He's just jealous of you and Elle. No one would believe that he was with Elle anyway."

"Yeah, Nicholas, the group he was talking with didn't seem to pay any attention to him."

"I know, but I don't like anyone, especially him, talking that way about Elle."

Eric and Matt tried to change the subject, but I was furious. All I wanted to do was find Oliver and beat his face in.

**

The smell of Cora's coffee woke me the next morning. It didn't make me sick, but it still bothered me. I took my shower and went downstairs. I felt hungry. I grabbed a bagel and cream cheese and sat down at the kitchen table. The news was on and was focused strictly on the snow that covered the city. From the reports, we had about a foot of snow. It was forecasted to snow lightly most of the day with another inch possible. I tore off a small piece of the bagel and ate slowly as I watched the news. I was not as angry as I had been the night before with Oliver. Actually, again I felt pity for him. He was once the most popular guy at school and now had sunk so low that he was spreading rumors.

Driving to Elle's was surreal. I hadn't noticed how everything looked in the snow the night before when I was riding with Eric. Everything was covered by a thick blanket of snow, making it look wrapped in heavenly clouds.

Elle's driveway was not cleared yet. I figured this would be the case, so I had brought my shovel. I parked on the street and began clearing their driveway off. I was just about done when the garage opened up. Elle was standing there all bundled up.

She was wearing red snow pants, a large puffy tan jacket and a pair of purple snow boots that matched her scarf and hat. She was adorable. She resembled a little kid whose parents got her ready to go out in the snow, not a typical teenage girl who was worried about her appearance. But then, she was not typical.

She grabbed a shovel and helped me finish clearing the rest of the driveway. I pulled my truck into the cleared driveway. The morning sun disappeared behind snow-filled clouds. The snow began to fall again in very large flakes. We spent the rest of the morning playing in the snow. We made snow angels and snowmen. Every so often when my back was to her, she would sneak up and tackle me. She kept knocking me into the large snow banks that had formed around her house. If it had been anyone else, I would have moved past them with ease, sending them into the banks, but she had no problem tackling me—I made sure of that.

Elle had become such an important part of my life now. I couldn't imagine being without her. It used to be just Cora and me, but now it was Elle and me.

We went inside to warm up. Her mom brought us some hot chocolate while we curled up on the couch underneath a blanket to get warm. Her dad wasn't home. He was gone on business, which was normal.

Elle wanted to go back out to play some more. We spent the rest of the time lying in the snow and looking up at the snow-filled clouds. Elle's head found my stomach. The large flakes were falling onto us. While lying with her in the snow, I remembered something my mom used to say to me: "Nicholas,

God makes each snowflake by hand. None of them are ever the same."

Elle must have been made just for me, my perfect snowflake.

TINA MCBRIDE
CHAPTER TWENTY-ONE

No sooner had the snow arrived than it was gone, bringing spring. The next couple of weeks brought new life all around me. Things began to grow. All of this growth inspired me. I decided that I would try to take my relationship with Elle to the next level. We had been inseparable for a while now, so the next step in my mind was for an actual date, and then hopefully next she would become my girlfriend. I dreamt of holding her so close that I could feel her heartbeat next to mine. My lips would be pressed against hers. Time would melt away around us. Nothing else would matter except for the two of us in that moment.

"So do you want to get some dinner tonight?" I was leaning next to her locker while she got out her book for Coach Hoff's class.

"Sure, we can get some pizza and watch a movie."

"No, I was thinking about going to a restaurant."

"Would this be an official date?" she asked without looking at me. The way she said it made me wonder if her question was a good thing or a bad thing, so I stalled.

"Well, if you don't want it to be, it doesn't have to be."

Her face twisted. She didn't like what I was saying. "Nicholas, if you want it to be a date, just say so."

"Okay, then. I am asking you on a date."

She smiled and shut her locker. She looked right at me with her beautiful, big smile. "Well, great! It will be our first official date."

Coach Hoff had already started class when we got there.

"So I will pick you up at 6:30," I whispered to her after we got seated.

"Sounds great."

In the back of the classroom, Oliver was staring at me, which was unusual. He had been acting like I didn't exist for a while now. He didn't look like himself; his perfect blond hair was unkempt, and he was wearing something you would typically wear after football practice. It was not the preppy, pretty-boy clothes that he normally wore.

"So you have a real date finally. Took you long enough," Eric said while admiring a couple of girls walking by us after school.

"I knew I shouldn't have told you."

"Knock it off, Nicholas. It's not like I am going to announce it to the world." Then he jumped and skipped around like he was in some sort of musical and started to sing, "NICHOLAS KELLER IS GOING ON A REAL DATE WITH ELLE CANAN. CAN YOU BELIEVE IT IS A *REAL* DATE?"

I tried to catch him, but he was just out of reach. Chasing him would only draw more attention to him, so I scrambled toward the door to get on the bus and away from him.

When I got home, Cora was sitting on our porch swing reading a book.

"Nicholas, how was your day?"

"I have a date tonight."

"With?"

"Elle."

"Well, that's a relief," she said. "I was afraid that after all the time she has been working on you, you picked one of your groupies instead." She laughed.

"Groupies? Whatever, Cora."

"What time is your date?"

"I'm picking her up at 6:30."

"Do you need the truck?"

"Yes, please. If that's okay."

"That's fine with me."

I was shocked by Cora's reaction to the date, but I should have expected that she would do the opposite of how I thought she would react. She had become very unpredictable this year.

I stopped and got a dozen daisies—Elle's favorite—on the way to her house. I had been planning this date ever since I saw her for the first time. The date seemed like a daydream, but this time it was real.

I walked up to her door and rang the bell. A minute passed, which felt like an eternity, and the door opened. Mr. Canan was standing there. My newfound confidence was quickly erased.

"Good evening, Nick."

"Oh, good evening, sir. Is Elle home?"

The birds that were singing in the background seemed to stop right when he spoke. "I would like to have a word," Mr. Canan said.

I was expecting him to invite me in, but instead he walked out the door onto the porch, shutting the door behind him. My stomach started to tense up. I had to fight back the urge to grab my Tic Tacs. I took an invisible deep breath.

"Nicholas, you are taking out my little girl. When you take her out of my house, I expect you to take care of her and treat her like a lady—nothing less than that. Can I count on you to do that?"

"Yes, sir."

"And Nick, if you hurt her, I will hurt you. Do you understand?"

"Of course."

"Okay, then we have an understanding." He opened the door and I followed him in.

There, standing at the top of the stairs, was Elle. She was wearing jeans that hugged her figure and a red blouse with a low neckline, which made my heart begin to race. Her silver necklace sparkled. Her hair had large wavy curls in it. She was mesmerizing. This was going to be a night that I would never forget.

I gave her the flowers, which I had completely forgotten about for a brief moment. Her face turned a slight shade of pink. Without words, her mom took the flowers into the kitchen and brought them back in a vase, setting them on the end table closest to us.

"I will put them in your room, dear, when you leave. You two have fun."

Elle breezed by me. I gripped the door so I would not stagger from the smell of her perfume. I wished I could slow things down whenever I wanted to, because I wanted this night to last forever.

"Elle, you look stunning," I said once we were in the truck.

Her beautiful eyes fixed upon me. "Why thank you, Nicholas. You look dashing yourself."

Chills went down my spine. I had missed out on so much over the years, but waiting this long made this date even more special.

"So where are we eating?" she asked.

"We are eating at Wendell's. It's a restaurant by the park."

"I know where it is. It's over on Erie Street next to Memorial Park in Montgomery."

I nodded. I forgot that she had lived here her whole life. Then for a brief moment I became nervous that she had been there already.

"So you've been there?" I asked.

"No, never. Dad says it's too expensive and it's a long drive." She must have seen the look of concern on my face. "Oh, but I am very excited to eat there. Speaking of my dad, I hope he wasn't too horrible."

"No, he just wanted to make sure I got you home at a decent hour."

She smiled. "Okay, good. I was worried. I tried to get him to not talk to you."

The long driveway to the restaurant was lined with large, mature dogwoods, which were starting to produce white blossoms. There was a man dressed in black slacks and a jacket next to a sign that said, "Wendell's Valet Service," under the canopy-covered entrance. The valet opened Elle's door and then came around and opened my door, saying, "Welcome to Wendell's, and please, sir, leave the truck running." I got out. The valet handed me a ticket and drove off.

Elle was waiting for me by the door, which a doorman was holding open. We walked in together. I puffed out my chest, feeling proud to be with Elle on a date. I could do anything; I was invincible. Before I had a chance to look for the hostess, a short man with slicked-back hair and a full mustache spoke from behind a small podium. It reminded me of Homecoming.

"What name is your reservation under?"

"Keller."

"Oh, yes. Keller, party of two. Right this way."

We followed the man through the restaurant. It looked like it was straight out of a '20s gangster movie. There was a large bar right in the middle of the restaurant, surrounded by tall wooden chairs. Behind the bar there were hundreds of bottles on display in a large, wood-framed glass cabinet. A small crystal chandelier hung above the bar. Off in the corners were lounging areas, complete with red leather couches and dark wooden tables. Dark wood and deep rich colors were everywhere. There were not many booths or tables in the restaurant, making every spot very intimate and quiet. Most of the tables and booths were filled.

The man led us to the back of the restaurant. Our table had two sheer curtains on both sides, creating even more privacy than the low-lit restaurant already provided. The table was covered by a long white tablecloth with matching lace napkins. I could smell the oil burning in the glass lamp centerpiece. Around the lamp was a wreath of simple white flowers. I couldn't ask for a more perfect setting for our first date.

"Madam," the man said, pulling out the chair for Elle. "Sir," he said to me, motioning toward the open chair across from Elle.

On the table were traditional fine dining settings. I was familiar with them because Cora set the table like this every once in a while when she fixed a fancier meal, normally during holidays. It was her way of taking me to a nice restaurant without leaving the house. I wished she were here to enjoy this too. This was part of the reason why we moved to this town, so we could experience these types of things.

The man handed us the menus and rambled off the specials. I didn't listen; I just nodded. I couldn't help but stare at Elle. He stopped talking. Elle was staring at me like I was supposed to say or do something.

"Nicholas, he would like to know what you want to drink."

"Oh, I'm sorry. Water will be fine. Thank you."

The man nodded and walked away. Elle must have given him her drink order already. We looked at the menu for a minute after he left, and then Elle put her menu down.

"Nicholas, I have a question. Where are the prices on the menu?"

I glanced down and saw that there were no prices. "I'm not sure, but don't worry about the cost. It's my treat."

"No, my dad gave me money. He doesn't want me to grow up thinking that men should pay for everything. He wants me to be independent, regardless of the fact that my mom told me he always refuses to let her pay for anything, ever."

"Well, how about this—I asked you out this time, so I will pay. Next time you can ask me out, and then you can pay."

She smiled. "What makes you think that I would ask you out?" She pulled up the menu, covering part of her face so only her eyes were exposed.

"Well, that's what I offer to all of my dates that I bring here."

"Nicholas Keller," she said in a motherly tone. I smiled at her; she smiled back. "Okay, I will pay when I ask you out—*if* I ask you out, Mr. Keller."

"Very funny, Ms. Canan."

We both laughed. The server who brought out our drinks was a girl who looked to be about the same age as us. We ordered our food and she brought it out quickly. The food was delicious. Cora was an excellent cook, but this melted in my mouth—or maybe it was so good because Elle was sitting across from me. I guess it wasn't fair to judge Cora's cooking ability when Elle was around; she always made everything better. I think they could have served me a grilled cheese sandwich, and I would have thought it was the best thing I had ever had.

"Would either of you like dessert?" our server asked.

Elle immediately spoke up, "No, thank you."

I smiled, "No, I'm fine, thanks."

"I will bring out your check," she said, clearing the table.

"So how was your food, Elle?"

"It was better than I thought it could be. I think it was the best dinner I've ever had. How was yours?"

"I was thinking the same thing. So are you ready to go?" I asked.

"I would like to use the restroom first."

"Okay, I will pay and meet you at the front door."

"Are you sure you don't want some money, Nicholas?"

I didn't even answer her. I just stared at her, showing just enough frustration to get my point across.

"Okay, okay. I just thought I would ask again. I will see you in a minute."

Elle got up. As soon as she walked away there were some loud voices over by the bar that caught my attention. It was dark, so I couldn't see what it was all about. Our server appeared next to our table. I was expecting her to leave the check, but she just stood there. When she didn't put down the check, I looked up and met her eyes. She looked like she was seeing a ghost or something.

"Are you okay, miss?"

"I just wanted to tell you that it's been an honor to serve you tonight. The manager has picked up the bill for you."

"I'm sorry, do I know you?"

She smiled and said, "You don't know me, but I know you. Someone who works here used to go to school with you and recognized you."

Her comments caught me off guard. Then it hit me. Someone here knew my secret and told the staff. Without hesitation I got up and walked with a quickened pace past the waitress and headed straight for the door. The people at every table I passed were staring at me. I avoided eye contact with everyone. I was getting close to the front door where Elle was already standing.

"Alex, Alex! It's me, Tina, Tina McBride!"

Suddenly, she grabbed my arm. I wanted to rip my arm away, but I didn't want to cause a scene. Elle's back was still toward me, so there was a chance I could get out of here without Elle knowing anything happened.

I looked directly into Tina's eyes. The years hadn't changed her much. "Tina, I know, it's been a while."

"A while? It's been five-plus years, and I owe you so much!"

"Listen, I don't have time to talk now. I promise that I will come back so we can catch up."

I moved past her and walked towards Elle, who was now facing us. I handed the valet my ticket at the door. I was hoping that Tina wouldn't follow me outside.

"So how did you know that waitress?"

"She was at the football game when I got hurt."

"Did she want an autograph or a date?"

"No, just making sure that I was okay."

"Well, I hope so. I would hate to have to beat up a girl on our first date."

I was too nervous to say something witty back; I was just concerned about getting out of there fast.

The truck pulled up. I opened the door for Elle, not waiting for the valet. I walked around to the driver side of the truck. I glanced up and saw that the doors of the restaurant were full of people staring at me. I got in, hoping Elle didn't look over to see all the people. Luckily, she was looking in a small compact mirror, putting on some lip gloss.

Driving away, panic set in. What was I going to do? People now knew who I was and that I was living here in Winsor. I had to tell Cora, but if I did, we would be gone tomorrow, no questions asked. We had some close calls before, but never someone actually recognizing me. This was a first. If I told Cora, it would mean never speaking or seeing Elle again.

"Nicholas, are you okay? You look like there's something wrong."

I looked in the rearview mirror and saw that I had lines on my forehead from the thoughts I was having. I relaxed, eliminating the lines. "Yes, I'm fine. I just need my Tic Tacs."

Elle had been around me enough to know about my sickness. She took the pack I had in the cup holder and took out three for me. "Here."

I reached out to take them from her, but she pulled her hand back and said, "No, just open your mouth." She then put them into my mouth one at a time. Her hand brushed my cheek slowly on the last one. Normally this type of thing would get me feeling nervous, stirring feelings that I was looking forward to, but I was too concerned about being recognized to allow these feelings to affect me.

"Maybe the food was a little too rich for you, Nicholas."

I smiled. "Yeah, that has to be it."

"Nicholas, if you aren't feeling well, we can finish our date another night. This won't be our last one." Her face was full of concern, looking closely at me. I had to fight the nausea, which was overwhelming, because I would probably be gone tomorrow.

"No, Elle, I'll be fine." I tried to look as normal as possible.

"Are you sure?"

"Yes, of course. I'll be fine."

"So, what's next?" she asked.

"It's a surprise."

It was just a thirty-minute drive to the small town of Newton. I was anxious to get out of the truck into the night air, hoping for some more relief. We pulled into the Eden Park entrance, where the Krohn Conservatory was having their annual butterfly exhibit.

"Nicholas, I can't believe you are bringing me here. I love butterflies!"

"What are you talking about?"

"Nicholas Keller, don't play dumb!"

We pulled into the conservatory's parking lot.

"Nicholas, my parents always used to take me here during the butterfly show. This place means a lot to me." She didn't know it yet, but this place meant a lot to me too. "But Nicholas, I don't think it's open after 5 p.m."

"Don't worry. I have it under control."

The Krohn Conservatory was a large glass building that resembled an old-world church. We walked up to the big glass doors, which opened for us.

"Hey, Keller. Hello, Elle," Matt said.

"Matt, why are you here?" Elle asked.

"My mother is the exhibit sponsor. Keller, you have two hours. Have a good time." Even months after football, the guys still used my last name instead of calling me Nicholas. Matt walked into the office and disappeared.

"Nicholas, this is amazing," said Elle, smiling.

She grabbed my hand and pulled me down the stairs to the rainforest exhibit. Everything was covered with different types of exotic plants. It had been a long time since I had been here, but it still looked the same. The same mini-river cut right down the center, filled with different types of colorful fish. We walked down the concrete path that ran along the stream. Off in the distance there was a two-story waterfall that fed the stream. Elle stopped to look at every plant, not wanting to miss anything. She didn't speak, but she flashed a smile from time to time to make sure I knew she was really enjoying herself.

We got to the massive waterfall and stood on the bridge that went across the stream right in front of the falls. The spray of the water felt good. We stood there hand in hand.

"I love this place so much, Nicholas. It takes away all of my worries."

The words sparked my worries again. I got out my Tic Tacs.

"Still sick?" she asked, looking concerned again.

"Yes, a little, but being here with you sure helps. Come here." I took Elle's hand and walked her back behind the waterfall into a narrow stone passage that went all the way to the other side of the waterfall. The roaring sound of the water was quieted behind the stone wall. The stone passage was lit by several yellow built-in lights along the top of the wall.

I stopped her halfway through the tunnel. I took her other hand, turning her to face me. "This is why I brought you here. When I was young, my dad used to bring me here. He would give me a quarter and tell me to hide it in the stones. He told me to make a wish, and if the quarter stayed hidden for at least a month, the wish would come true." I pulled two quarters out of my pocket and handed her one.

"So am I supposed to say the wish out loud, or is it like a birthday wish?"

"Either is fine."

"I will say it out loud then. I'm so happy to have met someone so wonderful, honest, and handsome. My wish is that I will get to spend a lot more time with him." She walked a couple of feet away from me and put the quarter up on a stone as high as she could reach. Elle walked back over to me.

"I wish that you will always remember this night no matter what happens." I placed the quarter between two stones right next to me.

"You definitely got your wish, Nicholas, because I will never forget this, ever." She took both my hands. "I promise I won't forget.... Okay, let's go look at the butterflies now." She led me down the path to the butterfly exhibit.

The rest of the evening was a complete blur. I became so preoccupied with having been recognized that I couldn't concentrate on anything else. I could only think about what I was going to tell Cora. The car ride home was quiet.

"Nicholas, are you sure everything is okay?"

"Sorry, still feeling sick."

"Okay, good. No, I mean, I thought that it was something that I did or said."

"No, Elle, you didn't do anything."

Her dazzling smile appeared. "That's a relief." She squeezed my hand.

We pulled into her driveway. I got out of the truck and walked around to the passenger side to open the door for her. The nausea I had been feeling was now accompanied by my nerves. This could be the last time I would ever see Elle. We walked up the path to the front door.

"Elle, I just want you to know how much I enjoy being with you. And no matter what happens, I want you to know how much I care for you."

"Nicholas, I feel the same way."

Just then the front door opened. Mr. Canan was standing there, arms crossed.

Elle whispered, "Save that thought." She winked and walked in past her dad.

"Goodnight, Mr. Keller," he said.

"Goodnight, Mr. Canan," I said, and he shut the door.

When I got home, Cora was sitting on the couch watching an old black and white movie. "So how was your date?" she asked.

"It was okay."

"What? Just okay? What went wrong? Was the food at Wendell's bad or something?"

"No, the food was good, and Elle loved The Krohn Conservatory."

"Well then, what?"

In the back of my mind I could hear our moving truck's engine starting up. "Something happened at dinner."

Cora's face became serious. "What happened?" she asked.

"I got sick at the restaurant."

Her face became motherly. "Come on. Let's get you to bed. I'm sorry you got sick on your date." She gave me a gentle pat on my back. She followed me upstairs, and I went straight to bed.

EMERGENCY EXIT
CHAPTER TWENTY-TWO

I didn't sleep well the entire weekend. I didn't get to see Elle all day Saturday or Sunday because she had relatives in from out of town. She tried to convince her parents to let me come over, but they wouldn't budge. It wasn't both her parents—it was just her dad for sure. I couldn't sneak over to see her at night because two of her cousins were sleeping in her room. The stress from Friday night lingered throughout the rest of the weekend. But no matter how bad it got, I still didn't tell Cora about what happened at Wendell's.

When my alarm finally went off Monday morning, I jumped out of bed just like I had the past two mornings and looked out the window to see if anyone was outside. No one was there. No press, no people, nobody. So for now I wouldn't have to tell Cora, and I could stay here with Elle.

I got onto the bus exhausted from lack of sleep. I just needed to see Elle; then everything would be better. I put my knees up on the seat and put my headphones on to block out all of the sounds around me. I closed my eyes. The bus jostled and bounced. The motion rocked me into a light sleep. A big bump jarred me awake. We had gone over the first speed bump before school. I sat up, pulling my headphones off. I couldn't open my eyes. I was still so tired. The bus slowed, pulling in between two other parked buses. The door opened. It took me a second to realize that there were people rushing *onto* the bus, not *off* the bus, and they weren't students or teachers.

"Where is he? He's got to be here!" Several voices shouted. The people storming the bus were carrying all different types of cameras.

"There he is!"

"It's him!"

There were flashes of light and a lot more shouting. I was stuck in my seat with nowhere to go. They were shouting questions at me.

"Alex, where have you been? Why have you been hiding?" During the questions the lights kept flashing, making it impossible to see. I covered my face from the cameras. The mob had me cornered in my seat. I heard a familiar voice cut through the shouting people from the back of the bus. It was Coach Miller.

"Keller, this way!"

I couldn't tell where he was exactly, so I fell out of my seat and pushed toward the back of the bus. Coach Miller had the emergency door open.

"Quick, Keller, jump!"

I jumped off the back of the bus. Coach Miller and Coach Hoff were now pushing the door closed on the reporters.

"Run to my office as fast as you can. We will come for you when it's safe," Coach Miller shouted.

I turned toward the building, and on cue my muscles tensed and the fire erupted in me. I ran toward the school and everything blurred around me. I had already turned the corner, so nobody could see me running this fast. The back door was propped open waiting for me. I ran in and down the dark corridor, turning into the varsity locker room. The lights were out except for Coach Miller's office. I slammed the door behind me. I quickly turned off the lights and pulled the shades shut; then I slid down the door onto the floor. My heart was pounding out of my chest. The horrible fire burning in me was out of control. I could feel the fire creeping up my throat, searing it, leaving a bitter taste that made me gag. I scrambled to my knees, trying to control myself. I started searching the desktop for a phone. In my haste, I knocked it off the desk along with a bunch of other items. I felt around on the ground and found the phone. I picked up the receiver.

I dialed our home number, but nothing happened. I kept trying to call, but I wasn't able to get through. This was the perfect time when a cell phone would have come in handy. Cora's restrictions were backfiring. I heard voices coming into the locker room. The door began to shake and it swung open. The light turned on, briefly blinding me. It was Coach Miller and Coach Hoff.

"Keller," Coach Hoff said. "Coach told you to *wait* in his office, not to go and trash it!"

"I'm sorry. I was searching for the phone in the dark." Not only had I destroyed his desk, but I had also managed to knock a stack of papers off his filing cabinet along with a couple of football trophies.

"It's okay. You must come with us now. I already called your mo—" Coach Miller stopped mid-sentence and corrected himself. "I called Cora. Let's go, son. The reporters are gone." Coach Miller helped me to my feet.

We walked through the halls, which were empty except for a couple of teachers who looked like they were on guard duty. I entered a conference room near the guidance office. It was empty.

"Keller, please take a seat."

I sat down on one of the plush black leather chairs that surrounded the large oval table. It had enough chairs for twenty people. I waited for only about thirty seconds, and then a steady parade of people came into the room. Most were dressed in suits and dresses. I recognized a couple of our school's principals but didn't know anyone else except for Coach Miller and Coach Hoff. Last through the door was Cora. Her face was cold, showing no emotion. She was still dressed in the pink and black workout clothing she had been wearing when I left for school. She may have been under-dressed compared to everyone else, but her presence commanded attention. The crowded room became silent.

"Are you okay, Nicholas?" she asked me, turning her back to the crowd.

"Yes, I am. I'm so sorry," I whispered.

"We will talk about this later. I'll take care of everything."

"Ms. Keller, my name is Richard Spears. I am the superintendent here at Winsor." He was not what I would expect a school superintendent to look like. He looked more like a game show host. His hair had at least an entire can of hairspray on it to keep it in place. He had on a suit, but he was wearing a bright orange golf shirt underneath it. "I just want to say what an honor it is to meet you."

Cora smiled but stayed silent.

"We want you to know that the board and the faculty will do everything in our power to make Alex's school experience normal. We will do whatever it takes." Hearing him call me Alex flooded me with anxiety.

"First of all," Cora said firmly so no one would doubt her authority, "his name is Nicholas, and while I appreciate your offer, there is no need. We will be leaving immediately."

I stood abruptly. Everyone in the room flinched at my sudden movement. "I would like to have a moment with my—with Cora."

"Well, of course. Everyone out," Superintendent Spears ordered. Everyone left the room.

"What is it, Nicholas? Can't this wait? We can talk about this when we are in the truck."

"No! Right now, Cora. I have been hiding for the past five years, never allowed to make friends or have relationships. And now I finally have friends and possibly even a girlfriend, and you want me to just run away again. I am not going to give that up. I'm not going to do it! Not right now."

"Nicholas, I'm trying to protect you. You have to—" Cora's commanding demeanor was gone.

"No, I don't have to be protected anymore. The reporters may have been a reason to run when I was younger, but now I am old enough to handle it."

"Nicholas, there's more that I'm trying to protect you from. You have to understand."

"Like what? Make me understand."

Cora didn't answer.

"Okay then. I would like to wait until the end of the year before we make the decision to stay or leave. And this will be a decision that we will both make."

Cora stood.

"Okay?" I said.

"Yes, of course. If that's what you want, then that's what I'll, I mean, we'll do." Cora walked to the door and opened it. I was stunned that it was that easy to convince her to stay. I was expecting more of a fight.

The majority of the people that had been in the room before came in again. Cora spoke directly to Superintendent Spears.

"Nicholas and I have decided that we are going to take you up on your offer. But if any of those reporters get to him or anything else happens to him, I will have you and this school in court so fast it will make your head spin. Do I make myself clear?"

His smile disappeared. "Of, of, of course, Ms. Keller," he stuttered. "We are going to have to keep Nicholas in this room for a while so we can make sure the staff is aware of what needs to be done to keep him safe. Is that okay?"

Cora looked my way and I nodded yes to the request.

"Well, okay, we will get to work." Superintendent Spears regained some of his composure.

"One more thing. I would like to pick him up from school at a different time and location each day. No more riding the bus. I don't want anyone to find out where we live," Cora said.

"Can't they just look you up?" a tall, skinny lady said in a snotty tone. She was standing right next to Superintendent Spears like she was second in command.

"No, all of the addresses that we put on Nicholas' school files are false. We live outside the school district," Cora replied sharply, putting the woman in her place.

The woman responded, "Is there *anyone* who knows where you live?" She now sounded like a mother concerned for her own child.

I spoke up, "Only two people—Eric and Elle—but neither would tell anyone."

"We'll make sure of that," Superintendent Spears said, "but where will he be picked up each day?"

"Never mind about that. Just allow Nicholas to come and go as he pleases, because I don't trust any of you," Cora said.

"Ms. Keller, we are all honorable people here," he said. The room started to buzz.

"Superintendent Spears," Cora said. The room quieted. "Don't take this the wrong way, but it is amazing what money will do to people's loyalty."

"Okay," he said. "We will do anything and everything for the 10-10 Hero, whatever it takes." Superintendent Spears said *10-10 Hero* like he had been dying to use the name that the media had given me over five years ago. Hearing him say it was like nails scraping down a chalkboard.

"Thank you, Superintendent Spears. That will be all," Cora said in a dismissive tone.

The room emptied again, leaving just Cora and me. Cora sat down next to me, putting her hand on my arm. I was prepared for it to burn me because of how I treated her earlier, but instead it was gentle and caring.

"Nicholas, I'm not mad at you at all. I'm relieved. The last five years have been all about protecting you and keeping you safe. I was prepared to hide again, but for the first time in five years, you spoke up. I know, normally it is a bad thing for us to disagree, but this time it's a good thing because it's not just me anymore—it's us. I will still try to protect you, but at least now we can make these decisions together." Cora's eyes were filled with relief.

"I'm sorry," I said. "I know you are only trying to protect me from things I don't see or really understand, but please know that I love you. I am so lucky to have you in my life."

Cora leaned forward and hugged me with such strength it knocked the wind out of me. "Nicholas, I am lucky to have you too. I love you!" She leaned back. "But you're going to have to tell me everything when you get home." She smiled.

"So how will I get to school and get home?"

"Let's start with getting you home for now. Right before sixth period, I want you to go to the side garage where trucks back up to make deliveries and wait."

"You want me to skip seventh period?" I asked Cora.

"It's only art class and you're getting an A."

"Okay, but then what?"

"Don't worry, you'll know, but I have to go now to take care of some details to make sure this works. Will you be okay here?"

"Yes, I'll probably be going back to class soon anyway."

Cora stood. She leaned forward and gave me a quick hug, and then she was gone. I was alone in the conference room, waiting. I walked over to the only window in the room. I could see the front entrance. It seemed just like yesterday that Cora and I were walking in to register me for the first day of school. But now, past the main entrance, I could see the growing number of media at the entrance of the parking lot. Police had blocked them from gaining access to the lot. I sat back down and thought about everything I had just done. It was all done for Elle.

I wondered who at the school knew what was going on with me. That was a stupid question. Of course, everyone did. News in a school spreads faster than wildfire, and with the press outside, they would have to know something was up. What was Elle thinking?

I sat in that conference room through my first four periods. What was taking them so long?

The door opened and in walked Joy Lemmins. Oh no, anyone but her. "Well, hello there, Nicholas. How are you today?" she asked.

"Well, I've been in this room for about two and a half hours. How do you think I am?"

"Oh, I'm sorry, deary. I just found out that they left you in here. If I had known earlier, I would have kept you company while the grown-ups were working hard to get things ready for you," she said.

"Ms. Lemmins, why have I been in here so long?"

"Superintendent Spears called an emergency faculty meeting to talk about your special situation."

"What was said at the meeting?" I asked.

"Well, everyone."

"No, I didn't ask who was there; I asked what was said."

"I'm getting there, silly. You see, he wanted to get everyone together so he could first explain who you really are. I have to say, I knew you were a special boy. I knew that right from the beginning." She was twirling her frizzy blonde hair around her finger.

"Once he was done with your history, which we all knew very well, he gave us our assignments—how we are supposed to help you blend in and make the rest of your year as easy as possible, so you can stay here at Winsor. You are one of the most important students we have ever had. Even though one time we had these twin boys who starred in a bunch of commercials.

"Mrs. Kitchen and Coach Miller should have finished talking to the last group of teachers by now. They should be here any minute."

Mrs. Kitchen was the tenth-grade principal. She was very strict. Well, that's at least what Eric said. He had been sent to her office a couple times this year for being late. Even though she would always give him Saturday school, he still insisted that the school would spin out of control without her.

"Nicholas, now for some counselor talk. Please, when you leave here, embrace who you are. There is no need to hide anymore; embrace the new you."

The door opened. It was Mrs. Kitchen and Coach Miller.

"Mr. Keller, we have spoken to all of the staff. Superintendent Spears would like us to let you do whatever you want, but let me clarify that statement. Rules still apply to you. You must attend all of your classes. Do you understand?" Mrs. Kitchen said.

"Yes, ma'am," I said.

"You may be late and leave early. You don't have to check in when you get to school, but you do have to check in before you leave. You may check in with any of the three of us."

"He can just check in with me to make things easier," Joy Lemmins blurted out like she was hoping whoever said it first would be the lucky winner.

"Thank you, but any one of us will do fine. Mr. Keller, I have tried to call Ms. Keller, but she is not home, so I would like you to know that we will be getting extra security to keep the press off of the property. That should help you to come and go from school more easily."

"Thank you, Mrs. Kitchen," I said.

"Coach Miller, will you take Mr. Keller to his fifth period class?"

"Let's go, Keller."

I got up and followed him out the door, thankful to get away from Joy Lemmins.

"Let's stop by my office first to get your bag," he said, patting me on the back.

We got to the locker room just as the fifth period bell rang. All of the stuff that I had knocked over was just piled up on his desk, still not in order.

"Coach, sorry about your desk."

"No problem, son." Coach handed me my bag and put his hand on my shoulder. "Nicholas," he used my first name, which shocked me, "people may think they know who you are, but only you know who you are and what you can be. I will always be here for you."

"Thanks, Coach."

"Head on up to Coach Hoff's class," he said.

"Don't you need to walk me?" I asked.

"Do you need me to wipe your nose too? Get out of here." He smiled.

SPLIT PERSONALITY
CHAPTER TWENTY-THREE

In the hall, people were talking about me, whispering, "It's him." I ignored them. Finally, I got to Coach Hoff's class. Elle was not at her desk yet. I sat down to wait for her.

"So who are you—Alex or Nicholas? Do you have a split personality or something?" It was Oliver, of course. Now that my secret was out, he had gotten back some of his courage to bully me. "So what else have you lied to us about? Maybe you're really twenty years old."

I turned and he was right next to my desk. My muscles started to react to the threat, but then a voice said, "Oliver, go sit down. Just because he kicks your butt in football and is more famous than you, doesn't mean you need to be an idiot."

The class laughed. He turned around and Elle was there, defending me again. There was no smile on her face, no hint of her normal cheery self.

"Oh, the girlfriend is being the hero for the hero. Not too tough, Keller, or should I call you Taylor?"

"Sit down, Rails, or you can bully others in detention for the next two weeks," Coach Hoff said, walking in.

Oliver gave me a dirty look and said under his breath to Elle, "I know you wish you could be with a real man, not a liar like him." Elle didn't respond; she just sat down.

Coach Hoff started class. I was feeling better, even with Oliver being his usual self again. I knew that Elle was right behind me, and that made everything better. In a few short moments we would be alone under the stairs.

"Okay, class, see you after lunch." I turned to Elle, but she was already getting up from her seat. Jennifer and Julie were next to her.

"Elle, can we talk?" I asked.

Jennifer and Julie looked at her and she nodded. They walked out of the class. She had no expression on her face; her eyes were hollow. The classroom was completely empty except for us.

"I'm so glad to see you. I want to tell you—"

"You want to tell me what? Another lie? Listen, Nicholas, if that is even your name, I thought that you trusted me. I thought we had something special."

"We do, but it is complicated, Elle."

"Obviously I wasn't special enough. Nicholas, I would never do that to you. If you have any respect for me, you will never speak to me again."

She was gone and my stomach sank. I did all of this for her and now nothing. I sat back down in my seat. How could I go on living this life here without her? The darkness that used to fill my dreams was now all around me, suffocating me.

I skipped lunch. I couldn't be around anyone. I had eaten two packs of Tic Tacs. They weren't really helping, but at least they were getting me through the rest of the day. I didn't pay attention to my newly attained celebrity status. Everybody wanted to talk about what had happened during the earthquake. I didn't speak. I ignored everyone, walking away from them if they tried to talk to me. I even had a couple of people ask me for autographs. Some of the teachers were worse than the students.

I hadn't seen Eric all day. At least I knew what to expect from him. He would make some smart comment about how popular I was, but then he would stop and treat me normal again.

Only five minutes were left in my sixth period class. Cora wanted me to go to the delivery door and wait. She said I would know when it was time to leave. The bell rang. I got my stuff from my locker, checked in with Coach Miller, and walked down to the delivery area. I couldn't concentrate; I was fixed on Elle's comments. My heart ached for her. The pain was overpowering, making it hard for me to stand. She was everything to me, and now there was no hope, no light, just the darkness.

"We are going to have a fire drill, so make sure to exit the building in a calm, orderly fashion," Mrs. Kitchen announced over the PA.

The fire alarm sounded, filling the halls with its ringing. This had to be what Cora was talking about. Classes started to file outside, surrounding the school. It was a large human shield. I looked for a helicopter, but there wasn't one. A man in a delivery truck was waving to me. I rushed over to the truck; the back door opened.

"Nicholas, get down in the back and hold on." It was bumpy in the back of the truck. Luckily, I was able to hold onto the racking, which was filled with boxes on both sides. I had been in the back of the truck for five minutes when we finally stopped. I couldn't see where we were. The driver grabbed a bag next to his seat and left. I stood there for another couple of minutes before the driver got back in, and we drove off again.

"Excuse me, where are you taking me?"

"I have a couple more stops, and then I am dropping you off near your house. Cora figured that if I kept making my deliveries, no one would think you were with me." Sure enough, he continued making his deliveries. His two stops were more like ten.

An hour later he said, "Okay, Nicholas, here's your stop." Weary from holding on during the bumpy ride, I was happy to hear it was time to get out. I opened the back door and hopped out.

"See you tomorrow, kid."

Tomorrow? Was this my new bus service? What had I gotten myself into? Without Elle, was all of this really worth it?

The front door opened before I could touch the doorknob.

"Hello, Nicholas, how was school?" she asked just like every other day.

"It was okay, I guess." I was confused.

"You have some explaining to do," she said.

Cora then made me relive the last four days. I started by telling her about my date in full detail, then all of the stuff that happened at school, and how everyone now wanted to talk about what had happened during the earthquake. I ended the story with what happened with Elle. Cora just listened, nodding her head every so often.

"I know it's hard, but it will get better. Are you hungry?"

"No, I'm not hungry. I just want to start packing. I know you have a backup school for me. Let's go." I was close to losing it. I sat down and took some deep breaths.

"Nicholas, I know this must feel like the worst day ever, but you made the decision to stay, and this time I agree. You may have done this for Elle, but now you have to stick with it. Nicholas, something deep inside you made this decision, and you need to find out why."

She continued, "And don't worry about Elle." I looked up at her in disbelief. "Girls sometimes act irrationally. Give her some time. Your secret is a lot for anyone to handle, even Elle. Think about it. You have had over five years of living with it, and you still don't like it. She has had only five hours. Give her time.

"Okay, now you have to eat. You need your strength. Go up to your room and I will bring you something."

The black fog had lifted while I was at home, but the hole in my chest was still there. I hoped Cora was right about Elle just needing time. If not, I was back to square one.

Cora came into my room with a full plate of mini hamburgers. Of course, they had a couple of Cora's gourmet twists to them with fresh veggies and hunks of melted cheese.

"Now, I hope you like them. Drink this Sprite for your sick stomach. It should help." She sat down next to me on the bed and turned on the TV.

"So what do you want to watch?"

"Don't care."

"Do you mind if I watch the early, early news? There is a recipe I was wanting to get."

No sooner did she turn on the channel than I heard, "The 10-10 Hero is believed to be attending Winsor High School under another name."

Cora quickly turned it off. "Well, I guess I should have seen that coming, but it doesn't mean we have to watch it." She turned on the old movie channel. A black and white Western was playing.

"Cora, how am I going to get to school and home again every day?"

"I am going to drive you to a different bus stop each day. There are thirty buses and thousands of stops between them, so there's no way the media can cover all of them. And then you will be coming home with Steve on his delivery truck."

"The delivery truck?"

"Yes, the delivery truck. Steve has been making deliveries to the school for twenty years. There is no way for him to be linked to you or me."

"But how am I going to get out to his truck? There can't be a fire drill every day."

"Of course not. He picks up the school's deliveries in a large cart when he backs up to the dock. You will hide out in the cart and he will load you into his truck."

"Cora, why didn't I do that today?"

"I didn't want anyone in the school to know how you were getting home. So please don't tell anyone, even if it is a teacher, friend, or principal. Especially don't tell that dingy counselor, Joy Loving."

"You mean Joy Lemmins."

"Loving, Lemmins, whatever. She is unbalanced. We have been able to keep you hidden for five years; keeping you from the media should be a piece of cake. Well, I better start fixing dinner."

She left me alone. I set the plate of half-eaten burgers down and put my head on my pillow.

I awoke when Cora called me down for dinner. Cora had fixed a three-course meal. I wasn't hungry, but she had made my favorites: Caesar salad; pot roast and mashed potatoes with glazed carrots; and apple cobbler for dessert. I was still full from the burgers, but I ate everything.

"Cora, how can I give Elle time when all I want to do is call her to explain?"

Cora put down her fork and knife. "You don't want to ignore her, but you don't want to crowd her either. Calling her would be a bad idea. If you need to communicate with her now, write her a letter."

"And do what with it?"

"Well, that's for you to decide. You can give it to her or just throw it away. Either way, it will make you feel a little better, and it will also give her some space. But remember, if you want to give it to her, you need to wait because she needs time. She will let you know when it's time to talk."

"But when—"

Cora stopped me mid-sentence, answering my question. "Don't worry. You will know when she wants to talk."

I walked back up to my room. I grabbed a pencil and paper and started to talk—write—to Elle.

Dear Elle,

There is so much I would like to tell you. First, I am so sorry. You were right. I should have trusted you enough to tell you everything. For the last five years, I have always avoided any type of relationship with anyone, but after I met you, I was not able to keep myself away. I just wanted to be near you. Your beautiful smile melted away all of my defenses. In the beginning, I wanted to tell you everything, but I didn't know how. I know it's no excuse, but I haven't had much experience in this area.

I want to answer a question you asked me. Remember when you wanted to know how I liked the last town that I moved from? I didn't know why I couldn't answer you, but now I know. The last town I lived in was lifeless, black and white, forgettable. Come to think of it, every town I've lived in for the past five years was like that. The reason they were like that was because you weren't there making everything come alive. I can't imagine a place without you that I would like.

Please forgive me!!!! I will answer every question you ask.
Yours,
Nicholas

MY WAY
CHAPTER TWENTY-FOUR

"Nicholas, wake up. Come on, get up. You can't need any more sleep. You've been asleep for 12 hours."

I felt so alive, no sickness at all. I showered and dressed. I met Cora at the bottom of the stairs. She handed me a bagel and cream cheese and a cup of apple juice. I ran back upstairs to get Elle's letter. Last night I was positive that I was going to throw the letter away, but now I was sure I was going to give it to her. I was confident that giving her the letter was for the best. Cora was already in the truck waiting for me.

"Are you okay, Nicholas?"

"Yeah, I feel great, Cora. I don't know how to explain it. This is the best I've ever felt."

"Well, that's good, considering the day you had yesterday." Cora was staring at me. She looked concerned. I couldn't blame her. Last night I was dying, and today I feel more alive than ever.

"Not sure why, but I'm feeling like I can take on the world. So where are you taking me to get on the bus today?"

"I'm taking you to a bus stop on Hanover Court. I've got all of the stops mapped out for the rest of the year. Those poor reporters," she snickered.

"Okay, the bus should be coming now," Cora said as we pulled up to the stop. Sure enough, the bus was at the end of the street.

"Nicholas, don't worry about anything. Everything will work out."

"Okay." I knew she was right.

I walked over to the bus stop with the rest of the kids. Cora waved. I smiled and waved back. The bus driver didn't seem shocked to see me, but everyone else on the bus was. I sat down and the bus began to buzz with excitement.

"Hey, Nicholas."

"Hey, great to see you."

"Are you going to be riding our bus?"

Smiling, I tried to acknowledge everyone who talked to me. It was weird but today, instead of sinking down in my seat and trying to hide, I embraced the idea of everyone wanting to talk to me.

We went over the first speed bump before the school. That's when I saw what looked like a large festival. There were news vans, tents, and trailers everywhere. People were swarming like ants. There were several police officers directing traffic. As a reflex, I ducked down in my seat. To my surprise, the people on the bus saw me and reacted in their own way. They put their backs up against the windows to block anyone from seeing inside the bus. They were protecting me. When we got through the sea of news people, everyone relaxed and sat back down in their seats. It made me feel so good that everyone on the bus would protect me.

We pulled up to the bus drop-off, and unlike yesterday, I was able to get off the bus without being mobbed. I walked toward the school, but then without thought, I turned and headed toward the sea of reporters. What was I doing? I had to confront them. I had to speak to them, but why? What would I say? What was the point of me going down there? The school and the students were willing to do so much to protect me, to make sure I was safe, but I didn't want them to have to protect me. It wasn't fair for one student to cause this much trouble for everyone. I couldn't be that selfish.

Halfway between the buses and the reporters stood one lone police officer. He was the barrier between them and the school. His eyes were focused on the growing blob of media that oozed in every direction, trying to get as close to the school as possible.

When I was a couple of feet away from him, he turned and said, "Hey, you don't belong down here, kid!"

"I'm sorry, officer, I forgot something down there."

He put his arm up to stop me.

"Trust me, I forgot something." I walked by him and I didn't look back. I was so close to them now. It was too late to turn back. When I got to the edge, a couple of reporters saw me. Electricity ran through the group; a wave of reporters surrounded me, shouting all types of questions. Okay, I'm here. Now what?

I cleared my throat and the crowd went quiet.

"Hi, my name is Alexander Nicholas Taylor Keller."

The crowd erupted into a chorus of questions. It was deafening. I held up my hand like a teacher does to quiet a classroom, and to my surprise, it worked.

"If you would like me to continue, then you must be quiet." The majority of them quieted down and shushed the other reporters who were still talking.

"As I said before, my name is Alexander Nicholas Taylor Keller. I have been in hiding for the last five and a half years. My aunt and I decided that it was best for me to hide so that I could have a normal life. As you can see," I motioned to the crowd surrounding me, "we were right.

"We moved here earlier this year and I have been attending Winsor High School all year. The entire school has been great to me, even willing to help me avoid you. But I can't allow the school to treat me differently than any other student. It's just not fair. I know you have questions for me, and that's fine because I will answer as many as I can. That's the reason why I came down here this morning, but it has to be my way. I will only take questions in writing, sent to the school and addressed to me. I will also do interviews by written request only." All at once the group exploded with questions. I held up my hand again. They quieted, but not as quickly as before.

"But if you continue to stay out in front of the school or show up anywhere else to find me or harass any of my friends, I will not answer any questions. I will go back into hiding, and this time you will never find me. You have one day to leave here." I turned and walked toward the school. They shouted more questions at me, but I ignored them. They followed me up to the police officer. He struggled to push them back, but managed.

"You forgot something, huh?" the police officer said.

"Yes, I did." All of my actions were automatic. I was on cruise control. Something inside me was controlling everything. I knew that if I followed it, everything would end up perfectly.

I patted my jacket where Elle's note was safely tucked away. Closer to the school, I could see two people standing outside by the main entrance, waiting for me—Principal Kitchen and Superintendent Spears. Mrs. Kitchen was smiling and Spears' face was beet red. He looked like he had swallowed a whole bottle of hot sauce.

"What do you think you are doing, young man? We just watched you on the morning show." Spears spat out the words like they were venom.

"Talking to the media," I said.

"Well, I can see that. You should have talked to me, I mean us, about that decision. We went to great lengths to keep your secret and to keep the media away, and now on the first day with the new restrictions, you go out to greet them. What were you thinking?"

"Well, Superintendent Spears, the way I look at it, I just saved the school a lot of money because I won't need all of this extra security. I am just like any other student now."

"But, but—" He looked like he was going to explode.

"Thank you, Mr. Keller, for thinking of the school," said Mrs. Kitchen. "We are both happy. Right, Superintendent Spears?" He didn't move or even acknowledge Mrs. Kitchen.

"Well then, off to class, Mr. Keller, and please don't be late again or next time, detention," she said with a smile.

The first four classes went smoothly, no problem. I talked to everyone who talked to me, and even some who didn't. I still felt so alive. I even carried on a conversation with Melissa and Erin in biology. Their perpetual jabbering didn't bother me at all for once. At last, no secrets. This new freedom was exhilarating. I headed to Coach Hoff's class, excited to see Elle and give her the note.

The hall between fourth and fifth period was unusually packed with people. Standing in front of Coach Hoff's classroom was Oliver with a couple of his friends. It didn't matter who was out front because all that mattered was seeing Elle. Could this be the day when Oliver just smiled, or better yet, turned away?

"So you think you're some big shot being on TV?" He was speaking a lot louder than his normal bullying. I realized he was doing this out here on purpose for everyone to see. He got what he wanted; everyone was watching us. His audience.

"Oliver, what do you want?"

"I don't want anything. I just want *you* to get out of *my* school. You're a big fake, Nicky—oops, I mean Alex, or whatever your name is. Some hero. Who knows, you could have lied about that too. And your parents are probably still alive and well." He began to laugh.

The force and speed with which I pinned Oliver against the wall knocked his friends to the ground and petrified him. There was no fire inside me; I was completely in control. My heart was pounding hard, but not quickly. My rage was controlled—no sudden jerks of movement or any sudden force of power. My strength and speed were smooth and precise.

"Oliver, you may call me Nicholas if you'd like." He struggled, but my forearm was under his chin, holding him firmly in place. "You shouldn't worry about what people call me, and just because they put you on a couple of billboards does not make this your school. You shouldn't worry about me so much. You should probably worry about yourself." While I held him there, I couldn't see his friends, but I knew they weren't going to try anything. They were backing up, putting distance between themselves and Oliver.

"Oliver, you're a loser," someone yelled from the crowd. I let Oliver down from the wall.

"You think you have what it takes, Keller?" He coughed. "You think you are captain's material? Then I challenge you to the rite of passage."

Several people around us were giving him evil looks and saying things under their breath. I looked through the crowd making sure Elle was not there to see what had just happened. The last thing I wanted her to see right before I gave her the note was this ugly incident or Oliver challenging me to the rite of passage. Coach Hoff was walking straight down the hall toward the classroom. He looked at me and gave me a big way-to-go, that's-what-I'm-talking-about wink. I turned back toward Oliver, but he was gone.

I walked into the classroom. I received a round of applause from some of the students already in there, but then my heart sank. Elle wasn't there. I searched the room and saw Jennifer and Julie, but no Elle. For the first time all day, I grabbed my

Tic Tacs and took two. Where was she? Why was she not in class? My confidence faded. I felt like everything I had done was for nothing if there was no Elle. Coach Hoff dismissed us immediately for lunch. I had every intention of going to eat in the lunchroom because I felt like being around people, but the staircase now seemed to call to me.

I sat alone under the stairs, eating my lunch. I was so ready to see her and give her the letter I had written, but now I didn't know if I could. What if she was changing classes or changing schools? I was being ridiculous. Her parents would never move her because of me.

The door opened, but then there was silence, no sounds of anyone going up the stairs. I heard a few soft footsteps, and then she appeared in front of me. I blinked my eyes several times to make sure she was not an illusion. It was her. She wasn't smiling, but she didn't look upset. I jumped to my feet, banging my head on a step. I grabbed the letter from my jacket and handed it to her. I didn't say anything. Even if I wanted to, I didn't think it was time to talk.

"Nicholas, you can come over tonight," she said, then turned and walked away.

I felt better after lunch, even though she didn't talk to me or look at me during class. Having confronted the media that morning, I decided not to bother riding the delivery truck home. It didn't seem necessary anymore. I walked out to the bus and noticed that there were half as many news vans and tents as before. The only remaining crews were breaking down their mobile newsrooms. Feeling good, I sat back in my seat, but sank down just in case it didn't work with everyone.

Cora was waiting for me at home with her arms folded. "So you've decided to do whatever you want now?"

"What are you talking about?" I asked.

"Going and talking to the media—what else could I be talking about?"

"You told me that I had to find my reason for staying here," I reminded her impatiently.

"Yeah, and how does talking to the media help that?"

"I don't know. It just felt like the right thing to do."

"Nicholas, I am trying to protect you and you are making it difficult."

"What are you protecting me from now?"

"This may work for a little while, but when they realize you're not going to do interviews, they will be back and will try to find you." Cora looked as angry as Superintendent Spears. Was she trying to control me too? "Nicholas, you still have to do what I say," she continued. "Just because we aren't moving, doesn't mean you can do whatever you want."

"So whatever happened to both of us making decisions together?" I asked.

"That option flew out the window when you decided to talk to every news person without talking to me first. You are going to do what I tell you to do, and that's that," she fumed.

"Cora, you are not my mom!" The words left my mouth full of anger and regret.

"You're right, I'm not Beth—" Cora stopped mid-sentence and stormed into the house.

I went upstairs to my room. I could hear a distant storm approaching. The thunder rumbled and the flashes of lightning were faint, but close enough to light up my dark room. The thick clouds made everything grey, eliminating all of the colors around me. I had a weird feeling that the storm was an indicator of things to come.

Cora came to my door and knocked. I didn't have a chance to answer before she said, "There is food in the fridge when you are hungry."

"Cora," I said, but there was no answer. She was already gone. It's amazing how great and alive I felt this morning, but now I didn't feel that way. The storm was getting louder. I didn't feel like eating—I was still too angry—but I had to eat. It was going to be a long night. Plus, I couldn't ask Cora for the truck for fear of starting another conversation that would end with her forbidding me to go to Elle's. I would have to walk.

In the fridge was a plate that looked like a Thanksgiving feast with all of the fixings. I grabbed just the turkey off the plate and some bread to make a sandwich. I took my sandwich to my room. I ate my dinner in the seclusion of my room and turned my thoughts back to Elle. Cora and I would be okay, but I wasn't sure about Elle and I. She wanted to see me, but who knows what that meant? I could only hope that our visit tonight would be the first step toward getting past this.

THE PAST
CHAPTER TWENTY-FIVE

I was counting the minutes until I could leave. I looked at the clock. Only 8:30—two more hours until I would be with Elle. I closed my eyes, concentrating on her. I slowly drifted to sleep. My muscles tightened and I stopped breathing. Was I asleep? I couldn't breathe; it felt like a 1,000-pound weight was crushing my chest. I struggled to move my arms and legs. I started to panic because I couldn't get air. I thought I was done with these types of dreams. What was going on?

I tried with all of my might to raise my arm to push the weight off of me. I managed to squirm away, to free myself from the weight. The crushing sensation was now replaced by a peculiar tingling in my arm. The tingling felt like small bee stings with a warm feeling radiating from them.

Cora had hold of my arm, shaking me to wake up. Still disoriented I yelled, "What's happening? What are you doing to me?"

"You were dreaming and hit the lamp off your nightstand."

I looked down beside the bed, and my lamp was shattered into hundreds of tiny pieces.

"Lie still and let me check your arm."

The stinging feeling was a gash from hitting the lamp. The warm sensation was blood running down my arm. She held my arm tight, picking the pieces of the lamp out of the cut.

"Doesn't look like you need stitches. Now you stay still until I get something to clean this cut."

I watched Cora glide out of the room. It was 10:00 p.m. I sat up.

"Where do you think you're going? I have to clean it out," Cora said, coming back in holding a first aid kit.

"It's fine. I have to be somewhere."

"No, you don't. That cut needs cleaning and it's a school night."

"Cora, please understand. I have something very important to do. I have to be somewhere. May I go?"

"Does this have to do with a certain girl that wasn't speaking to you?"

"Yes, it does."

"Okay, I will still need to clean this first and then you may go." She quickly cleaned the cuts and put a bandage on it.

"Okay, Nicholas, you're all set, but please don't be too late."

I was going to have to run fast; it was already 10:15.

"Nicholas, one more thing. We are going to have a talk about those dreams because there's something I need to tell you about them. Also take the truck tonight. I don't want you to be late."

"Thanks, Cora, and yes, we will talk."

I ran down the stairs and grabbed the keys off the kitchen table. The rain had stopped, but I could still hear and see the distant thunder and lightning. The humid spring air formed a thick fog, making it hard to see. Luckily our truck had fog lamps. Without them, it would have been faster to run than to drive in this fog. The drive took longer than usual, which gave me time to think about what I was going to say to Elle. I parked a couple of houses down from hers.

All of the lights were off in her house, making it invisible in the fog. I walked to the back of the house, ducking under each window just in case her parents were still up. I saw some light cutting through the fog—a light from her room. The window was open. I maneuvered my body through the small opening and landed quietly in her room. The familiar smell of vanilla was in the air and it calmed my nerves.

I turned to see that none of her lights were on, just a nightlight by her bed. That was the light I had seen from the backyard. She was sitting in her round chair in the corner of her room. She was wearing pink pajamas and a pair of fuzzy purple socks. I wanted to tease her about her socks but held back because I was sure this wasn't the time for that. Even in her pajamas she was still breathtaking. Her hair was pulled back with two sticks that looked like fancy painted chopsticks, holding it up in a bun. She also was wearing her glasses. I had only seen her in glasses one other time.

I walked slowly to her, but she didn't look up. What was I supposed to do? She sat still, never making any movements or acknowledging my presence. I wanted to say something, but I was not sure what to say or do to make this better. I knew that I had to make her understand everything, but this was not the time to do that. She needed more time to deal with everything. She would speak to me when she was ready, and I was prepared to wait. I sat down next to the chair and leaned my head against it. Time moved fast, even in the silence of her room.

She stood up after two hours and walked to her bed. I stood up quickly. She got into bed and looked at me. Her eyes told me it was time to go.

"Can I come back tomorrow night?" My heart pounded, anticipating her answer. It seemed like an eternity before she nodded yes.

"Goodnight, Elle, and thank you for letting me come over." I pulled myself up through the open window.

The next night was exactly like the first—mostly just sitting in silence. I was happy being near her, even if we didn't talk. If this was how it was going to be, I would happily accept it just so I could be around her. Cora didn't stop me from going to Elle's house, and she never brought up my dreams either.

I arrived at Elle's house at 10:30 on Thursday night. Her parents were still up watching TV, so I took more time sneaking around the windows before sliding down through her open window.

"Why did you keep those secrets from me?"

I spun around, surprised to see Elle right in front of me instead of in her chair. All of her lights were on, and she was still dressed in the clothes she had worn to school. She had been crying.

"Nicholas, before you answer me, you'd better tell me the truth from now on because you have only one more chance." She sat down on the edge of her bed.

"Please, Elle, I know that there are going to be parts that you will want to ask questions about, but you have to let me tell you everything first."

"Okay," she said.

"Before I start, my football injury was fake." I quickly continued before she could respond. "When we were at the restaurant, someone recognized me. It was Tina, out of all the people to see me. Tina McBride was one of the people that I pulled out of our collapsing school during the 10-10 Earthquake. When she saw me, of course she wanted to talk to me, but all I was trying to do was escape so that my secret would stay hidden. You see, for the last five and a half years I have been taught to avoid being the center of attention, taught to blend in. That is why I had to fake my injury, because I was getting too much attention on the field. You may know the part of my past that everyone seems to think they know, but I'm going to tell you what really happened that day during the earthquake. I have never told anybody this, not even my Aunt Cora.

"I was in fifth grade. It was October 10th, the day the earthquake struck the New Madrid Fault Line. Everyone remembers where they were when it happened. A couple of students and I had just been called in from recess to Ms. Rush's class when the quake hit. There was a loud sound like a train running into a brick wall. I can still hear it now. The walls and windows began to shake, and the ceiling started to fall in. I managed to run through the falling debris and make it outside, but when I realized that Mark, Tina, and Ms. Rush weren't behind me, I ran back into the collapsing school without thinking.

"I saw Mark first. He was on the floor with a large cut on his leg from concrete that had fallen on him. I managed to get him up and outside. The earthquake had stopped for a moment, so I ran back in to find the others. I couldn't tell where the classroom was because of the extreme damage that the quake had done. I yelled for Tina and heard her crying under part of a fallen wall, which was braced up by some desks. I got down on all fours, crawled in, and saw Tina trapped and covered in blood. I pulled her out from under the wall using all of my strength. Her screams sounded like she was dying, but I dragged her free.

"When I got back outside, some of the teachers and students were coming over toward us. Then the first of the major aftershocks hit. People were yelling and screaming again, but instead of fear, I just thought of Ms. Rush still trapped inside. I started to run back inside, even though everything was still shaking. I think some of the teachers closest to me yelled for me to stop and even tried to stop me, but I went in anyway. This time the partial walls that were still standing were swaying from the aftershock. I was yelling for Ms. Rush, but heard no answer. I spotted her large wooden desk covered by parts of the ceiling. I made my way around the twisted metal and fallen walls. I saw her leg sticking out from under her desk. She must have ducked under it when the earthquake hit. She was lying there motionless. I reached under the desk and pulled her out. I couldn't drag her over the debris because she would have gotten hurt worse. I didn't want to leave her to go get help because, with the aftershocks, I was sure she would probably die. So I reached down and picked her up.

"I'm not sure how I had the strength to do it, but I did. The school began to shake from another aftershock, and I knew it was about to collapse. I moved swiftly through the broken school. Right as we cleared the building, it caved in on itself. There I stood, holding Ms. Rush in my arms in front of what used to be our school."

I paused for a moment to catch my breath, and then I continued. "That morning, there were strange looking lights in the sky, which everyone had been taking pictures of before the earthquake. I later read that those lights are called earthquake lights. They sometimes form before large seismic events. So someone who had been taking pictures of the lights took a photo of me holding Ms. Rush. Cora and I still don't know who took it, but that picture changed my life and sent me into hiding.

"No one at the school realized how big the earthquake was at first. I didn't know yet that while I was getting them out of the school, thousands of other people were dying, including my mom and dad. I spent most of the day waiting at the school for my parents to come and get me, but my Aunt Cora showed up instead.

"Several news people showed up at my house when they heard what I had done and saw the picture of me holding Ms. Rush. They asked me why I ran into the school, and I answered, 'Because I had to save them. It was my responsibility.' I had no idea what I was saying. I was only ten years old. The next thing I knew, the picture was everywhere with the caption, 'Alex Taylor, the 10-10 Hero.' Then reporters from all over the world wanted to talk about what happened and about my mom and dad. The world became obsessed with making me a hero, even though thousands of people died and there were hundreds of other heroes out there.

"A week later, my Aunt Cora woke me up early and took me to visit my parents' graves, and then we disappeared. She told me that she wanted me to have a normal life and my mom and dad would have wanted that too. So for the past five and a half years, we have moved every year to a different town and school in order to protect me and keep my identity hidden. That's why I used my middle name and my mom's maiden name.

"But things changed when I got here. Everything just clicked for me. All of a sudden, I was good at football and I made actual friends. Then there was you. Cora and I would have normally moved after all of the attention I was getting, but I didn't want to leave you. I knew that I would eventually have to move away and never see or speak to you again, but I was selfish. I did everything in my power to postpone moving just so I could be with you longer."

I wasn't looking at Elle. I was looking at the ground, scared to look up. "Elle, I am so sorry for not telling you the truth. You are the last person I would ever want to hurt. You are the reason why I am still here and why I confronted the reporters. I couldn't imagine not seeing you." I looked up and her eyes were filled with tears.

"Nicholas, I am the one who should be sorry. I was the selfish one. The things you have gone through are things I could never have done."

"So does this mean you forgive me, Elle?"

Crying and laughing at the same time, she threw her arms around me.

FIRST DATE
CHAPTER TWENTY-SIX

"Cora, I have something to tell you," I said while getting ready to leave for school.

"You don't need to thank me. I knew she would come around. If not, I would have gone over there and straightened her out." She did a small curtsy.

"No, it's not about that. It's about a secret I have been keeping from you."

She looked at me with an expression that said, "Please, I know everything, even if you think it's a secret."

"I have been attacked two times since we've been here."

Her expression changed to panic. "What do you mean attacked? By Oliver?"

"No, there's a truck that has been following me around ever since we moved here. The first attack happened on the practice field, and the other one was outside our house when I was waiting for Eric."

She didn't move. "You mean the fallen tree outside the house?"

I nodded.

"Why didn't you tell me sooner?" she asked.

I didn't answer because it was obvious—I didn't want to leave Elle.

"We will talk about this later." She disappeared upstairs.

What? I just got done telling her that I had been attacked twice, and all she said was, "We will talk about this later"? That seemed to be her answer to everything now.

**

Cora still insisted that I should ride different buses to and from school. She said she wanted to make sure that the media didn't find out where we lived, but I had a feeling it had more to do with the pair of killers, which we were supposed to talk about but never did.

Another small wrinkle that came up after my impromptu meeting with the press was the amount of mail being sent to the school. I didn't think about how many letters would flood the school for me. Every day there were thousands. Cora did her best to keep up with them; she tried to answer as many as possible. Superintendent Spears made sure to tell me how much the letters were costing the school. He threatened to make us pay a handling fee, even though just a couple of days before he had been willing to lock down the school with extra staff, security, and police on my behalf. I guess the cost of that was fine, but not extra mail. I told him to call Cora and take it up with her, which he, of course, never did.

My celebrity status had died down at school. People still wanted to say hi, but it was nothing compared to that first day when the media showed up. Eric was still my biggest fan and campaign manager. Oliver had disappeared. After the fight between the two of us, he vanished into thin air. He was better at hiding than I was.

Elle and I were still eating under the stairs by her request.

"Elle, will you go out on a real date with me?"

"Was our first date not a real one?"

"Well, I don't count that one as a date, because I spent the whole time worrying instead of concentrating on you as much as you deserve. This next one will be free of any stress. So how about tonight?"

"Sounds good, but could I meet you somewhere else besides my house?"

"Elle, is everything okay?"

"Everything is great . . . it's my dad."

"Oh, your dad. I bet he's not my biggest fan right now."

She was looking down at a run in the carpet that she was helping along.

"Elle, say no more. I don't need to know."

"No secrets, Nicholas." I was hoping that she would keep this secret. I didn't want to hear how much her dad hated me. "My dad just isn't sure if I should be spending so much time with someone who has so many secrets." She hesitated, then looked up and smiled. "But don't worry about him. I can make up my own mind about who I go out with." She reached over and squeezed my hand. Her soft warm touch filled me with reassurance.

"So where do you want me to meet you for our first official date?" she asked, still holding my hands.

I pulled away so I could regain some composure. "Meet me at 8:30 at Hunters Green Golf Course."

"Where?"

"Hunters Green Golf Course. Do you know where that is?"

"I do, but this is going to be a date, right?"

"Yes, Elle, one you won't forget."

**

I walked over the small hill at Hunters Green Golf Course, which overlooked the clubhouse and the parking lot. The only car in the lot besides my truck was Elle's little blue car. She was outside leaning against it. It had been a warm April day, but the evening brought a cool breeze. Luckily, there was no rain today. Elle was wearing a white shawl over a pink blouse. Her long flowing skirt danced in the wind. After almost a year of seeing her on a regular basis, I was still in awe of her. She saw me and ran to meet me halfway.

"Are we allowed to be here?" she said in a hushed voice.

"Yes, don't worry. The staff left at 7:00."

"Wait, let me guess. Someone's parents own the place?"

I laughed. "Yes, Eric's parents."

"For a guy who has only been here for eight months, you sure have a lot of connections," she replied. I smiled.

The stars had started to come out. Elle grabbed my hand and I led her through the course. We walked through a small wooded area toward a large clearing.

"Where are you taking me, Nicholas?"

"You'll see."

We walked out of the woods onto the fairway of one of the holes. "Are you taking me out for some late-night putt-putt?"

I pulled her toward the seventeenth green, where the flag was waving in the breeze.

"Oh my goodness, Nicholas." She dropped my hand and went running to the green. Earlier, I had set up a blanket and scattered a dozen candles all over the green. The closer we got to the hole, the brighter the candles seemed to shine. I had taken a couple of daisies and put them in a vase next to the blanket, along with some food and drinks.

"I can't believe you did all of this for me." She walked around to each candle, looking at each one as if they were all different presents waiting to be unwrapped.

"I wanted to show you how much you mean to me, Elle." Once I said those words, butterflies filled my stomach.

"Nicholas, it's so beautiful."

The backside of the seventeenth green sloped down dramatically. Farther past the green was a clearing, which revealed the lake that the course was built around. The moon was reflecting off the lake. I sat down on the blanket. Elle sat down right next to me.

"The lake is so beautiful. You are so wonderful to do this for me, Nicholas. Just when I think I've got you figured out, you do something like this."

"Is this a bad thing?"

"No, absolutely not. This is the nicest thing anyone has ever done for me." She laid her head on my shoulder.

"So what's it like?" she asked.

"What's what like?" I whispered back.

"Being a hero."

"Well, I don't really think of myself as a hero."

"Well, you are. Those people would have died if it weren't for you."

"A lot of other people died, and I wasn't there to save them."

She took my hand and turned my head to look into her eyes. "There was nothing you could do about them dying. It was not your fault. Your parents are proud of you. I am sure of that."

Hearing Elle talk about my parents overwhelmed me. I had never thought so much about my parents around anyone other than Cora. It was easier to do what Cora had taught me—move on and don't talk about it. A couple of tears fell slowly down my cheek. They never had a chance to hit the ground; Elle's hand was there to catch them.

"Everything is okay," she whispered. For the first time in my life, I felt like that was true. We gazed out over the water for a while, just enjoying each other's company and the beautiful view.

"Okay, I brought some fruit for you, and I brought your favorite drink."

"Grape pop?" she asked.

"Yes, indeed," I said.

"Nicholas, everything is so beautiful. I would have never imagined that my perfect date was going to be at a golf course. How did you come up with this?"

"When my dad was younger, he worked on a golf course. He met a girl who worked there with him. Their first date was sitting on a golf course, looking up at the stars after work. That girl was my mom."

Without warning, she wrapped her arms around me, startling me. Her lips pressed firmly against mine. My muscles tensed from the shock. I stopped breathing, and the butterflies in my stomach were on the move. When the initial shock of what was happening was over, I began to relax and started to enjoy every second of it. The world stopped and was now revolving around us. I didn't want this to ever stop. Her soft lips felt like warm silk. She pulled away and looked into my eyes.

"Are you okay, Nicholas?"

"Yes, of course. Why?"

"You don't look fine."

"I'm not sick, I'm, well, um . . . that was the first time I have kissed someone, except when I stole a kiss in fifth grade on a field trip, but that doesn't count."

"I'm surprised that you have never been kissed before, because I want to kiss you all the time." She gave me that crooked smile that she did from time to time.

The rest of the night was incredible. We spent it staring up at the stars together. We shared one final kiss before she got into her car. I drove home feeling invincible. I floated up to the front door and unlocked it, creeping inside, hoping not to wake Cora because I was home an hour later than I had planned. There was a note on the table that read, "Nicholas, I'll be home later. See you in the morning. Love, Cora."

I walked upstairs still on a high from the night with Elle. The phone rang. I answered, "Hello?"

"Nicholas, it's Elle. I got home safely."

"Thanks for calling me."

"No problem," she said. "Nicholas, are we going out tomorrow?"

"Yes, of course."

"Would you come with me to the quarry party? It's the last one of the year. I want you to be my date." The dread that I felt about the quarry party was absent. Oliver had not been at school for a week, and his challenge was nothing more than an empty threat. The rite of passage was not going to happen for the first time ever.

"Elle, nothing would make me happier."

"Okay, it's a date. Meet me at my house at 7:00. Talk to you tomorrow. . . . Nicholas?"

"Yes?"

"Thanks again for tonight. It was wonderful."

"You're welcome. Goodnight, Elle."

"Goodnight."

As soon as I hung up the phone, it rang again. I picked it up quickly, "Hello?"

"Nicholas?" a rough voice said.

"Yeah, who is this?"

"Don't forget I challenged you."

"Oliver, I am not doing it. Do you understand?" I tried to be as threatening as I could over the phone. I failed.

"You will or I will make you pay. Your girlfriend has more guts than you do—maybe I should have challenged her."

He hung up. The fire in my belly burned. I knew that Oliver was not going to back down. This was his last chance to get back at me.

CORA'S SACRIFICE
CHAPTER TWENTY-SEVEN

"Nicholas, get up. Hurry!" I could barely focus on Cora, who was running around my room, grabbing my clothes.

"Put these on. We have to go now."

"Go? Where are we going? Cora, we aren't moving. I won't go," I said, determined.

"Nicholas, we are not moving. I need to show you something. Remember when I told you we would talk about the dreams and attacks later? Well, it's time."

"Can't it wait until morning?"

"No, I need to show you now." She threw my clothes at me. "Get dressed. We leave in two minutes."

I got dressed and staggered down the stairs. Cora was waiting for me, keys in hand at the door. I followed her out, shutting the front door behind me. She was in the truck before I was off the porch. I got in and she backed quickly out of the driveway. It was still dark out. I couldn't have been asleep long; the dashboard clock said 5:14 a.m.

"So where are we going?"

"Not now, I will wake you when we get close."

"Wake me? How far is it?"

"It's ten hours away."

"Cora I have to be back because Elle and I—"

"Nicholas, there are more important things right now than Elle."

"Cora, pull the truck over right now. There is no way we will get home in time. I have to be back because Oliver will do something stupid if I don't show up." I had my hand on the door handle ready to jump out at the next stop. There was no way I could let Cora take me.

Cora stopped the truck. She put her hand on my leg. "Nicholas, you have to see something; it can't wait until later. Believe me, I would rather not have to take you, but I have no choice. After you told me about the people in the truck attacking you, I knew it was time for you to find out. I finally have everything ready for you."

"What's ready?" I demanded.

"Nicholas, please. I promise you will be home in time for whatever you're going to do tonight."

I loosened my grip on the handle. She would never lie to me. Cora started driving. I tilted my seat back and fell asleep.

**

We were driving through a dark forest, winding through some steep hills.

"We're almost there," said Cora. I looked at the clock; it was 2:45 p.m.

"Where are we now?" I asked.

"We are in West Virginia. Nicholas, before we get there, I need to tell you something that I have been keeping from you, something from my past. I was hoping I could keep this from you forever, but now I am being forced to tell you everything, and I hope it doesn't hurt you the way it did me." When she spoke it sounded hollow like she was rehearsing lines from a play.

"When I was your age, I fell in love with a boy named Marcus Fray—you may remember him." I did remember him after she said his name. He had been with Cora at every family event that I could remember.

"He was my true love. We were inseparable. When we both considered colleges, he wanted to apply to the same schools that I did. Marcus and I both got accepted to Vanderbilt. Mom and Dad weren't too thrilled about me going to the same school as Marcus. They wanted me to be free of him so I could focus on my studies, but they reluctantly let me go off to school with him. Vanderbilt was better than high school for us. We were the 'it' couple by our sophomore year. He was student body president, and I was president of my sorority and captain of the dance team. We planned every social event for the school. It was just how I dreamt it would be. Everything was perfect.

"Sophomore year, Mom and Dad died in the automobile accident on Christmas Eve. After the funeral, I stayed with you, Beth, and Joseph for the rest of my winter break. Near the end of the break, they brought me to where I am taking you tonight."

The paved road became gravel, barely suitable to drive on. The forest was now right on either side of the truck with no room for another vehicle to pass.

"After the break, I went back to Vanderbilt. I tried to forget everything that I saw and learned here with your parents. I focused on making things return to how they had been before, but it wasn't working. So I decided to dedicate myself to school, just like my parents had wanted me to. I quit my sorority and the dance team, which didn't bother Marcus at all. He proposed to me on April 12. We were supposed to get married as soon as we graduated."

Cora stopped and wiped away the tears that were streaming down her cheeks. She cleared her throat and continued, "Marcus was so good to me after the accident. He supported me in every way. He even stepped down as class president so he could be there for me whenever I needed him. I never wanted him to do that, but he did it anyway, as well as making many other sacrifices to be with me." Cora's speech became very broken.

"On October 10 of my senior year, the 10-10 Earthquake hit. I left school immediately after I heard how severely it had hit our town. One of my friends from high school, who was a teacher at your school, called. He told me he was waiting with you because Beth and Joseph hadn't come for you, and he didn't feel right about putting you on the bus to the shelter. Marcus wouldn't let me leave without him because Beth, Joseph, and you were like his family too. Marcus' family had moved back to California a year earlier, so he had no family here when the quake hit.

"When we got close to Mt. Vernon, I was stunned by how much chaos and devastation the quake had caused. It resembled a town that was bombed in one of the world wars, barely recognizable. I was lucky to be able to get to you at the school. There were so many damaged streets. If I hadn't known all of the short cuts and side streets, we would not have gotten to you as quickly as we did.

"I don't know if you remember that your house was mostly spared from any significant damage from the quake, so we settled in at your house. That's when the media started to show up, wanting to talk to you about that picture. I didn't know what to do, especially when we found out what had happened to Beth and Joseph." Cora stopped and took in a deep breath, calming herself.

"Then I got a visit from some people. I asked Marcus to watch you while I talked to the people by myself. Marcus wasn't too happy about them being there, because one of the individuals was Chase Letterby. He disliked Chase because Chase was always trying to get me to dump Marcus, which I would never do. The other two people were Jerry Hill, who just died recently, and Ester Theasing—yes, the same Ester Theasing from Winsor.

"They came to tell me that I had to go into hiding to protect you, and that it had to be just me, no one else, especially not Marcus. Ester provided us with enough money that we would never have to worry about money again. Jerry was responsible for erasing our pasts and creating our new lives. And Chase was, well, always on call, our personal doctor in case we needed any medical help or a quick getaway.

"So that night I started a fight with Marcus while you were asleep. For his own safety, I wasn't allowed to tell him anything about us having to leave. I told him that I didn't want to be with him anymore, that we were over. It was the worst thing I ever had to do. I told the love of my life that the only reason I said yes to his marriage proposal was because I had been upset about my parents' death, that I hadn't been thinking clearly, and that it was a big mistake. He begged me to change my mind, pleading with me for hours. I went on to say things I will not repeat to you, and he eventually left early the next morning."

Cora looked like she was on the verge of a complete breakdown, but like before, she took a deep breath and continued. "Three days later, we visited your parents' graves and disappeared."

"Why did you do that? I would have been okay. Who cares if the media kept bothering me? That would have been better than you and Marcus not being together. I could never leave like that, especially if someone asked me to leave Elle. I wouldn't do it."

"Nicholas, I had to protect you. I had to make that sacrifice."

"Sacrifice your future to protect me from what? A couple reporters?"

"No, the reporters were just a small part of it. What I had to protect you from was something larger and more dangerous than you know."

She pulled off the gravel road onto what felt like a newly paved road. The road was extremely well maintained for being in the middle of nowhere. "We are here. I will explain more with a little help once we are inside, Nicholas."

A house, which was a little bigger than a guardhouse, was positioned right next to a large metal gate. The gate connected to a tall metal fence, which shot off in both directions, disappearing into the woods. Cora stopped next to the house. A side door opened, and a man dressed in what looked like a hunter's outfit came out. Cora rolled down the window.

"Hello, Mr. Weathers," she said.

The unkempt man spoke in a frail but friendly voice, "Well, Ms. Cora Keller, it's been a long time. It's so nice to see you. And who do you have with you?" He leaned forward and looked inside the truck.

Cora spoke, "It's Alexander—"

He finished her sentence, "Nicholas Taylor Keller? Well then, by all means, go on in. The others have already arrived."

Cora rolled up the window.

"What was that all about? Who was that old man?" I asked.

"He's the caretaker."

"For what, a wildlife park?"

"No, for this."

THUSIANS
CHAPTER TWENTY-EIGHT

Cora turned around a bend. There was a large, open paved lot, where two helicopters sat on either side of an entrance carved into the side of the mountain straight ahead of us.

"What is this place? Is it a mine?"

Cora got out, ignoring the questions, and walked toward the entrance. I slipped my shoes back on and caught up with her.

"Nicholas, it's very important that you follow me very closely." She turned and walked into the entrance. I followed her. A couple of steps into the entrance it became darker than I thought possible. The light from the entrance vanished. I could hear Cora walking ahead of me, but I didn't know how far ahead of me she was. The walkway started to slope gradually downward, leading us down into the mountain.

I heard Cora counting out loud, "142, 143, 144 steps, then the door."

Without warning, I was blinded by an intense, bright white light. I squinted through my hands and saw Cora's silhouette standing in a doorway. The light coming from the door was overpowering.

Still barely able to open my eyes, I walked slowly through the door, holding my hands out to steady myself. Behind me, Cora shut the door with a loud, hollow bang. "We can wait here until you get used to the light."

A minute passed and I started to see our surroundings. We were standing on a platform that was connected to a steep set of stairs that went down the middle of a large round tunnel. The wall was smooth and white with no visible seams. The tunnel was lit by large lights hanging down the center.

"Nicholas, it's just a little farther. Once we are there, we can talk." She started down the stairs. I followed. The stairs went on as far as I could see.

We had been walking down the stairs for what must have been about fifteen minutes when I heard a faint rumbling sound coming from below us. The farther we descended into the mountain, the more the sound grew in intensity. It was becoming so loud that even if I had wanted to talk to Cora, she wouldn't have been able to hear me. I felt like my ears were going to explode. Then I saw the end of the stairs.

Cora walked quickly down the last couple of steps, and I followed closely. She walked into a room that was a couple of feet past the end of the stairs. The loud roaring sound was muffled once we were inside. The room was made out of some sort of shiny metal. It looked like copper. Straight ahead was a large door with no visible doorknob or handle. On the right side of the room, there were twelve small metal wheels attached to the wall in a straight line parallel to the ground.

Each one had a ring of letters surrounding it and a marker, which lined up with a different letter depending on how you moved the wheel.

Cora started at the first wheel and worked her way down the row, carefully lining up each marker with a different letter. The farther she got, the quieter the roaring became. When she made it through all of the wheels, the sound was gone. The only sound now was coming from the door. It was making a series of clicks that sounded like it was being unlocked from within. Then a handle appeared out of the door. Cora pulled the lever and the door opened. She walked in, and I was right behind her.

We were standing in a large stone cathedral cut from the belly of the mountain. The ceiling was high and vaulted like in an Italian cathedral built by the greatest architects of its time, but this cathedral was cut entirely out of stone. All of the ornate decoration and details were carved. The walls were as smooth as glass.

There were twelve individual stone seats cut out of the ground, rising up from the floor at the front of this magnificent cave. Each seat was unique from the others. The front of this stone cathedral had the most splendid altar I had ever seen. It looked like a large stone fireplace, but it took up the entire front wall. It was made out of flat rocks stacked on top of each other; the rocks' jagged edges stuck out to make a rough finish. Water was cascading down from the ceiling over the front of the rocks. The water disappeared into the ground below. In between the rocks was an iridescent yellowish-white light that illuminated the altar, making it glow.

I looked down and noticed that I was standing in a very shallow puddle. The ground was wet with several puddles. It looked like it had just rained.

"Cora, where are we?"

"Remember in the truck when I said your mom and dad took me somewhere at the end of my winter break? Well, this is that place."

"Okay, but where are we? Why have you brought me here?"

"We are in the central chamber of the Thusian Vault."

"The *what*?" I asked.

"The Thu-see-en Vault. The reason I brought you here is for you to understand the changes you are going through on the inside as well as understand your past and your future."

Chase Letterby and Ester Theasing walked out of a door directly across from where we had entered. Ester came over to Cora and put an arm around her. Cora didn't flinch; she actually welcomed it, which was completely the opposite of how I expected her to respond.

Chase walked over to me. "Hey, Nicholas, it's good to see you. How's that cracked vertebra?" He smiled and patted me on the back. My head was swimming.

"What's going on, Cora?" I asked, hoping she would wake me up from whatever this was, but Ester spoke instead.

"Nicholas, this is going to be hard for you to understand at first, but please give me a chance to explain what this is all about. Then Chase will speak to you about your dreams and your newfound talents."

Chase walked over to Cora, and he replaced Ester's arm with his own. Again, Cora didn't fight him. She leaned against his chest, using his arms like a crutch. She looked ragged and exhausted.

"Nicholas, I will start from the beginning, just like I did for Cora when she first came here. Roughly 2,000 years ago, the Thusians were created. There were a thousand original Thusians. Their sole purpose was to protect the human race from the evils of this world, no matter the cost—most of the time sacrificing their own lives in the process. They are like guardian angels.

"As time went on, the Thusians' numbers began to dwindle. So the Keeper—the Thusians' king—declared that, for the first time, Thusians would be allowed to marry non-Thusians in order to hopefully repopulate the Thusians' numbers and continue to protect mankind. This plan was very successful, because the Thusians' numbers grew into the hundreds of thousands in no time, but the Thusians' ways were not passed on to everyone with Thusian blood.

"The Keeper also acted as a librarian for the Thusians. He knew all of the history and, more importantly, the bloodline of the Thusian families. The Thusians looked to him for guidance, but when the numbers grew too large, a group of Thusians decided that the Keeper was no longer able to do his job effectively. They formed a governing body, the Divine Council, to make decisions and manage the growing population. After the formation of the Council, the Keeper tradition was eliminated.

"The Council consisted of twelve individuals selected by the Governor of the Council." She motioned to the twelve stone seats. "For years, the Council was successful and just, but it eventually became corrupt. They thought the Thusians' numbers had grown too large to govern. So they gathered 100 of the brightest and strongest Thusians and created a secret group called the Seekers. Their sole purpose was to kill Thusians who did not know about their connections to the Thusian heritage. If they didn't know their purpose, then they should not be allowed to live.

"The Seekers would create circumstances through which targeted Thusians would be most likely to sacrifice their lives. This was the way the Council thought they would purify the Thusians. People with any Thusian blood would be compelled to sacrifice themselves for others during certain events, even if they didn't know about their Thusian heritage.

"Hundreds of years went by with the Council and Seekers working hand in hand. Then the Council became powerless to control the Seekers. The Seekers started to eliminate all Thusians, regardless of what the Council wanted, because they thought no one was pure enough to be a Thusian. Even the old Council was slowly killed off by the very Seekers they had created. It was Thusian genocide. But with the birth of America came the hope of a new Council. I am the Governor of the Divine Council now. Both of your parents were on the Council, and so was your grandmother." She paused long enough for me to ask a question.

"So my whole purpose in life is to be a sacrificial lamb, to die for someone?"

Ester answered the question like I had asked her about the weather. "Yes, Nicholas, when your time comes, it may require that. Thusians are usually drawn to dangerous occupations where they risk their lives daily for others, such as being police officers, firemen, paramedics, or in the military. But at the end of the day, no matter what their occupation, all Thusians may have to give up their lives for a final sacrifice, just like your parents did."

My heart raced. It felt like it was pounding in my throat. "What do you mean just like my parents? They died in the earthquake."

"Nicholas, they died as a result of the quake happening and being Thusians, but not during the actual quake. Your father died while saving three small children from a collapsed house, and your mother died saving two co-workers at her office. Luckily, they managed to save everyone they were attempting to help."

"Luckily? Luckily? Are you kidding? They died saving complete strangers, but what about me? Why didn't they think of me?" I was seething with anger and the fire in my stomach was burning red-hot. Cora was now in front of me, trying to calm me down, but I didn't want to be calmed.

"Nicholas, they didn't have a choice," Cora said calmly. "When a Thusian is called to make a final sacrifice, something inside takes over. We can't control it. Like when I had to protect you and keep you safe from everything, I couldn't fight it. It was my sacrifice. Neither could your parents."

"But why was your sacrifice just protecting me, and why did they have to die?" I yelled at Cora.

Chase stepped forward, shielding Cora and Ester from me. Chase was a lot bigger than me, but I knew he would be no match for me right now.

"Nicholas, you need to calm down. I know it is a lot to take in all at once, but remember, we didn't kill your parents."

"You didn't, but this crazy Thusian curse did. How do you expect me to be calm when one day I will probably have to sacrifice my life for a complete stranger, leaving my family behind?"

"Not everyone's sacrifice is a death sentence. Not everyone's sacrifice is for a stranger either. Maybe one day you might have to sacrifice your life for a friend or Cora or even your girlfriend, Elle."

Hearing Elle's name was like an instant tranquilizer for me. If I had to give my life for her, it would be the easiest decision I would ever have to make.

"Nicholas, now that you are calming down, I think that Ester and Cora would like for me to discuss with you some of the things you might be experiencing." Chase didn't wait for a confirmation. "First of all, the dreams when you feel like you're suffocating, paralyzed, or being surrounded by something— this is normal for most Thusians. It should only last a couple of months and then it's gone."

A couple of months, was he kidding? I had been having those night terrors for the last five years, but I didn't see the need to tell him that.

"The night terrors begin for Thusians around the time of realization. Realization is when we first get or realize our talents. Talents are usually broken into one of two different areas: either physical or mental. But just because there are two categories, doesn't mean the talents in one category are all the same. For example, Cora, Ester, and I all have mental talents. Cora's talents are in risk management, which is why she always knew how to keep you safe and hidden. My talents are in the area of medicine. When taking care of someone, I am always able to make the right decision about how to best treat them. Ester's talents are in finance. She always knows how to make large sums of money.

"Your talents, on the other hand, are obviously physical in nature. You will not be able to use them on demand; it doesn't work that way. Over time, you will know the limits of your talents. I know what you're thinking: 'Why do I have these talents?' They are to aid you in your final sacrifice, which you will have to make one day."

"Actually, Chase, I have a different question. Who was Cora keeping me safe from? I don't think any of the media wanted to hurt me."

Chase didn't speak. Ester walked up to his side, and Cora stood on his other side. They were all facing me, forming a wall.

Ester spoke, "Remember the Seekers I mentioned? Well, they are still out there, and they are still trying to eliminate Thusians, trying to eliminate all of us. And from what Cora explained to us, it seems that you have already been attacked by two Seekers."

I nodded.

"Ever since the Keepers were eliminated, there has been no real way for the Seekers to keep track of the family bloodlines.

The members of the Council were the only ones who knew and tracked most of the bloodlines of the Thusians. So now the Seekers watch the media, along with other things, for any act of heroism or unusual luck. So after the earthquake when you got all of that media attention, we knew it was only a matter of time before they came looking for you."

"So let me get this straight," I said. "I am part of an ancient group of guardian angels called the Thusians, and I have super powers that will force me to eventually get killed or leave everything behind for some great final sacrifice that I have no control over? All the while, an ancient death squad formed by the Thusian Divine Council is out to kill me. Did I forget anything?"

Chase laughed. "Wow, Nicholas, you did a great job of summing it up. Maybe next time you should give the talk."

"Chase, this is not a laughing matter," Cora scolded him, walking up and putting her arms around me. "Nicholas, I am so sorry I didn't tell you this earlier."

"So this means I can't tell anyone about this?" I asked, knowing the answer.

"Absolutely not," Ester said. "Telling someone would put their life in terrible danger."

I couldn't believe it . . . more secrets.

Ester showed me around the rest of the place, explaining more of the history of the Thusians. She took me into the room where they had been waiting for us when we first came in. It was a large round room, but not as tall as the cathedral; its ceiling was only two stories high. It was filled with books and papers. Ester explained to me that this was all of the

Thusian history that they had been able to recover from the old vault in Europe.

She had Chase and Cora come into the library with us, and she closed the door, which looked identical to the large metal one in the copper entrance room. When the door closed, the rumbling sound returned.

"Nicholas, can you hear that sound? That is part of our security here. You see, when both doors are closed, the main chamber is filled with rushing water. That's why everything was wet. The vault was cut just below a river that runs through this mountain. So when the doors close, the ceiling opens and allows the river to fill the space, thus protecting our secrets. If someone tried to get in and didn't know the right combination, the tube leading down to the vault would flood. If they came prepared for water and got through the door, the current would be too strong and would suck them into the underground river. And if somehow they got through the river and tried to enter into this chamber, it would flood, and the water would destroy all of the records, keeping our secrets safe."

Ester picked up a book off of the nearest rack. "Nicholas, the paper on which we keep our records is formulated to instantly become pulp when water touches it." She walked over to a bookcase and pulled on it. It opened up, revealing more wheels and letters like at the entrance. A couple turns of the wheels, and the water sound stopped. "So it's always important, once you're in the vault, to open the records room door so that the chamber won't flood. Either the chamber door or the records room door needs to be open at all times while anyone is in here. It may seem like a big risk to take, but our secrets are more important than any one life. Maybe one day someone will have to sacrifice their life to protect the Thusians' secrets. We can never be too careful."

We all walked out of the records room. Chase went over to the door through which we had entered and opened it. Ester closed the door to the records room, and we walked out of the vault. Cora was very close to me.

"Nicholas, if you have more questions, please don't be afraid to contact me. I will be happy to talk," Ester said.

My head was spinning from spending a couple of hours down in the vault. "I do have a question. Why tell me and show me all of this right now?"

"Because you need to know the dangers that we face every day as Thusians," Ester answered, and then started up the stairs.

Once we were at the top of the tube and outside, Cora spoke, "Chase, can we borrow your helicopter?"

"Of course," he replied. "You and Nicholas can take it back to your house. I will be happy to drive your truck back. You don't look like you're in any condition to drive anyway."

"Do you have a phone in there that I can use?" I asked.

"Of course," Chase said. We boarded the luxury helicopter. I grabbed the phone and dialed Elle.

"Hello?" a faint voice said.

"Elle, thank goodness you picked up. Oliver is still challenging me to the rite of passage. He called me last night."

The voice changed. "This isn't Elle. She is away right now." It didn't sound like her dad or mom.

"Who is this?"

"Just someone who has been trying to kill you for some time now."

"Who is this?" I demanded.

"You know who I am, and I bet you are still at the Thusians' secret vault," he laughed with a dry cough.

"You better not do anything to Elle, or I'll kill you and your friend."

"I love young Thusians," he said sarcastically. "I haven't done anything to her directly, youngster. Your little girlfriend was taken by Oliver a short while ago. I sure like him."

"When I get there—"

He interrupted me, "What? Are you going to come after me? Ha! That's not how this works. *I* come after *you* pathetic, weak Thusians. If I were you, I'd be more worried about your little girlfriend. Soon, she and Oliver will be headed to an icy, cold death at the bottom of that quarry lake. What a shame, really. I have been planning this death for you for such a long time. I'll be seeing you soon," he laughed, and then the phone went dead.

"Chase, get on the helicopter now," I yelled.

THE RACE
CHAPTER TWENTY-NINE

"Chase, you and Cora go the quarry, and make sure you stop Oliver. I will go to Elle's house to make sure she isn't there."

"It's a trap; you know that. Let's all check her house, and then we can go to the quarry," Chase suggested.

"Chase is right. We should stick together," agreed Cora.

"No, we have to split up. That is the only way we can make sure to cover all of the places. You will drop me off by her house and then fly to the quarry. That's the only way we can be sure." Both Chase and Cora nodded reluctantly.

We landed in the park right next to Elle's subdivision. The cool breeze was refreshing, and the sun felt good on my skin once I was out of the helicopter. The sun began to set behind the park's large trees, casting long, ominous shadows across the field. The sound of the helicopter was fading away. I was halfway through the park, near one of the picnic areas, when I felt a sharp, stinging pain radiate from my lower back. My knees buckled and the world began to spin. My head hit the ground and everything went black.

"Wake up, Alexander!" a frantic female voice shouted. "Alexander, you must wake up! Alexander Nicholas Taylor, open your eyes!"

My eyes felt like they had 100-pound weights holding them shut. The female voice stopped begging, seeing my eyes start to open. Everything was blurry. I had to blink several times to clear my vision. I was not in the field any longer. I was lying on a bench under one of the park's shelters. My head was in the lap of the strange woman who was pleading for me to open my eyes. My body throbbed. I felt like I had been hit by a truck. The woman was looking at me with her compassionate green eyes. She was rubbing my head, comforting me, which helped to distract me from the pain radiating from my back. This woman's skin was radiant and lightly tanned, but not by the sun; it must have been native to where her family was from. Her brown hair was in small braids on either side of her slender face, pulled back behind her head. Her light pink lips were together, making a shushing sound like you would do to a baby to get it to calm down.

"Who are you?" I asked, trying to sit up, but she kept my head where it was with little force.

"My name is Genevieve, and his name is Riley," she answered calmly.

I looked over and saw a tall, slender man standing a couple of feet away, looking around the park. He reminded me of a younger Coach Miller.

"You were attacked by a Seeker named Xavier and one of his friends," Genevieve said. "Luckily, Riley and I have been watching you for some time, keeping you safe."

I sat up, panicked. "You have been trying to kill me!" My head was spinning. I knew for certain that these were the two people who had been following me.

She spoke softly but firmly. "We haven't been trying to kill you; we have been protecting you."

"Each time I was almost killed this year, you were there, weren't you?"

"Well, of course we were there," Riley said, "but you didn't need our help. Your Thusian talents saved you."

"Are you bodyguards sent by Ester or Chase? Another line of defense that I didn't know about?"

"We have nothing to do with Ester or Chase," Riley replied. He had a thick Irish accent that sounded like it had been slightly Americanized. He went back to watching over the park.

"There is no time for talking, only time for you to listen," Genevieve said. "Xavier would have killed you if we hadn't shown up. We heard him telling you that you were too late and that you would never make it in time to help her. Who was he talking about? You have been mumbling something about Elle, a car, and a dock. What does that all mean? You have to tell us."

I closed my eyes, focusing on the voice growing louder in my head. It was the same one that I had heard on the phone earlier. The harder I concentrated, the louder the obtrusive voice got. Then the voice was clear.

Oliver and Elle are on their way to the rock quarry, and there is no way you will be able to get to them in time before they die. I knew you would come here and check her house. How predictable.

Sending the others away to the quarry is exactly the kind of thing that gets you Thusians killed so easily—always trying to be the hero. Just so you know, there is no way to save her, the voice said.

It continued, *To be honest Alexander, I think she may have some Thusian blood in her too because of the way you were drawn to her. Killing her now will save me from having to come back and kill her later. The hero of the 10-10 Earthquake has been more of a challenge to kill. You survived the earthquake and my first couple of attacks, so I had to kill you in person. And what a shame, I spent all that time cutting the supports on the dock.*

His voice rang in my head. *There is no way to save her.* It grew so loud that my head throbbed with pain. In an instant I was standing. Adrenaline surged through my body. All of my pain was gone. The fire burned and my muscles tensed.

"Oliver has taken Elle and they are going to die!" I said, running out of the shelter past Riley. My surroundings immediately blurred. I had to get to the quarry in time to save Elle. If this was my turn to make a final sacrifice, I would willingly die for Elle.

TOO LATE
CHAPTER THIRTY

It was completely dark outside of town. There were no streetlights, but I could see perfectly. I was only a mile away from the party. The handwritten map that Eric had used back in August was as clear in my head as if I was the one who drew it.

I got to the quarry entrance and ran down several gravel roads before I saw the light from the party ahead of me. I saw everyone yelling and cheering, staring right at the dock. There were even more people here than at the last party. The quarry seemed 100 times brighter than the last time; I could see everything clearly. The only movement near the dark grey lake was coming from a primer grey beater that Oliver was using for his rite of passage. The car began to slow down, and then it stopped just a few feet from the end of the dock. Then, in slow motion, the part of the dock that the car was on collapsed, and the front of the car crashed into the water. The remaining part of the dock flipped over on top of it, and the taillights disappeared under the water. Was I too late?

I was at the edge of the water pulling off my shirt before any of the people there had a chance to move. Chase and Cora were running toward me from the helicopter, which had landed in an open area off to the side of the lake. Why hadn't they stopped this from happening? I dove into the dark, icy cold lake. My lungs seized, not prepared for the cold. My body quickly adjusted to the water temperature. Once in the water, I was able to move toward the car with no resistance. I was able to grab handfuls of water that felt firm, like a grip. I sank my fingers into it to help propel me through the water quickly. I pulled with all of my might, and I sent myself hurtling toward the car.

The water was dark, but my eyes pulled all of the light from above, allowing me to see everything clearly in the dark, murky water. I was moving quickly toward the car. Through the pieces of the dock I could see that the car was almost completely filled with water. I gave the water one more thrust with my hands, and I hit the car with such force that it sank deeper into the depths.

I dismantled the pieces of the dock that surrounded the car like they were made of toothpicks. Inside, Elle was struggling with her seat belt to get free. Oliver was bloody and unconscious, floating next to her in the water-filled car. The windshield imploded, filling it completely with water. The car raced toward the bottom. I caught the hood near the windshield, keeping it from sinking any farther. Elle's eyes fluttered. She was close to becoming unconscious, barely struggling anymore with her belt. I grabbed her seat belt and ripped it off of her. I pulled her out and pushed her to the surface. I could see her break the surface of the water, and her legs began to lightly tread water. Then I went back and grabbed Oliver's broken body and pulled him up with me toward Elle at the surface. I broke the surface of the water right next to her as she went under again, unable to keep herself afloat anymore. I pulled both of them up on my chest and swam them to the shore in a matter of seconds. People from the crowd reached out to take Oliver from me and pulled him ashore. I carried Elle out and gently laid her on the ground.

"Elle, can you hear me? Elle, please!" I begged. One of my hands was cupped under her head and the other stroked her cheek.

She spoke very quietly, almost inaudibly, "Don't leave me, Nicholas." Then her cold body went limp. I listened to her chest and felt for a pulse. She had a faint pulse and her breathing was shallow. She had no visible cuts or broken bones.

I grabbed my dry shirt, which was within arm's reach of us, and wrapped her in it, trying to keep her warm. Shouts and screams were coming from all around me. I pulled her up onto my lap to keep her close and to try to warm her. Why did this have to happen to her? I would do anything to switch places with her.

I started pleading, "God, take me, not her. Please, God, let her live."

"Nicholas, you have to let go now. I will take care of her," Chase said. I knew I had to let her go, but I couldn't let someone take her from me. Not again.

"Where were you? Why didn't you stop this?" I screamed at him.

"Nicholas, let her go." Eric was prying me off of her now.

I let go and fell back to the ground. There was so much commotion around me. People were yelling and screaming. Chase worked on her for what seemed like forever. Eventually, Elle was being loaded into a nearby ambulance. I staggered to my feet to follow her. I got up to the back door and tried to get in, but someone grabbed me from behind. I didn't have the strength to fight back.

"Nicholas, stop. You can't go with her. You have to get checked out yourself. You have blood all over your back," Eric said, holding me back.

"I have to go with her! I have to! Let go of me!"

"Nicholas, it's okay." I turned and saw Cora and began to cry uncontrollably.

"Cora, please let me sacrifice my life for her. My life is nothing without her. Please, help me, please."

"Nicholas, it doesn't work that way. Shh, it will be okay." Cora moved me away from the crowd.

"Where were you? Why didn't you stop this from happening?"

"Nicholas, it's a big quarry; we had to look for the party. We only found it when it started to get dark outside. Plus, Chase needed to stop and get supplies from the hospital in case we needed them, which we did."

"If you hadn't stopped, you could have prevented this all from happening, and you wouldn't have needed those supplies."

"Stop, Nicholas. We aren't to blame. We didn't know what we were going to encounter."

I fell toward her and wrapped my arms around her. "You're right. I'm sorry."

"Come over here and let Chase take a look at your back before he leaves for the hospital."

"No, I must go to the hospital to be with Elle. Chase can check me out later," I said. Cora nodded, understanding. She got some gauze, cleaned my wound, and taped the gauze over it.

Once in the truck, I was able to take in the scene around me more clearly. There were dozens of squad cars and emergency vehicles throughout the enormous crowd of people at the party. Some of the people were talking to the police, and others were huddled in groups. Then I saw them for a brief second—Genevieve and Riley and their sea green truck.

"Cora, look out there. Those are the two Thusians that saved me." When I looked back at where they had been, they were gone.

"Nicholas, what are you talking about? Saved you from what?"

"I will tell you later. Let's get to the hospital."

Chase was already working on Elle by the time Cora and I got there. I couldn't see what he was doing, but there was a room full of doctors and nurses assisting him. Both of Elle's parents were sitting in the waiting area. Mrs. Canan's eyes were swollen; her head was resting on Mr. Canan's shoulders. Mr. Canan was like a statue—pale, not moving, just staring off into space in shock. Cora stood next to me while I stared through a small window into the room, hoping to see something.

After about an hour, Chase came out of the room and went straight over to Mr. and Mrs. Canan. He sat down across from them. I couldn't hear what he was saying, but they both listened to him intently. Then they all stood, and Mr. and Mrs. Canan followed him into the room. Chase then came back out to us.

"Chase, is she going to be okay?" I asked.

"Nicholas, she is in a coma, but she is stable. I think she will be okay, but it's going to take some time," he said. "She is lucky you got there when you did. I don't think she would have made it any longer in that frigid water.

"Nicholas, do you want me to take a look at your back before I assist them with the boy you saved? They said they need help with him."

"You aren't going to help with him, are you?" I asked, horrified. "Chase, you have to stay with Elle. You are here because we needed your help with Elle, not the person who took her and put her in danger."

"Someone took her?" The three of us spun around to see Ester Theasing standing behind us. "Who took Elle Canan?" she repeated her question to us.

"Oliver Rails did, but it should have been me. His plan was meant for me. I was supposed to be in the car."

"Nicholas, what are you talking about? What plan?" Ester asked.

"Xavier was planning to kill me."

All three recoiled at the mention of Xavier's name. Chase spoke first, "Did you say Xavier?"

"Yes."

"Okay, start from the beginning," Ester said.

"Xavier was at Elle's house and answered the phone when I called. I went to check on her at her house, while Chase and Cora went to the quarry to stop Oliver. I was attacked in Swaim Park by her house. When I came to, there was a woman and a man there named Genevieve and Riley. They stopped Xavier and his friend from killing me. I then recalled Xavier telling me that he had cut the dock supports so that the dock would collapse when the car drove onto it. Oliver and I were supposed to crash into the lake, but when Oliver took Elle instead, Xavier changed his plans. He decided to kill me in person and let them die in the lake, since he thought Elle might be a Thusian too."

I looked at Chase. His face had lost all of its color. Ester and Cora looked like they were both in deep thought.

"Ester, should we go into hiding?" Cora asked.

"No, Cora, there is no need to do that. He had his chances and missed them. He would never try again out in the open. But this changes everything. I must speak to the Council immediately." Ester then disappeared down the hall.

Chase was still pale and visibly shaken. His golden tan was gone.

"Can someone tell me what's going on?" I asked.

"Nicholas, Xavier is a very dangerous Seeker. You are lucky that Genevieve and Riley showed up," Cora said.

"Nicholas, he is one of the most feared Seekers out there," Chase said.

"Who are Genevieve and Riley?" I asked both Cora and Chase.

"I'm not sure. Do you know, Chase?" Cora asked.

He blinked repeatedly, and some of the color returned to his face. "Xavier is here. Did you see what he looked like?" Chase asked.

"No, Chase," I responded. He was clearly focused on Xavier. I really didn't care who Xavier was, or who Genevieve and Riley were for that matter. I just wanted Chase to take care of Elle and make sure she got better. Everything else was an afterthought, something for later. "Listen, I don't care who this Xavier is. You take care of Elle. Do you understand me, Chase?"

Chase nodded. He turned and started to walk back into her room.

"Chase," I called after him. "Go ahead and help Oliver. This was mostly Xavier's fault anyway."

RECOVERING
CHAPTER THIRTY-ONE

Elle was recovering in the hospital, still in a coma. I refused to leave the hospital. I had to be there when she woke up. Doctors came and went, but I continued to sit there, waiting. From time to time, Chase checked on her and gave me an update. Her parents were there around the clock too. They took turns going home to sleep while the other sat by her side.

Mr. Canan never spoke to me. I was sure he blamed me somehow for what had happened to Elle. Mrs. Canan was the complete opposite. She was nice, telling me that she would call me right when Elle woke up if I wanted to go home. I politely declined each time. She seemed as concerned about me as she was about Elle.

I spent most nights drifting in and out of consciousness. I was exhausted and still hurt from the attack I had suffered in the park. Fatigue set in, making it difficult to do much of anything. Luckily, Chase was able to get me into the showers that the doctors use at the hospital as well as a room in which I could lie down and relax. Still, for the most part I stayed in the waiting room right outside Elle's door. Cora brought me new clothes to wear each day. She also brought home-cooked meals for me, the Canans, and the staff at the hospital. Tic Tacs were the only thing that could give me some relief from the nausea brought on by my lack of sleep.

"Nicholas, Nicholas, wake up!" I must have dozed off in the waiting room because Mrs. Canan startled me.

"Is Elle awake?"

"Yes, dear, she is. She's awake and she wants to see you."

I stood up, still feeling lightheaded from sleeping. Outside it had become dark; I must have been asleep for a while. I followed Mrs. Canan to Elle's room. This was the first time that I had been able to see her since that night in the quarry.

When I entered the room, I saw Chase surrounded by a couple of adoring nurses, which was not surprising. Elle was sitting up, sipping a drink. For having just come out of a coma, she looked incredible and full of life. When she saw me she cried out, "Nicholas." She began to weep. I sat down on her bed next to her. She leaned forward and buried her head in my chest. I held her tightly.

"I thought I would never see you again," she sobbed.

"I am here. Everything is okay."

Holding her made all of my aches and pains go away. I rocked her back and forth while she cried. As she got quieter, I could hear some sniffling from behind us. It was Mrs. Canan. She had been crying along with her daughter. Chase and the nurses left the room to give us privacy.

Elle pulled back and looked into my eyes. "You look worse than I do," she laughed, wiping away her tears. I smiled at her. Even lying in a hospital bed, she could still make me smile.

Mrs. Canan said, "He has been here the whole three days, waiting for you to wake up, never leaving. Nicholas and Cora had Dr. Chase Letterby come to take care of you."

I looked into her eyes. "When I pulled you out of the water, you told me not to leave you, so I didn't."

She took both of her hands and raised them to my face. She pulled me close and kissed me tenderly. All of the sounds of the hospital were gone. Her fragile lips sent a feeling of reassurance through me that she was going to be okay.

Elle's father showed up a short time later. I left so her parents could be alone with her. Later, Elle's friends showed up to see her. Mr. Canan came out of the room and walked right up to me. I braced myself for the worst. He stood in front of me for a few seconds and then stuck out his hand. I grasped his hand with mine, and he shook it firmly, which was his way of saying thanks.

I called Cora.

"Is everything okay?" she asked.

"Yes, Elle's awake."

"I will be right there."

When she arrived, we went and stood in Elle's room with the rest of the visitors. Her friends and family kept asking her what happened that night at the quarry. She never really answered; she just ignored them. I made eye contact with her from time to time. Her eyes told me to be patient and that we would be together again soon.

There were only a few friends left when a police officer showed up. The room went quiet when he entered. Mr. Canan pulled the officer to the side of the room to talk.

"Can everyone leave now? Elle really needs her rest," Mr. Canan announced to the room. Cora and I started to walk out with the rest of her visitors.

The police officer stopped me. "Excuse me, are you Alexander Taylor?"

I nodded, cringing, still not used to being called by my other name. Cora instinctively stood closer to me for protection.

"My name is Officer James Montgomery, and I want to say that it's an honor to meet you, young man. You are one of the reasons why I joined the police force five years ago." He shook my hand. I smiled, and then Cora led me out of the room.

"Can we go get something to eat?" I asked Cora once we were in the hallway.

"Of course we can," she said as we walked toward the elevator.

"Nicholas?"

I stopped right before I hit the down button for the elevator and turned around. Mrs. Canan was hurrying after us.

"Officer Montgomery forgot he needed to speak with you, Nicholas."

"Is he in trouble?" Cora asked.

"No, of course not. He just needs to ask him a question or two about the other night."

"Can't it wait? He's tired," Cora said.

"No, I am fine. I can answer his questions now," I reassured Cora.

I waited outside of Elle's room for Officer Montgomery.

"Well, thank you for everything, officer," I heard Mr. Canan say. "If you need anything else, please let me know."

Officer Montgomery came out of the room and walked over to where I was standing. "Mr. Taylor, may I ask you a question or two?"

"Yes, sir."

"When we questioned the witnesses at the quarry, no one saw you at the party or entering the water. Most of the people thought you must have been in the car with Mr. Rails and Ms. Canan. Were you in the car?"

"No, sir, I was not in the car. I entered from the shore next to the dock right when the car hit the water. Everyone was probably in shock that the car fell into the water. That's why they didn't see me swim out."

"Incredible! The hero of the 10-10 Earthquake saves two more lives right here in Winsor. A hero once again."

"Is that all, officer?" Cora asked. "Nicholas is tired."

"Yes, that's all. Thanks!"

"Excuse me, do you know how Oliver is doing?" I asked.

"He's stable right now," Officer Montgomery said. "He lost a lot of blood, and he had some pretty serious head injuries. If it weren't for you and Ms. Canan, he probably would have died."

I pulled him to shore, but what did Elle do?

Officer Montgomery continued, "He's in a drug-induced coma, but Dr. Chase Letterby is optimistic about his chances of a full recovery. Amazing—even after he put your girlfriend in danger, you were still willing to risk your life for him."

"Let's go, Nicholas. You need to get home and rest."

"One second." I turned and walked back into Elle's room. I walked up to Elle, who was lying back in her bed. I ignored both of her parents, who were sitting in chairs next to her. I leaned down and kissed her.

"I will be back tomorrow. Get some rest," I whispered into her ear.

ELLE'S STORY
CHAPTER THIRTY-TWO

Elle was released from the hospital a week later and was put on strict bed rest at home. Cora and I didn't speak about Xavier, Genevieve, Riley, or anything else that had happened that night. Elle and I were both exempted from the last month of classes, so school was over for us. Every time I came to visit her, one of her parents would sit in the room with us.

The day she was finally able to get out of bed was also the day of Winsor's prom. I brought her over a rose corsage that Cora had made for her and a movie for us to watch. She was down on the couch when I got there. Her dad was out of town on business, and her mom, to my surprise, left us alone. She must have been truly better, because her dad hadn't left once for business until today.

"I got this for you." I handed her the corsage.

"Nicholas, you didn't have to get me this."

"What kind of boyfriend would I be if I didn't get you a corsage for prom? Plus, Cora worked on it all day."

She smiled. "Well, thank you, and tell Cora it's beautiful."

"I will tell her."

She smiled, patting the couch for me to sit next to her. I sat down and she curled up against me.

"We are finally alone," I said.

"Yes, isn't it nice, Nicholas?" Her fingers had intertwined with mine. She had our hands resting on her chest. I could feel her heart beating strongly, and it stirred memories of the night that I pulled her from the water.

"What's wrong, Nicholas? Are you okay?"

"I'm fine. It's just that the last time I felt your heart, it was barely beating. I almost lost you."

She sat up and smiled. "But thanks to you, I am here. Everything is okay."

"Elle, why did you get into Oliver's car?" That question had been eating away at me for some time. Now that we were alone, I could ask.

"On the day of the quarry party, Oliver showed up at my house in that old car. He was looking for you. He told me that he had challenged you to that stupid game of chicken—you know, the rite of passage. I told him that you weren't going to do it and that he should just leave us alone. He told me he was going to find you and show everyone once and for all that you were nothing more than a coward. I lost my temper. That's when I opened the car door. I began yelling at him, telling him to leave you alone and that I wouldn't let you get in the car with such an idiot. He grabbed my arm, pulled me inside, and took off driving. I could barely get the car door shut before he sped down the road.

"He began mumbling something about how I should have ended up with the captain of the football team because the most popular girl always does, and how you had ruined everything for him this year. He was losing it. I put on my seat belt, scared he might wreck the car. I even tried to calm him down, but he didn't respond to me. I demanded that he let me out, but he still wouldn't stop. He told me that he would take me to the quarry party and pull onto the dock with me inside the car. He would stop on the dock and tell everyone that you were too scared to do the rite of passage, so you sent your girlfriend instead. I was hoping you would see that I wasn't home and then come to the quarry. Luckily, you did.

"We drove around the town for a long time before he headed toward the quarry. I never had an opportunity to jump out because he never stopped completely. He wasn't going to go to the party without me, his trophy. When we got to the party, he was smiling. He was getting ready for his big speech. He drove slowly down the dock, stopping near the end. Then the car went head first into the water before I had a chance to get out of my seat belt and escape. Oliver was not wearing his seat belt, so he went head first into the windshield. He was badly hurt and covered with blood. He was lying sideways in his seat, unconscious. The car started to fill with water so I grabbed him and propped him up to make sure he wouldn't drown. I tried to get my seat belt off, but it wouldn't unlatch. Then the windshield broke, completely filling the car with water. Right before I passed out, I felt my seat belt go loose and then I shot to the surface. I remember seeing you, and then everything went black."

"Elle, you should have just let Oliver go looking for me. I can take care of myself."

She kissed me, shutting me up from the lecture I was about to give her. She looked into my eyes. "Nicholas, I would sacrifice everything for you. I love you."

"Elle, I love you too."

END OF BOOK ONE

Are you a fan of
THE HERO CHRONICLES?

Be the first to get fan exclusives and insider Thusie information by engaging with *The Hero Chronicles'* author online.

Visit the links below to talk directly to Tim Mettey, stay up-to-date on his writing process, get insight into the world of *The Hero Chronicles,* and even catch some sneak peeks of future books.

Join other Thusies around the world on:

Facebook.com/tim.mettey

Twitter.com/TimMettey

Pinterest.com/timmettey

#Thusies #TheHeroChronicles

THE HERO CHRONICLES

TRUST

TIM METTEY

BOOK TWO OF *THE HERO CHRONICLES*

"A tremendous sequel with an unexpected twist!"
- Leizbel, 13

OBSESSION

Chapter One

It had been nearly three months since I was told that I was part of an ancient group called the Thusians, the secret guardians of mankind destined to sacrifice our lives at any given time. I would have thought that after finding this out everything would have become really complicated for me, but it hadn't. It was nice and quiet.

Everything I went through to get to this point was worth it, because now I had Elle. I still couldn't believe how such a wonderful, amazing girl ended up with me. We were inseparable during the summer. Unfortunately now I was keeping more secrets from her. It was for her protection, but I still hated it.

Elle and I were lying in my front yard under the shade of the towering oak trees, enjoying each other's company like we had done most of the summer.

"Nicholas, what's wrong?" Elle asked for the hundredth time.

"Sorry, I'm just preoccupied today."

"It's okay. I just wanted to make sure it wasn't me."

How could it be her? She was nothing but wonderful, my reason for living.

"Elle, it's not you. You know that. I'm just thinking about the last interview I did. It wasn't very good."

Last year when I confronted the mob of reporters at the school's entrance, I told them if they would leave me alone I would do interviews. To my dismay, Cora, my aunt and guardian, made sure I did every interview they requested. It had now become the thing I dreaded most. I had to relive the worst day of my life, the 10-10 Earthquake, like it was some recurring nightmare from which I couldn't wake up.

"Sorry, Nicholas, I know how much you hate doing interviews, but at least that was your last one until next summer."

In addition to me only doing interviews in the summer, Cora had told the media that I would only answer questions over the phone. She also required that they never say where I live or where I go to school, even though they were camped outside of my school last year telling the world all of that information. Cora thought, better safe than sorry.

Cora had even talked to Ester Theasing, the head of the Thusian Council and a friend of ours, about doing the interviews to make sure it was safe for me because of Xavier and the Seekers who were trying to eliminate me and any other Thusians. Ester didn't have a problem with it.

Chase Letterby started visiting us more midway through the summer. After the attack last year he left as soon as his doctor talents were no longer needed. No one had heard from him for a while. Even his regular TV appearances had stopped. But as more time passed during the summer, he started to frequent our house again. Cora didn't seem to mind his company, despite his countless attempts to get her to go out with him. He was fixed on the one woman he couldn't have, Cora.

Elle and I continued to lie beneath the trees. She went back to reading her book while rubbing my head. Her hand moved slowly through my hair, making me forget all of my worries. With every pass, a wave of relief went through me. I had positioned myself on her lap facing our driveway, so I could watch my new obsession. A large house was being built next door. It was hard to believe that the lot had been completely wooded just a month ago, and now the house looked close to being completed. Cora was not happy about the new house and the new neighbors that came with it. She still wanted our privacy, and the trees surrounding us had given us ample protection, but now they were gone. She even tried to buy the lot, but it had been sold exactly a week after we moved in last year.

The workers swarmed over the site like ants working hard on their hill. It was amazing to see such a large home being built so quickly. For some strange reason it was fascinating to me. I had no interest in design or architecture, but it still captivated my attention.

Cora and I had been in five different houses in six years, but never a brand new house—one freshly built just for us. Our new neighbors were about to get the fresh start I had wanted after the earthquake, but never got. Maybe that was the reason for my obsession.

NEIGHBORS

Chapter Two

"Nicholas, Coach Miller is here to see you," Cora yelled up to me. I was in my bedroom lying on my bed, daydreaming about Elle, who had gone home. He had told me that he was going to visit during the summer, but I wasn't really expecting him to show up the first week of football tryouts.

"Coach Miller, would you like something to eat or drink?" Cora offered as I walked down the stairs.

"No ma'am, I'm fine. Please call me Aaron."

Cora smiled and walked into the kitchen, leaving both of us standing in the hall. I felt awkward around him. I still felt so guilty for faking my injury last year. It was like I let him down, even though the team won the state championship.

"Son, can we talk?"

I walked him into the family room. I sat on the couch and he took a seat across from me.

"So, how has your summer been?"

I eeked out a "Fine."

He nodded his head as if to say he understood and that

we didn't need to continue. "I hope you've considered my offer. The team and I really need you."

How could this legend need anything from me? I'm just a quitter.

"You would be one of my varsity assistants, if you agree to it."

I didn't say anything.

"You know, this is the first time I have ever asked a student to help with the team." He paused and took a deep breath. "After everything with Oliver, they need a real leader, one they can look up to." Coach Miller's voice was quieter when speaking of Oliver. Did he feel sympathy for him? He was staring at me, waiting for an answer.

"Okay, Coach, I will think about it and let you know in the next couple of days."

He smiled as though I had said yes. "Great, Nicholas. And remember—if you ever need to talk about anything, I will always be here for you. We have more in common than you know."

What did that mean? I smiled and he stood. I walked him to the door and he left.

Later that evening, I joined Cora on the front porch. She was doing a crossword puzzle, and I was daydreaming again about Elle, which was always my favorite pastime. I tried to picture what it would be like to have no secrets at all, just to live a normal life with her. We would go off to college, get married and maybe even start a family. It felt so good to just sit there with these thoughts comforting me, allowing me to forget about everything that had to do with Thusians, Seekers or Xavier. The sun had already started to set, sending in a cool, calming breeze that welcomed in the night. It was refreshing after the long, hot day. I closed my eyes and listened to the wind moving through the trees, rustling the leaves on its journey by.

A loud, wrenching sound shattered my peace. It was like a lawn mower going over a piece of concrete. I sat up to see where it had come from. Then the sound happened two more times. Our porch lights flickered and then were extinguished, along with all the lights in the house. The loud noise had come from somewhere out by the street. Cora and I both walked down off the front porch to see what was going on. We saw the problem immediately. One of the large work trucks from next door had backed into an electric pole, knocking it over and sending it into the street. The workers were all scrambling around. One of the workers saw us and hurried over.

His tool belt bounced along with his belly. He was very out of breath by the time he reached us.

"Ma-ma'am," he stuttered, taking off his white hard hat. "I am so sorry for this inconvenience. We have already called the power company and they are on their way to resolve this situation."

Cora didn't say anything; she just politely smiled. He put his hat back on, tipped it and hurried back to the mess.

"Well, I guess we'll be without power for a while," Cora said.

I went upstairs to relax in bed. The Illinois Power & Electric trucks' lights were flashing through my window, illuminating everything in my room with a yellow glow every couple of seconds. It was soothing. The pulsing light put me into a hypnotic state.

I could hear Cora busy preparing something in the kitchen. My stomach was growling relentlessly. When I went down to the kitchen, I was shocked to see that Cora had not actually fixed anything. She had gotten take-out from a restaurant. She must have slipped out while I was in my room.

"Cora, what are you doing?" I asked, dumbfounded. She always made everything we ate. She prided herself on her delicious, gourmet meals.

"Oh, Nicholas, I didn't feel like cooking tonight. Besides, the power being out made it too difficult, so I just went out and got food." She never made eye contact with me; she just continued to set out dinner.

The power outage was just an excuse. She could cook a gourmet meal with a couple of matches and paper plates. About a month ago, she mentioned that I was getting to the point where I didn't need her anymore. She thought she was becoming useless. I tried to convince her that she wasn't, but I knew what she meant. She had spent so much time over the years keeping me hidden and protecting me, but now there was no real need for that. Ester Theasing had told us we would be safe from any more attacks, which reinforced Cora's thoughts of not being needed. This had to be the reason for the slow decay of Cora's vibrant personality.

The flickering candle light couldn't hide her depression at the dinner table. Her eyes looked sunken and hollowed, and her always perfectly-styled hair was falling down in several places. There was a knock at the door, snapping Cora out of her trance. When someone unexpectedly came to our house in the past, she would have normally become focused, but it didn't seem to be a big deal to her anymore. I knew Ester said we were safe, but I still kept up my guard.

"Nicholas, are you expecting anyone?" Cora asked.

I wasn't. Elle was at church and my friend Eric was over at his girlfriend's house. "No," I said.

Cora slowly walked toward the door.

"Nicholas, could you start cleaning up the dishes for me?" she asked when she was almost to the door.

I had gotten up and began to clear the plates when Cora rushed back into the kitchen, scaring me.

"Nicholas, run!" Cora said, in between yelling and whispering. I didn't know what to do. I was stunned.

"What are you talking about?"

"There's no time to explain—you're in danger. I will keep whoever they are busy at the front door. Go out the back and run straight to the Theasings' house. Tell Ester what's going on and then call Chase."

"Who's out there? What's going on?" I whispered urgently.

"There are Seekers here for you." She shoved me toward the back door. "Move, and when I open the door, you run for it," she yelled louder because I was still standing there stuck to the floor.

I dropped the plates onto the table. Both of them fell off the side, shattering on the floor. She crept to the front door and I ran to the back. I looked at Cora, and from where I was standing, I could see a woman peering into our window next to the front door with both hands up framing her face. It was too dark to see who it was. Cora was at the door, getting ready to open it. Then two loud thuds rattled our front door. Cora pulled away, startled, and then moved back into position.

What was I doing? I couldn't leave her. Cora was scared for me but I didn't feel anything. There was no fire in me warning of danger. But I still couldn't trust that feeling and leave Cora to face whatever was on the other side of that door alone, just in case I was wrong. Even though the fire was absent, I couldn't leave her defenseless.

Cora looked back at me and mouthed the words, "Go now." Before she had time to fully open the door, I was next to her. My fear of something happening to her made me get there faster than normal. She had the door a quarter of the way open. Realizing I was now standing next to her, she grabbed my arm and tried to pull me back. She started to slam the door with her free hand, but I stopped her.

"Cora, it's okay, I know them," I said, recognizing the two people in front of us. "Riley and Genevieve are the ones who saved me in the park."

Cora still had a tight grip on my arm and on the door knob. I opened the door all the way so we could see both of them on the porch.

"Wow, you guys have a funny way of answering the door. How about a little gratitude?" Genevieve said sarcastically.

"I'm sorry for scaring you, Cora," Riley said. His Irish accent was less obvious than last spring. I had never really gotten a good look at Riley before. He was tall and slender. He reminded me of a greyhound with his narrow face and wiry frame. Genevieve looked like a movie star, dripping with sex appeal. Her radiant skin was still lightly tanned. She was tiny but not like a little girl. Her brown hair was pulled back in complex braids. The nurturing way she had spoken to me in the park last year had been replaced by sarcasm, which sickened me.

"My name is Riley and this is Genevieve. We are fellow Thusians like the two of you. We have been searching for you both for many years, Cora. We caught up with you a year ago in Tatesville, and we followed you here so we could watch after you both. Luckily we did, because we were able to save Nicholas."

I looked over at Cora. The light had returned to her eyes. She was the Cora of old, vibrant and in control. She was in her protecting mode; she had a purpose again—to keep me safe.

The four of us just stood there in silence, waiting for the next person to make a move. Cora wasn't impressed by what Riley was saying or willing to let them get any closer to me. She had somehow managed to get her foot in front of me just in case.

"Maybe we could come in so we can talk," Genevieve urged.

Cora didn't budge. She wasn't going to let them into the house under any circumstances.

"Cora, can we invite them in?" I asked, but it was like I wasn't even there. Riley tried this time.

"Cora, you are right not to trust us, but please just give us a chance. We would like for you and Nicholas to come to dinner tonight at our house. We still have power. I thought it would be the neighborly thing to do since our workers knocked out your power."

Neighborly? The house I had watched being built all this time was theirs. The fresh start I dreamed of having belonged to these two.

"We have had dinner already," Cora said, showing her contempt. They weren't winning her over tonight, that was for sure.

Riley smiled. "Of course you have, but please come next door in a half hour, even if it's just to talk."

Cora's gaze was cold and hard.

I glanced at Genevieve, who was staring at me just as intensely. A sparkle appeared in her radiant green eyes that restored her beauty for a split second, but then it vanished. Riley grabbed her arm and pulled her away.

Cora turned to me. "We have to go now," she said, shutting the door and locking it, still watching them as they vanished next door. *Not this again*, I thought. I wasn't going to run from the very two people who had rescued me. If I was going to eventually die anyway, I wanted to at least spend as much remaining time as possible with Elle.

"Cora, I'm not going anywhere. You know this. What's gotten into you? They saved my life—that has to count for something. They're not the bad guys."

She turned to me. "I'm grateful they saved your life, but that's where it ends. I have a bad feeling that being around them will lead you into more danger or maybe something worse."

"Worse than my Thusian Final Sacrifice? You know, the one where I'll most likely die for a complete stranger? Cora, I am *not* moving and I *am* going over to their house to hear what they have to say, with or without you."

"Nicholas, if that's your decision," she paused, collecting herself, "I will go with you, but I want you to know that I don't support this at all."

LEFTOVERS

Chapter Three

Cora and I drove over to their house. She insisted that we drive even though they were right next door, just a two minute walk. Cora was definitely back in control.

Cora grabbed my arm before we got out. "Nicholas, even though you think you know them, we still can't trust them," she said. "You let them do all of the talking."

"Cora, they did save my life," I reminded her again.

"We're here, aren't we? But still, we can't assume anything. Please listen to me. I've been doing this a lot longer than you. I know what I'm talking about. You have to trust me."

I nodded. She was right, she had a lot more experience and I should listen to her. But deep down inside I felt like they were fine, like I was supposed to be with them.

We got out of the truck. The house was even more incredible up close. It was at least two times the size of our modest house. The house looked like it was a luxury log cabin or a ski lodge. There were windows and lights everywhere, making large, dramatic shadows. We walked up an ornate brick path lined with freshly planted trees, bushes and flowers.

Cora was about to knock on the oversized wooden door that should have been on the front of a castle rather than a home, when the door opened.

"I'm so glad you both decided to come over," Riley said, smiling. He had on a bright teal polo and a pair of khaki shorts. He looked like he was ready to go out on his yacht or something.

"Why, thank you, Riley," Cora said, walking through the door and handing him a bottle of wine that she had gotten from our pantry. Cora never drank alcohol—she thought it made people look and act unsophisticated—but she always had a bottle on hand for cooking purposes.

We followed Riley into the house. It was almost completely empty. The floor plan was open, with tall, vaulted ceilings, which made the large, empty house look even barer. We walked over to the only piece of furniture that I could see in the house. It was a large, round metal dining table set for four. Riley motioned for us to sit down. Cora walked over and sat facing the door. I sat right next to her.

"Genevieve will be out in a little bit and then we can start to eat, only if you'd like more dinner, of course. I got the food from a little restaurant in town, Marcello's. It's supposed to have the best Italian food around." He picked the same restaurant that Cora had gotten our food from earlier. We should have just brought over our leftovers to save them the trip. I laughed. I must have laughed too loudly, because Cora kicked me under the table and shot me a dirty look.

"I would also like to apologize for the lack of furniture; the workers just finished. Our furniture will be here tomorrow," Riley said, changing the subject.

"I don't mean to be rude, but let's skip the small talk. Why have you been searching for us?"

Cora had just told me to let them do all of the talking and then she went and asked him the million dollar question right away. Riley's face showed that he was shocked, too. I was sure he was thinking, like I was, that it was going to be a long evening of trying to figure each other out, like a courtship or a game of chess.

"Cora, if you don't mind, I would like to wait for Genevieve. Then we can discuss—" Before he finished, his eyes looked past both of us. I turned to see Genevieve gliding down the hallway, coming toward the room. She looked like a Greek goddess straight from Olympus. Her hair was pulled back in another elaborate style, different from the one just thirty minutes ago. She was wearing some simple silver jewelry that was a perfect accent to her dark skin. Her white dress was cut well above her knees. The fabric looked like it was made of a loosely woven silk. She was incredibly beautiful, but she didn't stir any emotion in me. Elle was the only one who stirred those types of feelings.

Genevieve sat down. "Okay, so what did I miss, kids?" Again, the way she spoke didn't match her elegant appearance. She was rougher and more sarcastic, not polite or nurturing at all.

"Well, Genevieve, Cora just asked why we have been trying to find them all this time," said Riley.

"Wow, you don't mess around, do you?"

Cora didn't look at her. "We are only here because you saved Nicholas, but if we don't get some answers right now, we are leaving," Cora said, starting to stand.

Riley motioned for her to stop and she slowly sat back down.

"Cora, we haven't really been searching for the both of you," Riley said. "We have only been searching for Nicholas."

Cora grabbed my arm under the table. By her grasp, I could tell she was preparing me to run.

"But before you go racing out of here, let me explain why only Nicholas. As I told you at your house, we are Thusians too. My family can be traced back to some of the original Thusians and my great-great-great-great-grandfather was even a Keeper. The Keepers were the ones who knew all of the bloodlines and history and made sure they were respected."

"Riley, we already know what Keepers are," Cora said.

He smiled and continued, "Of course you do. The reason why we were looking for just Nicholas is because he discovered his Thusian talents, going through his Realization, on the same day both Genevieve and I did, October 10th."

"I'm sure there were other Thusians who discovered their talents the same day as the three of you," Cora said. Riley was trying to link me to them and she was clearly trying to derail any effort for a connection.

"Cora, you're right, but we are the only three that discovered significant talents and are still alive today."

Cora looked partially satisfied with his answer. I looked

over at Genevieve, who was not paying attention. She was playing with the paper napkin on her plate, making it into some sort of flower, not interested in the conversation at all.

"Beyond the fact that we are all alive, I was also drawn to Genevieve and we were both drawn to Nicholas."

"You were drawn to me?" I had to say something because that sounded weird.

Everyone at the table was now looking at me. I even got Genevieve's attention.

"Yes, we were drawn to you, Nicholas," Riley said. He looked at Genevieve and she spoke up as if on cue.

"Yeah, we were," she said, like she had been coached on what to say.

"You see, we are all being drawn together. Nicholas, don't you feel it?" Riley asked.

Everyone was looking at me. My stomach started to feel sick with nerves. I grabbed a couple of Tic Tacs and popped them in my mouth.

"I do feel something, but I'm not sure what it is."

Inside of me, I could feel something drawing me toward both of them. I wasn't sure if it was gratitude for them saving me or curiosity, but something was there deep inside.

Riley smiled in triumph and Genevieve went back to her paper flower. I avoided looking at Cora. I was sure she wasn't happy with my answer.

"Of course he feels drawn to you. You two saved his life. That's the only reason why we came over here in the first place," Cora said. Then she looked at Genevieve. "And if I were a teenage boy, I would definitely be drawn to you the way you're dressed. It's nothing more than a cheap, physical attraction with you."

I couldn't believe she just said that. It was kind of funny, though Genevieve didn't think so at all.

"I don't have to take this crap, especially from a nobody like you." Genevieve stood up ready for a fight, her napkin flower falling to the ground. Cora remained in her seat. She didn't look threatened in the least.

"Genevieve, sit down now," Riley said firmly.

It took a minute or so, but she eventually sat down in her chair, picking up her flower from the floor and playing with it, but with less enthusiasm.

Riley continued to talk as if nothing had happened between the women. "After I discovered that the three of us had our Realization of Talents on the same day—and in such dramatic ways—I had to find Genevieve and now you, Nicholas, so we can find the 4th Thusian, which will help form The 7."

I glanced over at Cora. She looked puzzled by what he said.

"What is The 7?" I asked.

"The 7 is a group that was formed when the Council created the Seekers. The Seekers, you know, were used by the Council to eliminate the Keeper. That Keeper's name was Finn Wren. He was one of the oldest and wisest Keepers the Thusians ever had; he was in his 90s when he was finally killed. The Council used the Seekers to kill him in order to gain power, but not before he foretold about The 7."

"Wait a minute. I thought the Keeper wasn't able to keep track of the growing population of Thusians, because they were able to marry non-Thusians. And because of this population explosion, the Seekers were formed and used by the Council to eliminate the Thusians who didn't know about our traditions, right?" I asked, remembering what Ester had explained to me in the vault last year.

"Of course that is what you were told; that is what they told all of the Thusians. But the Council wanted the power for themselves, and they used the Seekers to take it from the Keeper. Anyone who stood in their way was killed by the Seekers." Riley looked at me to make sure he had answered my question. I wasn't sure if I believed him entirely, but it was an answer.

"But why would they need a group of people to kill one Thusian Keeper?" I asked.

"Keeper Wren had hundreds of loyal Thusians protecting him. It was a bloody period in our history," Riley answered.

I had no idea if he was lying or not, but I could tell that he believed what he was saying.

"Okay, now let me explain The 7 to you in more detail." He paused and looked at Cora and me, then continued. "The 7 consists of three Seekers and four special Thusians. The three Seekers represent evil, everything that is wrong with the world. The four Thusians represent the goodness in people, the part that is self-sacrificing with no thought of one's own well-being—everything the Thusians stand for. Together they make up The 7, representing the balance between good and evil."

I already saw a flaw in this; I was surprised Cora didn't speak up first.

"Riley, three Seekers and four Thusians aren't balanced. It favors good by one whole person." I didn't have a problem with that, but his explanation was still flawed, which drew into question his credibility. He seemed prepared for this question.

"Excellent point, Nicholas. I asked my dad the same question when he explained it to me when I was young. He told me that a group of three Seekers and three Thusians isn't balanced at all—it's uneven. Evil will always win when it's a fair fight, three on three. The expression that good always conquers evil isn't exactly true. Evil will do anything to gain an advantage, so that's why good needs extra help. Good values life and evil doesn't. So that's why there has to be a fourth Thusian to make it fair and balanced between both sides. Then once The 7 is formed, we will fight, representing both the Thusians and Seekers. The winning side will determine everyone's fate, giving us the opportunity to finally end the Seekers' terrible reign of terror over us."

I wasn't sure if that made sense, but I believed him. However, if it were up to me, I would want hundreds of Thusians fighting the Seekers, not just four of us.

"So that's why we have been searching for you, Nicholas. You are one of the 4. Now that the three of us are together, we can find the 4th. He or she will have more talents than we do, and once we're all together, we will all develop more talents as time goes on."

"This 4th, whoever it is, just started to get his or her talents now?" I asked.

"Well, actually no. He or she would have started developing them last year. Even though we didn't actually meet up with each other before you moved here, I believe that's when this person would have started gaining talents, because we were so close to each other. But I'm not 100-percent sure."

"Riley, I'm not saying I believe you, but how are we supposed to find this 4th? It sounds impossible."

"It will be difficult. We'll have to be careful while we're looking and hope whoever it is won't draw too much attention to themselves with their newfound talents. We have to get to them first, before Xavier and the Seekers do."

Then I thought of Elle. Could she be the one we are looking for? Could she be the 4th? As soon as I got to Winsor, I had been drawn helplessly to her. The love I felt for her was something deeper and more mystical than just a high school romance.

"Nicholas, I'm going to rely heavily on you in finding this person, because you have been here in the community and you have most likely met them or seen them already. You might even be friends with them. I've taken a job at Winsor High as a history teacher and Genevieve is going to pretend to be my wife. She will be scouting out any leads that we come across while we're in school. Nicholas, is there anyone Genevieve should start checking out?" he asked, eagerly waiting for my answer.

I wanted to say the 4th had to be Elle, but I restrained

myself. I still didn't know if I believed their story or if they could be trusted.

"I can't think of anybody right now, Riley."

Genevieve cleared her throat and said under her breath, but loud enough for everyone to hear, "Yeah right."

I looked at her. "What's that supposed to mean?"

Her beauty was once again tarnished by her tone. "I know you think we should check out your little girlfriend, Elle. I have been following you back and forth from her house for too long. Cora's got at least one thing right tonight. Boys always think their physical attractions mean so much more than—"

I stood and my chair fell backward, interrupting her. Everyone at the table jumped to their feet except Genevieve, who was not even paying attention to me, twirling her paper flower between her fingers.

"Elle is not just a physical attraction. She is someone I care about deeply, more than you will ever know or understand. I did consider her, but I wanted to think things over before telling you to start looking at her. I'm not sure I can even trust the two of you."

Genevieve stood and smiled at me like a little kid who was just teasing her brother until she got what she wanted.

"Thank you, Nicholas. That's all I wanted you to admit. You think she is a possible candidate. I will start checking her out." She turned and walked back toward the hall and added over her shoulder, "But I doubt she's the 4th."

I felt like chasing her down to give her a piece of my

mind, but all I wanted to do was get out of this place. The walls felt like they were closing in on me fast.

"Cora, we're leaving." I turned my back to Riley and walked to the door. "Don't contact us again. When I'm ready, I will contact you," I said loudly enough so that Genevieve could hear me wherever she was in the house.